ar cFadyen was born in Liverpool and has enjoyed a
uc   ful career in marketing. He lives in Hertfordshire
vit s wife, his three children and his retired greyhound.
it *Vhite Lies* is the first of three novels featuring DI Steve
Ca nael, the other two being *Lillia's Diary* (Book Guild,
20   and *Frozen to Death* (Book Guild, 2010).

By the same author:

Lillia's Diary, Book Guild Publishing, 2009

Little White Lies (large print edition), Magna Large Print Books, 2010

Frozen to Death, Book Guild Publishing, 2010

LITTLE WHITE LIES

Ian McFadyen

Book Guild Publishing
Sussex, England

First published in Great Britain in 2008 by
The Book Guild Ltd
Pavilion View
19 New Road
Brighton
BN1 1UF

Typesetting in Baskerville by
IML Typographers, Merseyside

Printed in Great Britain by
CPI Antony Rowe

A catalogue record for this book is available from
The British Library.

ISBN 978 1 84624 761 3

To Chris

Chapter 1

As the home side lined up to clap in the visitors, the non-playing members in the lounge made positive noises about the prospects of their team for the rest of the season. The air was full of speculation about the impact their new star would have against Newbridge in the Cup match the following week. It was the first game of the season and those who had watched could not fail to be impressed with the new young addition to the Moulton Bank Cricket Club.

That particular Sunday was just like most other Sundays in the small Lancashire village. In the council estate by the railway line, women were preparing tea, while outside their husbands were hard at work washing and polishing their cars. With the exception of those who had spent the afternoon at the Cricket Club, most of the residents of the more upmarket houses on 'The Common' were mowing their lawns and tending to their carefully clipped hedges.

Applegate Lane lay between the grand houses of The Common and the less sought-after homes by the railway line. Its residents included plumbers, shopkeepers, self-employed builders, bank clerks, sales reps, the village bobby, the head of the local primary school and a funeral director. It was to one of these houses that the talk of Moulton Bank Cricket Club would return that warm June afternoon.

After changing quickly, the teenager and his friend rushed

1

across Wigan Road, then along the bank of the river and into Tan House Row. As he turned into the lane he quickened his step. He could hardly wait to tell his father about his innings and the thrill of taking his first wickets for the village team.

Chapter 2

The Carmichael family had been connected to the police force for two generations. Donald Carmichael had joined the police in his native Dumfries, in the mid 1930s. Within 15 years both of his sons had dutifully followed their father into the profession. John, the eldest son, remained in Scotland, rising to the rank of sergeant and was stationed for the majority of his career only 15 miles away from his father in Lockerbie. The younger brother Robert was a little more adventurous and certainly more ambitious. He had no intention of living under the shadow of his father and brother and instead of joining up in Scotland he decided that he would move south, joining the Hertfordshire police force. Robert's career was in many ways the most distinguished. He rose to the rank of chief inspector but sadly was forced to retire in the early 1970s due to poor health, an occupational hazard in the 60s and 70s. With this pedigree it was no surprise when his only son Stephen also decided upon a career in the police. However, like his father, Steve wanted to avoid any comparisons being made between father and son, so he decided to make his career with the Met.

Steve left the police training school at Hendon at the end of the 70s. In his final report it stated that he was one of the brightest recruits, and that he had shown a natural aptitude for leadership. After spending two years at Mill Hill Police station, Steve transferred to the Fraud Squad where he spent a further three years and progressed to the rank of sergeant. Armed with a brace of commendations he then moved over to the Vice Squad.

Initially, Steve found vice the most rewarding area of all. He continued to shine and, at the age of 31, he finally achieved the rank of inspector. It was during his time in the Vice Squad that he first came across Nick Butler. Although Steve had known of Butler, it was not until he was assigned to an investigation into the illegal activities within a seedy north London nightclub that he had any direct experience of Inspector Butler in action.

* * * *

It had been Penny's idea for the family to move from their suburban house in Bushey to Moulton Bank, the village where she had grown up and which held such happy memories. She was sure that the pace of life in the quiet Lancashire village would benefit the whole family, particularly Steve who had changed so much since the announcement of Butler's promotion to the new Chief Inspector. Steve was not so sure. He had no desire to work under Butler but he also had great difficulty seeing himself as an inspector in a provincial force.

When the vacancy in Lancashire first caught his eye Steve's first instinct told him to keep it from his wife. However after spending only a few weeks under Butler, Steve finally had to concede that Penny had been right all along and he put in a transfer request. He had few problems at the interview and within a few months Inspector Carmichael, his wife and their three children were on the move to the north-west of England. Penny had insisted that they allowed the children to complete the summer term before they moved from Watford and on Friday 29 July, two days after the term ended Inspector Carmichael and his family arrived in their new home in Moulton Bank. Despite spending all Saturday unpacking, when Sunday arrived they were still surrounded by many of their possessions in an assortment of crates, boxes and bags.

'Do you think we'll ever get straight?' Penny asked as she surveyed the boxes and crates left behind by the removal van.

'Don't know,' Steve replied. 'At least we've got enough space.'

The new family home on Tan House Row was at least twice the size of the house which had been home to them for the last 15 years. On the ground floor there was a large family kitchen and three other rooms, which the estate agent from Mullion and Thorpe had described as the front parlour, the sitting room and the morning room. Upstairs there were five bedrooms and two bathrooms. However, the most appealing aspect of the house from Steve's point of view was the attic. This was to be his space, his sanctuary.

'These rooms are really pokey,' he shouted from the morning room. 'We could do with knocking these two through. What do you think Pen?' Penny didn't answer. She had gone out the back to marvel at the large garden, her main reason for persuading her husband to spend the extra £20,000 on this house, rather than one of the new executive detached houses on the Tan House development across the road. Steve went out to find his wife and repeated his previous question. 'Fine, that's a great idea,' he said to himself, when for a second time he received no response.

'Isn't this garden just brilliant,' said Penny, as she bent down to smell the perfume of a bright purple verbascum. 'I'm certain we'll all be happier here than we were in Bushey,' she continued. 'I know that it's not what you are used to, but the peace and quiet will do you good. You'll see!'

Before Steve had a chance to respond, they were interrupted by a high-pitched shriek in a distinctly strong foreign accent from the old lady next door.

'Here puss, come to mummy it's lunchtime.'

'Yes, the peace and quiet,' Steve mumbled. 'I'm enjoying it already.'

The Carmichael family then spent several more hours unpacking their belongings.

'Can we have a rest?' asked an exhausted Natalie.

'Good idea,' replied Steve. 'I need a break too.'

' I know,' chirped up Penny, 'Let's go for a walk. I could show you all the village.'

Ten minutes later the five new inhabitants of Moulton Bank closed the gate of their new home and headed off up the lane towards The Common and the open fields beyond. Penny could not help feeling that at last she had returned home and as she looked round her on that warm summer afternoon she had a feeling of inner contentment.

About 100 yards up the road they reached the T-junction and The Common, which had always been the 'posh' part of the village when Penny was a girl. Although the large detached houses which lay on either side of the road still pervaded an air of opulence, they no longer seemed as grand as they once had to the young girl who walked past them twice a day on her way to and from the small village school.

'That's my new school,' exclaimed Natalie as they turned the corner.

'It was my school too!' said Penny. 'Come on everyone, let's go and look.'

Jemma and Robbie exchanged a look ... which expressed more than any words could that wandering around a village was not usually what they would want to be doing on a Sunday. However, they had resigned themselves to the fact that their fate that Sunday afternoon was to follow their parents. Experience had taught them that, in the long run, compliance would prove to be far preferable to confrontation. That, however, did not prevent them from making their protest by ensuring that they walked at least 10 yards behind their parents.

Natalie was different. At the tender age of eight she had yet to experience the embarrassment of having to acknowledge that her parents existed. The thought of exploring her new school was met with great excitement from the baby of the family, much to the added annoyance of her elder siblings.

'Good heavens,' Penny shouted, 'it's hardly changed at all.'

They entered the school through a large blue gate.

'Moulton Bank C of E Primary School,' read Natalie from the large blue board on the side of the school wall. 'Headmaster, David H. Turner BA (Hons). Caretaker, Clive Penman.'

'My God,' Penny said, as she read the board herself. 'It can't be.'

'What's the matter Pen?' Steve said, his interest having been roused for the first time since they had left the house. 'What can't be?'

Before she could answer they were interrupted by the appearance of a man in his early forties wearing a scruffy pair of jeans and a T-shirt with a motif which read 'Ed's Diner … Eat Mo Pig!'

It had fallen upon Penny to manage the various arrangements for the children's new schools, and although she had done this with her usual thoroughness, she had only discussed Natalie attending her old school over the phone. All her calls had been with the deputy head, and up until that moment she had no idea that the current head was a childhood friend.

'Good afternoon,' said the stranger, 'can I help you?'

'Good afternoon,' replied Steve. 'We're just having a look at our daughter's new school.'

'Excellent,' replied the stranger. 'I'm the headmaster, David Turner. You're fortunate to find me here on a Sunday.

I don't normally come into school during the holidays but we only just broke up on Thursday, so I am sorting out a few things before I start my summer break. If you want I'd be happy to show you around.'

'Don't you recognise me then?' Penny asked.

Turner frowned. 'No, sorry, have we met before?'

'I'm Penny Lathom,' replied Penny.

'Penny! I didn't know you were coming back. It's great to see you.'

From his manner Steve could see that David, as he insisted they address him, was going to be quite different from Miss O'Dwyer, the head at Bushey Middle School, where all three of his children had spent the first years of their academic lives. Despite this, it was clear that he was a hit with Natalie, who described him that night as a 'Will Young looky-likey'.

'Would you like to have a look inside?' David asked Natalie, when he realised she would be joining the ranks of Year 4 in September.

Natalie, her parents and her two reluctant siblings spent the next 50 minutes being introduced to the six classrooms, the main hall, the kitchen, the dining room, and every inch of the school playground and its adjacent sports field. By the end of the tour, the numbers of disinterested parties had swelled to include Steve and Natalie. This development was not lost on Penny who tactfully declined David's invitation to take coffee and biscuits in his study.

'It's been great to see you again David,' she said as they finally departed the hallowed grounds of Moulton Bank Primary School. 'I'll see you around.'

'My pleasure,' David replied. 'Perhaps we'll see you in The Railway Tavern. That's where most of the old crew hang out.'

'That would be great,' Penny shouted as she quickened her step to catch up with her retreating family. Once she had caught up with the others they were all well out of sight of the school and its enthusiastic head. She was about to launch into a lecture on manners, when the most unimaginable odour enveloped them.

'What the bloody hell is that?' exclaimed Steve.

'It's disgusting!' shrieked Jemma.

'I think that we've just encountered the scent of Alcar sewage works,' Penny answered, trying hard to hide her amusement at the contorted facial expressions of the rest of the family. 'I'd forgotten about that unique perfume,' she continued. 'Don't worry, Alcar's at least five miles away. It's pretty rare for the smell to waft this way, as I recall.'

The remainder of the walk took the new inhabitants down memory lane, with the excited Penny as their guide. Penny's tour included such wonders as Martins Lane, where Penny collected conkers as a child, Wood Lane with its fantastic blackberry bushes, the site of the old basket works which had long since become a housing estate, and a large pond called Jackson's Pit, where Clive Penman had once ridden his bike when it was frozen. However, the high point of Penny's rosy fantasy was the village hall. Here Penny excelled herself with her reminiscences of Guide meetings, her first disco, and the time Gary Leeman and Robbie Robertson repelled an invasion of three troublemakers from the neighbouring village who had gatecrashed Sarah Mulholland's eighteenth birthday party.

It was at about this time that Steve told his wife that it was now almost six o'clock, and they had not eaten for some time. Steve also made the point of reminding Penny that he was due to start his new job in the morning, and as yet he did not have an ironed shirt to wear.

Fortunately for Steve, the tour had taken the family in a circle and it was only a couple of hundred yards back to their new home. Once they were back inside the house the family dispersed. Penny went into the kitchen, Jemma, Robbie and Natalie disappeared to their respective bedrooms, and Steve climbed the narrow staircase to his attic hideaway.

9

Steve had not trusted the removal men with any of his most private possessions. These had all been transported in the boot of his black BMW. Once they had arrived in Moulton Bank he had insisted that although the children should do their bit in helping with the lifting and carrying, nobody was to touch any of the carefully labelled boxes which housed his treasures. Not that they needed to be told. They had long since learned that 'Dad's precious things', as they were lovingly called, were better left alone. Now in the peace and quiet of his newly-found hideaway Steve took pleasure in admiring his collections of coins and military memorabilia, and the vast array of photographs and cuttings from his career. It was only now that he began to contemplate how he was going to approach his first day with Lancashire CID.

Chapter 3

Steve had always had an obsession with time. As a young boy he would set himself targets to complete various tasks, like homework projects or cycling to school. As he had aged this obsession hadn't waned. In fact Penny and the children often teased him when he'd give them such precise predictions of the time they would arrive when they were travelling long distances. So when at precisely 8:23 a.m. his BMW pulled into the tiny car park at the rear of Kirkwood police station Steve felt a great sense of pride. He was just one minute over his estimated travelling time, having completed the 23.2 miles in 33 minutes.

He took a deep breath and headed towards the entrance. He did not notice the two pairs of eyes that were focused on him from behind the blinds of the first floor window.

'What do you think Lucy?' asked Sergeant Watson. 'He looks a bit bloody keen for my liking.'

'He looks younger than I expected,' replied Lucy. 'And you've got to admit, he's a good deal smarter than Inspector Rowe.'

'Don't get all hot under the collar Bamber!' said Watson, with a smug grin. 'I'm told that he's happily married with kids.'

By the time the two officers had finished their conversation Steve was through the front entrance and into the lobby. He strode up to the front desk and in a clear authoritative voice informed the desk sergeant of his name and asked him to inform Chief Inspector Hewitt that he had arrived.

'Morning sir,' replied the desk sergeant. 'I was told to expect you. If you would care to take a seat, I'll let him know that you have arrived.'

Steve thanked him, but decided to remain standing.

After a couple of minutes, an elderly lady in a long winter coat and those comfortable-looking zip-up boots that seem such a necessary fashion accessory once you pass the age of 65 made her way to the front desk. In a frail voice she explained to the sergeant that she had lost her handbag. Steve was impressed by the sensitivity that the sergeant showed towards the old lady, who was obviously distressed and extremely confused. It was clear that the sergeant was well used to dealing with the public and that he had a considerate and caring attitude to the elderly. They were then joined by what Steve later described to Penny as 'two pubescent PCs with an even younger male prisoner'. With a great deal of difficulty, the PCs escorted their charge past Steve and the old lady and through a set of double doors at the far end of the reception area. Steve was not impressed with the PCs. He thought their appearance was scruffy and in his opinion they were displaying an unnecessary degree of force.

Once all three were out of sight the desk sergeant asked the old lady to take a seat and then disappeared in the direction of the PCs. Steve could only assume that he too had been unhappy with the actions of the young officers.

Steve and the old lady were now the only occupants of that part of the police station. The old lady remained quiet and still on the bench, as if she felt she had no place being there. Steve, through both nervousness and boredom, paced up and down, occasionally glancing at the various tatty notices that festooned the walls and the overpopulated public noticeboard. After what seemed like an age, but was probably only a couple of minutes, the double doors burst open and in strode the tall thin figure of Chief Inspector Hewitt.

Hewitt was a wiry man with a long thin face, small dark eyes and a small mouth. Dominating his face was his pointed dagger of a nose, which seemed to Steve to be totally disproportionate to the rest of his features.

'Good morning Carmichael,' he boomed. 'Sorry to keep you waiting.' Hewitt shook Steve's hand vigorously and before Steve had a chance to reply had turned and was walking back in the direction from whence he had come. He shouted back to Steve, 'Follow me.' Steve did as he was told, pausing only briefly to glance at the old lady, who remained motionless on the bench, oblivious to the presence of either officer.

Once they were through the doors and into the corridor Steve quickened his step in an effort to catch up with Hewitt. He did not want the first impression of his new colleagues to be that of a naughty schoolboy following on behind the teacher. However, Hewitt was a quick walker and he had already got a head start, and once Steve had caught up he had to walk at a very brisk pace to ensure that he remained in step. They went through at least three double doors before they reached a staircase. Here Hewitt turned quickly to his left and started bouncing up the stairs, two steps at a time. This completely threw Steve. He had not anticipated that they were to go up the stairs and had already taken two or three steps further down the corridor before he realised that Hewitt was no longer next to him. By the time he had managed to stop walking and return to the bottom of the staircase Hewitt was already halfway to the first floor.

Steve decided that he would continue the rest of the journey at his own pace, electing to take one stair at a time. When he reached the first floor Hewitt was already at the top of the stairs on the second floor. Without waiting Hewitt marched across the corridor and into his office, and by the time Steve was able to join him he was already seated behind his large mahogany desk and was ordering tea on his hands-free phone. Steve took a seat directly opposite his new boss. His chair was noticeably smaller and looked a lot less comfortable than the one being occupied by Hewitt, and he wondered whether this was a deliberate ploy orchestrated by his superior to ensure that his guests recognised their relatively lowly status.

When Hewitt had concluded his conversation he depressed a button on his phone and turned his attention to his visitor. 'Great to have you with us inspector,' he said. 'I'm looking forward to working with you. It's not often we're joined by an officer from the Met, particularly one with your experience.'

'Thank you sir,' replied Steve. 'I'm very much looking forward to working here.'

'We're a much smaller operation than you will be used to, but I think that you will be pretty impressed by the standard of policing here. Our clear-up statistics are quite exemplary at this station.'

Steve tried to look impressed even though he detested the concept of equating good policing with clear-up rates. In his experience some of the worst officers had the best clear-up rates. However, he knew that his record could stand up well to most in this respect, even if he didn't wholeheartedly agree with the means of the measure. 'I hope I can continue the good work,' he responded tactfully.

'I'm sure you will inspector,' continued Hewitt. 'It was one of the main reasons I supported your transfer. Although to be totally candid with you, there were those on the panel who were not convinced by your motives in moving to Lancashire from the Met.'

For the first time that morning Steve started to feel uneasy. Perhaps his new boss was shrewder than he looked, he thought. 'I'm not sure I understand what you mean.'

14

'Put it this way,' continued Hewitt. 'You're obviously an experienced and very able officer. Ambitious too. So why choose Lancashire? I would have thought that there would be greater opportunities in London than here. It doesn't quite add up, Inspector Carmichael.'

'As I said at the interview, my wife is from this part of the world. We felt that the environment would be better for our children. And to be honest, in the Met I felt like a small fish in a very large and sometimes murky pond.'

Hewitt seemed to like Steve's explanation. He nodded gently as if to show his approval. 'Sorry to seem suspicious, it's just that I have to be sure that your reasons for joining us are ... how should I say ... of a positive nature rather than the contrary. Do you get my drift?'

Steve nodded. 'I can assure you sir, that my application here was done for no other reason but to enhance my promotion prospects and improve my family's quality of life. There's no other reason', said Steve, hoping that this would conclude the questioning.

'I'm pleased to hear you say so, inspector. Be assured that I accept your reasons. In fact, again to be candid with you, I find it hard to understand how anyone could endure twenty years in the Met. In my opinion they have still to expunge themselves of some very dubious practices and I'm afraid to say some very dubious officers.'

Hewitt got up slowly from his chair and walked the few paces to the window. He made a small opening in the blinds with his thumb and forefinger and peered out into the car park. Steve elected to remain quiet, even though he sensed that his new boss was disappointed not to get a response of some kind.

'And how did you get on with Chief Inspector Butler?' Hewitt asked, without bothering to turn round. Before Steve had a chance to respond, there was a knock on the door. In walked a frail lady in her mid- to late fifties carrying a silver tray upon which was set a china teapot, two cups on saucers, a sugar bowl and a tiny milk jug, all with matching floral patterns. The tray was laid on the desk, the lady smiled kindly at Steve and then, without any words being spoken by either her or the two officers, she shuffled back to the door and departed. This interruption seemed to distract Hewitt from his questioning, much to Steve's relief.

'Do you take your tea with milk and sugar, inspector?' asked Hewitt.

'Both please,' responded Steve.

Once Steve and his superior had sorted out their drinks Hewitt, who by now had returned to his luxurious leather swivel chair, looked straight at Steve and said, 'I have been asked by the chief constable to trial a new initiative for him, and I would like you to manage this very important assignment for me.'

Steve's attention was aroused immediately. 'What sort of assignment Sir?'

'Well, the details are still being sorted out, but I can tell you that the role will cover the whole of the county and will require you to work with a very small team.'

'Any more clues?' asked Steve, who by now was thoroughly absorbed by the thought of heading up a county-based initiative.

'I'm sorry, I'm not yet at liberty to divulge the nature of the role. I am due to meet with the chief constable in a couple of days, after which I should be able to brief you a little more on the initiative.'

'I understand,' replied Steve, although he did not understand why Hewitt had even bothered to mention the role if he was unable to share any information about it.

'But in the interim, you must keep this between the two of us, do you understand?'

'Absolutely.' Steve who was at a loss to think what possible damage he could cause by reciting his entire conversation to anyone who would care to listen. As far as he was concerned Hewitt had said nothing that would be of any interest to anyone.

'The main reason I have mentioned this to you is to allow you some advanced notice, so that you can review the various team members in CID, and be ready to select two or maybe three at very short notice, to be with you in the assignment,' said Hewitt.

'I understand,' said Steve for a second time. By now he was absolutely convinced that the assignment was likely to either come to nothing or involve hours of tedious and laborious leg-work to nail a petty criminal, whose main crime was to have upset someone at the chief constable's local Masonic lodge.

Hewitt looked at his watch. 'Damn,' he said, 'I was planning to take you around the station myself. I didn't realise the time. I need to make a call to the chief constable. Would you mind terribly if I got Angela to escort you down to your office, and do the necessary?'

'Not at all,' replied Steve. 'That's absolutely fine with me'.

It transpired that Angela was Hewitt's secretary and the lady who had brought them tea. She also proved to be an excellent guide. During the rest of the morning Steve was shown around the station. Angela left Steve with Alan Pearson, the only other CID inspector on duty, with whom he spent a good half hour. Pearson was a well-built man in his late forties. He had a large round head, which sat on top of a thick strong neck. Steve instantly took a liking to Pearson. He was amused by his humorous tales of some of the other officers at the station. He particularly liked the stories about 'Huge-Tit', which was the station's pet name for the chief inspector.

After a hearty albeit not very exciting lunch in the canteen, Steve decided that he would take a stroll for 20 minutes and then return to have a one-to-one with his team.

First of all he met with Sergeant Marc Watson. Watson was

a local man born and raised in Lancashire and coincidently, like Steve, the son of an ex-bobby. He was slightly built and in his late thirties. He had been in the force since leaving school at the age of 18, was married, had two children and lived within walking distance of the station. During the meeting Watson explained to Steve that he was currently working on a number of cases, none of which were more serious than petty theft and minor break-ins.

The second officer that Steve met was a young DC called Lucy Clark. Although she had only been in CID for 18 months, she demonstrated all the attributes of a real high-flyer. She was a graduate with a degree in sociology. Despite being only in her early twenties she seemed very mature and was quite clearly interested in the humanitarian side of the job. She was a Geordie with pronounced accent.

'What cases are you working on at the moment?' asked Steve.

'I've been helping Sergeant Watson over the last six months, sir,' she responded.

'So you've not had any cases of your own?'

Lucy looked surprised. 'Chief Inspector Hewitt has a policy with new DCs. We can only work on our own after we have completed our first two years. I've got another six months to go.'

'So there's no juicy cases at the moment?' Steve continued, in a feeble attempt to relax the young officer who was clearly a little uneasy in his presence.

'How do you mean?' asked Lucy, who was surprised by her new inspector's choice of words.

'You know, murders, bank robberies, that sort of thing.'

'No, sorry sir,' replied Lucy. 'Although I thought we had a case of murder a couple of months ago.'

'What do you mean? In my experience it's usually easy to spot whether it's a murder or not. What were the circumstances?'

18

'Well it was a middle-aged woman. She was found down a quiet country lane in one of the local villages. Sergeant Watson and I felt sure that she had been plied with drink and tablets. But we found no real evidence to prove anything amiss, and the coroner recorded an open verdict and the case was closed.'

'But an open verdict means exactly that,' said Steve. ' The case is still open.'

'Yes, but in this case the chief told us that we had no evidence and we were instructed to close the case.'

'And do you and Watson think you should just give up like that?' said Steve sternly.

'Well I did want to pursue our investigation but I was instructed not to,' she said with surprise. 'And we didn't have any hard evidence.'

'So why did you think it was a murder in the first place?'

'Well it may be nothing,' said Lucy, 'but she was found smartly dressed in a quiet lane. She had died of an overdose of sleeping tablets washed down with vodka.'

'And?' prompted Steve, who was starting to get interested.

'Well, if I was going to kill myself I'm not sure I'd get myself all dressed up and then do it in a quiet lane,' said Lucy. 'And no woman I know would ever wear shoes like that with such a smart outfit.'

'What do you mean?'

'Well they looked more like the sort of shoes she would wear in the garden rather than with the outfit she had on.'

'Where did you say all this took place?'

'I didn't,' replied Lucy, who by now was becoming more at ease with her new boss. 'But it happened in Moulton Bank.'

Steve couldn't believe his ears. A murder in Moulton Bank had been the last thing he would have expected. 'Before you leave tonight, get me the case notes. I'd like to have a look at them if you don't mind.'

*　*　*　*

The third member of the team that Steve met that afternoon was DC Paul Cooper. He was the most experienced of the bunch having served for 15 years in uniform before transferring to plain clothes. Cooper was a massive man standing well over six feet tall with wide shoulders that suggested to Steve that he could have once been a handy centre half or maybe a second-row forward. He had a crooked nose that had clearly been involved in more than one violent altercation and although he was actually not much older than Steve, his somewhat discontented face gave the impression that he was at least 10 years older than his new boss. Cooper was not a natural conversationalist and Steve found it much more difficult to strike up a rapport with him than with either of the other two officers he had met that afternoon. In fact, compared to Marc Watson and Lucy Clark, Paul Cooper seemed quite dull and ordinary. Nevertheless, at the end of their first meeting Steve had correctly concluded that Cooper would prove to be a solid, honest and reliable officer.

Just before Steve left for home, Lucy Clark came into his office and handed him the case notes relating to the death of Sarah McGuire. Of the three officers he had met that afternoon, she was definitely the one that Steve warmed to the most. Without reading more than the cover, Steve placed the file in his desk drawer.

Chapter 4

Robin Mayhew's drunken antics were legendary within a 20-mile radius of Moulton Bank. In the past 20 years he had been barred from most of the public houses in that region of east Lancashire. As a teenager he was a lively and popular figure, good at sport and in many ways a role model for the majority of the youngsters in the village. In his mid-teens he discovered the delights of cigarettes, girls and beer, and with the company of a select band of soulmates, he embraced wholeheartedly the 'laddish' way of life. At first this did nothing other than enhance his position with his peers and their parents, who looked upon this development as a temporary phase. However, over time his drinking partners either moved away or simply married and modified their behaviour, and as Robin's band of friends slowly dwindled, so too did the attitude of most of the village towards his adventures.

Apart from a brief dalliance with marriage, which lasted no more than 10 months, Robin had long since lost his appeal to the opposite sex. When his wife Debra had finally had enough and left, he used her departure as yet another excuse to drink even more. It's not easy to define the exact moment when Robin changed from a local hero to the village drunk, but by the time he reached his mid-thirties he had certainly completed his journey. Now that very same behaviour which had once been a source of great interest and amusement to the villagers was clearly viewed with embarrassment and irritation, and the once so popular Robin was at best now ignored, and by some treated with utter disdain. The only true exception to this was his old friend, the landlord of The Railway Tavern.

During licensing hours Robin could normally be found perched on his stool in the corner of the tap room in The Railway Tavern. On the day that Steve and Penny decided to go for a quiet lunchtime drink, Robin was in his usual place.
It had become almost like a ritual for Steve to partake in a quiet alcoholic beverage on Saturday lunchtime. In the 18 years since they had been married he must have only missed a handful of quiet Saturday liquid lunchtimes. Now that Jemma was old enough to be left by herself to look after her siblings, Penny was occasionally willing to be persuaded to accompany her husband. That particular Saturday was one such occasion.

There was a choice of only two public houses in the village, the Oddfellows Arms, which was a popular haunt of the residents of The Common, and The Railway Tavern, which was little more than two minutes' walk from their house. Steve and Penny selected The Railway Tavern.

At first the Carmichaels entered the lounge. Having waited for several minutes alone and without any sign of a barman to take their orders, they decided to move downmarket and try their luck in the tap room next door. With the exception of Robin, a noisy group of teenagers playing pool and two elderly farmers sipping brown ale in the opposite corner, customers were sparse. Unlike the lounge at least this part of the pub could boast the luxury of a barmaid. Steve was used to more vibrant surroundings, and under normal circumstances he would have suggested that they retreat to somewhere a little more lively. However, on this occasion his wife needed to visit the pub's washroom, and the speed at which the previously under-employed barmaid had shouted, 'What can I get for you both today?' made it difficult for Steve to avoid at least a brief introduction to the local beer.

'Try the dark mild, Steve,' Penny suggested. 'And mine's a half of lager.' With that she headed for the ladies, leaving Steve to confirm the selection to the attentive young barmaid, who wore a tight pale shirt. As he waited his eyes became transfixed by the barmaid's belly-button jewellery, which consisted of a large silver pin with three or four glittery tentacles, which gently swayed to and fro as she pulled the pump to release his pint. Steve stared at her navel for several seconds before realising what he was doing. The barmaid smiled when she realised Steve was paying such close attention to her. She was used to her customers enjoying her figure so she thought nothing of Steve's attention. Steve was worried that the young woman might perceive him as a lecherous old man, so he quickly moved his eyes upwards to her face. To his relief her features showed no sign of rebuke. She simply smiled again and rested two overflowing glasses on the bar in front of him. Steve returned her smile, paid for the drinks and then scoured the room for a suitable resting place. It was at this point that the red-faced man at the end of the bar seized his opportunity to enter into conversation with the new arrival.

'Are you new in the village?' he muttered.

'Yes,' Steve replied. 'We moved in last weekend.'

'I've lived in the village all my life, worst luck,' replied the drunk.

At this point Robin's elbow slipped, and his large round head with its mass of greased back hair came tumbling down into the fag-ends which occupied the enormous ashtray in front of him. His beer glass fell over, his weight then shifted to one side, and within a couple of seconds he was sprawled on the floor at Steve's feet.

'You stupid old sod!' shouted the barmaid unsympathetically. 'That's the second time this week you've fallen off that bloody stool.'

At first the drunk made no attempt to rise. Steve was about to bend down to assist his new acquaintance when Penny returned.

'Good heavens,' she exclaimed. 'What's happened here?'

'Don't worry yourself,' retorted the barmaid. 'It's only Robin making an arse of himself as usual.'

'Is he all right?' asked Penny, bending down to try and look Robin in the eye.

'Of course I'm not fuckin' all right!' shouted Robin. 'I'm going to sue the bastard brewery about those soddin' stools. I could have broken me bleedin' neck.' As he lifted his head, blood poured from above his hairline and down into his already bloodshot eyes.

'I think we had better call for an ambulance,' Penny suggested. 'This cut looks nasty.'

'You're right,' agreed the barmaid. 'That does look bad.'

It took about 20 minutes before the ambulance finally transported its passenger out of the car park of The Railway Tavern. Once it had departed, Steve and Penny resumed their position at the bar where the barmaid introduced herself as Katie Robertson, the landlord's daughter.

'You're Robbie's daughter,' exclaimed Penny. 'I went to school with your father, I should have known he would end up owning a pub.'

'Well, he's the landlord. The brewery actually own the place,' responded Katie in a matter of fact way. 'He'll be back soon. Why don't you both hang on? I'm sure he'd be pleased to see you again.'

'Sounds good to me,' said Steve as he emptied his glass. 'And we'll have another of the same while we wait.'

When Katie placed the repeat order on the bar, Steve was surprised to find the charge for this round was only £3.80. 'But you charged me £4.10 last time,' he remarked.

'Ah, but I didn't know that your wife was a friend of my dad's before did I?' she replied. Katie's eyes shone as she spoke and her cheeks rose gently to form two pink mounds either side of her broad grin.

Robbie Robertson entered the bar about 15 minutes later. He was a big man with broad shoulders and a distinctive round belly which hung over his tightly-belted jeans. 'Hi darling. Is everything OK?' he said to his daughter.

'Yeah, no probs,' responded Katie. 'Well, except for Robin falling off his stool and being taken to hospital.'

'Is he OK?' asked her father with genuine concern.

'Yeah, I think so. Just a bad cut to his head. Nothing too serious.' At that point the landlord of The Railway Tavern picked up a pint glass and started to pull himself a pint. 'Oh, I almost forgot,' Katie said, moving her head in the direction of Steve and Penny. 'That lady says she's an old friend of yours.'

Robbie frowned as he looked over towards the woman at the end of the bar. Then as he realised it was Penny, his face cracked open with a broad engaging smile. 'Good God,' he shouted. 'Penny Lathom!'

'Penny Carmichael now,' responded Penny. 'How are you Robbie?'

'It must be twenty years since I last saw you,' Robbie continued.

'Twenty-three years to be precise,' said Penny.

'So what have you been up to and what are you doing back here after all these years?' he asked.

'I've been living in London. I'm married to Steve. We have three children and we moved back here a week ago. I think that's a quick summary of the last twenty-three years,' she said with a smile.

'And you're in my pub and your glasses are empty,' said Robbie with a grin. 'Katie! Can you get some refills over here on the house.'

Steve couldn't help feeling a little superfluous to the conversation. But he didn't mind. His wife seemed genuinely excited to see her old friend.

'Oh I'm sorry,' Penny said, clasping Steve's arm. 'I haven't introduced you both. Robbie this is Steve, my husband. Steve this is Donald Robertson, Robbie to his friends.'

'Pleased to meet you Robbie,' Steve said as he shook his hand.

'Likewise,' replied Robbie.

During the next 30 minutes Penny and Robbie were engrossed in an exchange of news and reminiscences. Penny learnt that Robbie had married David Turner's sister Mary, that they had one child, Katie, and that Mary had died two years earlier after a long battle against cancer. Robbie learnt that having moved south with her parents, Penny had graduated from Hatfield polytechnic with a degree in computing, had married a policeman, worked for a merchant bank in the City until the birth of their first child and had now moved back to Moulton Bank as a result of Steve taking up a new position with the Lancashire force. He was astounded when Penny told him that her parents had retired to Spain and were enjoying a second childhood 20 miles west of Alicante.

'I seem to remember that your father was always critical of anything foreign,' Robbie said with his now familiar broad smile. 'Didn't he give you a right lecture when you asked him if you could come with us to France when we were kids?'

'I think that was probably a reflection of his mistrust of you, Clive Penman and Sarah Mulholland rather than his opinion of France,' Penny responded.

At the mention of Sarah's name Robbie's expression changed. 'Do you know about Sarah?' he asked.

'No,' replied Penny. 'What's there to know?'

'Oh it's a real tragedy I'm afraid. She married that Ken McGuire. I never understood why. The no good bastard.' Robbie took a deep breath. 'Well she was never happy and about two months ago she died. Suicide they say but I'm not so sure.'

'Oh Robbie, I didn't know,' Penny said with tears welling up in her eyes. 'I'm so sorry Robbie. I know how … er, how close you both were.'

At the mention of the death of Sarah McGuire, Steve had stopped drinking and was now listening intently. He had not discussed with Penny the conversation that he had had with Lucy, and her suspicion about Sarah McGuire's death. It had never occurred to him that his wife would have known the dead woman. Steve looked Robbie straight in the eye and asked, 'Do you think Sarah's husband was responsible for her death?'

'Yes,' Robbie said with real venom. 'Oh yes, he was responsible. He didn't kill her but he was responsible.'

Steve was just about to continue with his questions when a short, slightly built man located himself beside Penny. At first she didn't take any notice of their new companion, but slowly their eyes met and Penny calmly said to the stranger, 'Hello Clive, I wondered when I'd finally bump into you.'

'Hello Penny, how are you?' he replied in a broad Lancashire accent.

Forgetting the conversation which had gone before and without thinking Penny flung her arms around the shoulders of Clive Penman and gave him the sort of hug that Steve had only ever seen her give to either him, her parents or the kids. Penny realised very quickly that the manner of her greeting had created a degree of discomfort for Steve. In an attempt to balance out this act she released her grip on the new arrival and quite deliberately linked her arm with her husband's. 'Steve,' she said, 'I'd like to introduce you to a dear old friend of mine. This is Clive Penman.'

'You're the school caretaker aren't you?' asked Steve. 'I remember seeing your name on the board outside the school.'

'He's got about a dozen jobs, our Clive has,' said Robbie. 'Caretaker, taxi driver, builder, plumber. You name it, he does it.' Clive offered a dirty, nail-bitten hand to Steve, which

Steve shook with a slightly forced smile. 'Clive's been helping me build a wall out the back,' continued Robbie.

'And it's thirsty work so I thought I'd pop in for a quick half,' Clive replied.

'Is this one on the house as well?' asked Katie.

'It bloody well isn't,' snapped her father. 'He's not building the wall for nothing, so he can pay for his ale like everyone else.'

' Your usual?' asked Katie.

'Yes, but only a half,' he replied. 'I need to get back before his lordship starts moaning about my lack of progress.'

'Actually, you might be able to do me a favour,' said Steve.

'What's that?' replied Clive as he collected his half pint from Katie.

'We could do with some work doing on our new house. Would you be interested?'

'Yes, of course. I'd be happy to give you a quote,' said Clive. 'Cash in hand mind. I'd rather those buggers in the tax office didn't get their hands on any of it.'

Robbie roared with laughter, Clive looked confused and before Steve or Penny had a chance to say anything, Katie whispered something in Clive's ear that made his cheeks blush bright scarlet. 'Of course, I'd have to declare any work I did for you inspector,' he said jokingly.

'Well, when can you come round?' asked Penny.

'How about tomorrow afternoon?' replied Clive. 'Say three o'clock?'

'That's great,' said Steve. 'We live …' Steve was about to give the builder their address when he was interrupted.

'I know where you live,' said Clive. 'I'll see you tomorrow then.' With that he downed the last dregs at the bottom of his glass, slapped Robbie on the back and headed out of the door.

'Now he hasn't changed much since we were kids,' said Robbie. 'Most everything else has here, but Clive's pretty much the same.' Penny wasn't sure that she agreed, but she said nothing.

*   *   *   *

Sunday morning in the Carmichael household was always a stressful time. Steve had long since stopped trying to fathom out why, from Monday to Friday, it was possible for him to get up, get ready for work and be at his desk by 8:30 and for the children to be at school for 9:00, but when they had to be in church for a 9:30 service they were always in a rush. This Sunday was no exception. 'For heavens sake Jemma!' he bellowed. 'Will you get out of that bathroom. It's ten past, we'll be late if you don't get yourself shifted.'

The Sunday morning visit to church was a habit observed by Steve as diligently as the Saturday lunchtime drink. The Carmichaels had excused themselves from church the previous week on the grounds of the chaos after the move. This only served to make Steve more stressed than normal, a fact that had not gone unnoticed by the rest of the family.

'Do we have to follow this ridiculous charade?' muttered Jemma when she eventually emerged from her preening. 'There's only you and Natalie that believe in God. It's a chore for the rest of us.'

'That's not true,' countered Steve angrily. 'Your mum and I both think that it's right for all of us to go to church.'

Penny tried hard to look as though she supported her husband's views. A difficult task that she didn't quite pull off.

By the time the family reached the church it was 9:30. Steve slammed the car into the last empty space in the car park, and the Carmichael tribe walked briskly up the narrow path to the church door. Fortunately for them they managed to find a large vacant pew at the back. They had all only just managed to be seated when the service began.

Steve had found religion fairly late in life. Although his

mother had always believed in God, he had only started to form an active relationship with the Almighty when he was advised that his new-born baby daughter, Jemma, had a condition that was potentially life-threatening. In spite of Penny's persistent attempts to diplomatically argue that maybe it had been the skill of the surgeon rather than the hand of God that had ensured Jemma survived, Steve continued to insist that the family made this one sacrifice every week. The irony of the fact that Jemma was the main source of complaints about having to go to church every Sunday had not been lost on Penny, who found the whole situation mildly amusing.

The church was a typical rural English stone building, with fine stained-glass windows. From the outside it looked cold and uninviting, however inside it was surprisingly welcoming. Steve's first impressions were very favourable. He was particularly impressed by the fact that despite having the capacity to hold at least 200–300 people the church seemed quite full. He was not used to such congregations in Watford.

During the first hymn, Steve noticed a few faces in the congregation he recognised. The headmaster, David Turner was there with an elderly lady in her late sixties or early seventies. On the other side of him was Adrian Hope, the estate agent who had sold them the house. Steve guessed that the lady to Hope's right and the two small girls in matching purple dresses were his wife and children. Penny nudged her husband gently and nodded in the direction of the old lady. 'That's David's mum, on his left, and on his right is Adrian Hope. And I assume that must be his wife and children next to him.'

'So he can't be gay, Dad,' piped up Robbie, who had overheard his father and mother debating the sexual orientation of the estate agent during their first visit to their new house a few months earlier.

'Shh', said Penny, realising that the people in the pew in

front of them had probably overheard her son's comment.

'Who are the people the other side of Dave Turner?' asked Steve.

'The parents of one of your team,' replied Penny. 'Mr and Mrs Watson.'

'Really,' said Steve. 'He used to be the local bobby, didn't he?'

'Yes he was, but he must be well retired by now,' said Penny. 'He was getting on a bit when I was a teenager. They must be well into their seventies, maybe even older.'

At that point the hymn finished and Steve had to stop his questioning, as save the occasional cough, sniffle or put-on throat clearing, there was now no noise to block out his whispers. The village vicar, a man in his sixties, rose and walked slowly towards the open-winged golden eagle which stood at the top of six small steps, and over which lay a huge black bible.

'What's the vicar's name mum?' asked Jemma.

'He's called the Reverend Pugh,' answered her mother in a whisper.

'Did you hear that Natalie?' giggled her elder sister. 'The vicar's called Pugh.' Natalie didn't get the joke, but laughed anyway, much to the annoyance of the other occupants of the pew.

The congregation spent the next 10 minutes transfixed by the vicar's sermon, which was mainly aimed at extolling the virtues of the family and the importance of parental guidance through modern life's hazards. Then followed a reading from St Mark, delivered with confidence by Miss Linda Cartwright, an old classmate of Penny's, and the village postmistress. The second hymn of the service was 'The Lord is my Shepherd', during which the collection plates were passed down each pew by the ushers, one of which was Clive Penman.

'Good heavens,' said Penny when she recognised her old friend. 'I had no idea that Clive was an usher. He had less religion than me when we were young.'

When Clive saw the Carmichaels he also seemed surprised, but he smiled warmly at Penny, nodded a greeting at Steve, and then continued to the next row.

'Who else do you recognise?' asked Steve, when he felt that the singing was loud enough to drown his question.

'Let me see,' said Penny. 'Well I think I recognise the lady with Mr Hope. If I'm not mistaken that's Lisa McGuire. She's the daughter of Trevor McGuire, the ex-Bolton footballer turned petfood multi-millionaire. She's the sister of Ken McGuire, who Robbie was on about yesterday in the pub. I'm not sure about the others. It's difficult to make them out in this light.'

After the hymn had finished the congregation, like synchronised swimmers, unhitched their hassocks from their hooks, knelt in unison and bowed their heads while the vicar said a short prayer. This was followed by a number of public announcements including a car boot sale at the end of the month, a poetry recital planned at the school the following week, and the forthcoming exchange visit with the people of St Moulion, the village's twin from the Loire Valley. Then with great enthusiasm Reverend Pugh asked the gathering to raise the roof with their final hymn, and the whole congregation dutifully obeyed.

The service ended just under an hour and a half after it had started with a rousing rendition of 'He Who Would Valiant Be', which was a great favourite of Steve's.

When it was over the Carmichaels were one of the first to reach the exit. In front of them were the Turners and the Watsons. Having exchanged the customary one-minute pleasantries with both families, the Reverend Pugh then fixed his gaze upon Penny and her pursuing family. 'Good morning Penny, my dear. I'm so pleased you came this morning. I'd hoped that you would.'

'Thank you Mr Pugh,' she replied. 'I'm surprised that you recognised me after all these years.'

'I'd heard you were back. It's the main source of conversation in the village you know. And this must be your husband.'

'Pleased to meet you Reverend Pugh. I did so enjoy the service,' said Steve as he shook the vicar by the hand.

'Thank you Inspector Carmichael,' he replied. 'You must be a remarkable man.'

'How do you mean?' asked Steve, who was amazed not only by the question but also by the vicar's knowledge of his name and rank in the force.

'Why, to get Penny to come to church,' he replied with a knowing smile. 'As I recall Penny was never what you would call a regular with us. Although I'm sure her dear mother and father did their level best to lure her through this door. Your achievement is worth praise indeed inspector.'

'Oh please,' muttered Jemma under her breath to her brother.

'I can see your daughter takes after you in both looks and manner,' commented the vicar, much to the embarrassment of both Penny and her eldest child. Realising that he had spent his allotted time with the Carmichaels, the Reverend Pugh then turned his attention to the couple behind them.

Once they were safely belted in the car Penny spun round to address the children. And by the time the car had left the church all three knew that their various words and deeds over the past 90 minutes had not gone unnoticed by their now very exasperated mother. In an attempt to regain some normality Steve said cheerily, 'He seems a good sort of bloke.'

'Oh yes,' replied his wife. 'His faith is, to use one of his favourite verbs, remarkable.'

'I think that you mean adjective, don't you mum?' commented Robbie.

'Whatever I mean, he's a remarkable man. And that's for sure,' replied Penny.

Steve's instinct told him that there was more Penny knew about the vicar than she wished to share at that moment. He moved the conversation to new pastures and would revisit the subject with Penny when she was in a better mood.

*　*　*　*

Clive Penman arrived at the house at exactly three o'clock. Penny answered the door and ushered him into the hall and then through to the kitchen.

'Steve won't be a minute. He's in the attic playing with his new PC I think,' she said as she filled the kettle. 'Tea or coffee?'

'Coffee would be nice,' replied Clive as he looked around the room for an empty chair to sit.

'We're still in a bit of a mess, I'm afraid,' Penny said clearing a pile of unironed clothes from a chair. 'I don't know when we'll be straight. Sit down here.'

Clive had just sat down when Steve appeared.

'Hello Clive, how are you?'

Clive rose quickly from his chair. 'I'm fine, Mr Carmichael,' he answered.

'Please, call me Steve.'

'I was surprised to see you at church this morning Penny,' Clive said as he again descended into his chair.

'We never miss a Sunday do we?' interrupted Steve before his wife had a chance to reply.

'Well, only occasionally,' said Penny.

'That vicar's quite a character,' continued Steve. 'Being an usher you must know him better than most.'

'I suppose I do,' answered Clive 'He's a good man and an inspiration to us all. The whole village respects Reverend Pugh.'

'Inspiration, that's an unusual way to describe anyone,' Steve said. 'What makes him so inspirational?'

34

'Well he's done so much for so many of us. It's difficult to know where to start. And given the problems he's had over the years it's a miracle that he's managed to keep going.' As he spoke Clive's eyes stared down to the floor and his fingers nervously fidgeted with the sugar bowl which Penny had placed in front of him.

'What problems do you mean?' asked Steve, who was now well and truly engrossed in the Moulton Bank cleric.

'Well first there was the tragic death of his little girl. Then his wife departed,' said Clive. 'How he's coped with all that I just don't know.'

'Do you take milk in your coffee Clive?' asked Penny, trying hard to break up what was now quite clearly becoming another of Steve's famous interrogations.

'Milk and two sugars, please,' replied Clive.

'We met David Turner last week at the school,' Penny said. 'Who would have thought he would follow in his dad's footsteps and be head?'

'I didn't know that,' said Steve. 'Was his father the head-master when you were both there?'

'Yes, Mr Turner was the head,' replied Penny.

'He was a great head too,' said Clive. 'His death was a shock to the whole village, and is still a mystery to me. I think David went into teaching as a sign of respect to his father. And although Mr Turner is a difficult act to follow David's a good head and very well respected himself.'

Then came the question that Penny was dreading but fully expecting.

'So how did he die?' asked Steve.

'Oh, he died years ago,' replied Penny, who by now was desperate to bring the conversation to an end.

'It was on Sunday the thirteenth of June 1976,' said Clive. The precision of his recollection of the date took both Steve and Penny by surprise.

There then followed a brief moment of silence until Penny

35

said, 'I hadn't thought of Arthur Turner in years. Not until last Saturday when I saw David at the school.'

'Really?' said Clive with genuine surprise. 'There's hardly a day goes by that I don't think about him and wonder why he took his own life like that. You got away from here. It's different for those of us who stayed.' Penny could not help feeling that Clive's last remark was meant as a criticism.

'Another inspirational character then,' said Steve. 'Moulton Bank seems to have been blessed with its fair share of characters.' Then, turning to face Penny, he whispered, 'And if you don't mind me saying so, its fair share of tragic demises.'

The silence that followed made it obvious to Steve that Clive had heard what he had said and that both he and Penny *did* mind him saying. However, neither of them commented. Realising that he had perhaps ventured too far along the current line of questioning Steve tried to change the subject. 'So how long have you been an usher?' he asked.

'For about ten years,' replied Clive without any attempt to elaborate.

'You must find it rewarding to do it for so long?' Steve asked.

'Yes, I suppose I do,' said Clive. Then after a brief pause he continued, 'I find it very rewarding and I find the reverend a great source of strength.'

'A bit like Arthur Turner was when you were children,' Steve said as his nose for intrigue got the better of his sense of propriety.

'Yes, I suppose that you could say that the reverend is now the pillar of society in Moulton Bank. Just as Mr Turner was when we were kids before he ... er, his death.'

Clive was now clearly entering emotional territory. His voice trembled as he mentioned the reverend and Mr Turner in the same sentence. At this point Penny decided that Steve's interest was becoming too intrusive. 'Why don't you both go into the morning room and you can show Clive what we'd like him to do for us,' she suggested.

'Yes,' said Steve, realising for second time that day that his questioning had hit a nerve with his wife. 'Let's go through. Bring your coffee with you Clive.'

The two men wandered into the next room to discuss the details of the work Steve had in mind. At first Penny remained in the kitchen, listening to their conversation. Once she felt sure that Steve was confining his attention to the alterations she slipped out of the back door and into the garden to steal a quiet moment alone.

It took less than 10 minutes for the two men to complete their business. Steve showed the builder out of the front door and joined his wife in the garden.

'All done?' asked Penny, as he sat next to her on the large garden seat.

'Yes, we've agreed on a price and he thinks he should be able to get started on Tuesday,' Steve replied. 'If I say so myself, I'm more than pleased with the deal. It's less than half of what we'd have had to pay if we were still in Bushey.'

'Did you have to be so …' Penny struggled to find the right words.

'So what?' asked Steve.

'So bloody nosy!' said Penny, who by now was getting very agitated. 'And that remark about tragic deaths. That was totally insensitive.'

'I was just showing an interest,' said Steve.

'Well, please be a bit more tactful in future. Remember these are my friends and our neighbours. They aren't suspects,' continued Penny.

'I consider myself scolded,' said Steve with his hands in the air in mock surrender.

'You stupid sod,' said Penny, who by now couldn't maintain her attempt to keep a straight face. 'You've been questioning suspects for so long, you've started doing it in your spare time. You'll be doing it in your sleep next.'

'How do you know I don't already?' said Steve with a grin.

Having made her point, Penny leaned back on the bench and took another long look at her beloved garden. 'Do you think we'll be happy here Steve?' she asked.

'You know I think we will,' Steve replied as he gently took hold of her hand.

Chapter 5

If there was one thing that made Steve angry it was bad time-keeping. So when Tuesday came and went without sight nor sound of Clive Penman, he was less than impressed. It was not until the Friday of that week that Steve finally managed to speak to Clive. Despite trying several times to contact him on his home telephone and leaving messages with Robbie Robertson, it was by chance that he caught him when he saw him outside the school on his way home from the station. 'He has promised faithfully to be here *next* Monday,' Steve told Penny that evening. 'I hope for his sake he doesn't let us down again,' thought Penny, although she would have laid money on her husband being disappointed once more.

In those first days in Moulton Bank, while Steve was at work, the rest of the family tried to absorb themselves into their new surroundings. Penny made an effort to make conversation with the neighbours and to reacquaint herself with many of the people she had been close to as a child. As for the children, they all seemed to settle in fairly well. Jemma started spending time with a couple of girls called Nicola and Amy, who lived a few doors down the road. With the help of her new friends it had taken Jemma very little time to be introduced to other teenagers. She was an attractive girl with a bright smile and a good figure. Accordingly she quickly came to the notice of the local Romeos, particularly a boy called Jason, who had his own car and an interesting wispy goatee.

It had only taken Robbie about an hour on his first day to locate a game of football with some of the local lads, and from this he had forged a strong relationship with a boy called Andy.

Natalie had taken a little longer than the others to find a friend. However, with a little help from a neighbour who Penny got talking to, she was introduced to another girl of her age called Charlotte. Natalie was particularly pleased to meet Charlotte, especially when she discovered that Charlotte's mother ran the local riding school. For Natalie, being with horses was just about as close to heaven as you could get.

*　*　*　*

Monday 15 August started off badly for Steve. He and Penny had spent most of the prior evening clearing out their furniture from the back room. They had not managed to eat until nine and with no school the next day the children had gone to bed much later than usual. Either the alarm had not gone off, or more likely Steve had turned it off and gone back to sleep. Either way it was already 7:45 a.m. when Penny glanced at the clock. 'What time are you due in today Steve?' she mumbled from beneath the covers.

'Jesus Christ!' he shouted as he leaped out of the bed.

Normally Steve was very organised in the morning. In fact he considered himself a morning person, and often commented on the fact that he was always able to get out of bed, shower, shave and have a hearty breakfast before leaving home. This particular day was an exception. ' Shirt, shirt,' he moaned, as he rifled through his side of the wardrobe. 'I haven't got a clean shirt.

'It's hanging up in the lounge,' said a half asleep voice front the far side of the bed.

'What's it doing there?' snapped Steve.

40

'You must have forgotten to bring it up last night,' was the polite yet firm reply.

'Jesus Christ,' said Steve, for a second time, as he departed the bedroom door in his underpants and socks. There was to be no long shower or hearty breakfast for Inspector Carmichael that morning.

Steve arrived at the station at a little after 8:45. He had broken his personal best by a good five minutes to achieve that feat. However, he was not in the mood for congratulating himself on his achievement. He hated being late. The thought of his team sniggering at him as he arrived made him angry, particularly Marc Watson, who he had already spoken to about his own timekeeping. He slammed the car into its space, grabbed his briefcase and strode in at a pace even Hewitt would have had problems matching.

'Good morning sir,' was his greeting from Sergeant Wilkinson behind the front desk. 'The chief asked me to tell you to pop by his office when you arrived.'

'What?' replied the angry inspector. 'I'm ten minutes late and the chief's on my case. What sort of station is this?'

'I don't think it's to do with that,' said Wilkinson. 'There's been a report of an incident. I think that's why the chief wants you.'

'Incident? What sort of incident?'

'A suspicious death in Moulton Bank this morning.'

'Moulton Bank? I've just come from there. Did nobody have the sense to call me on my mobile?' Steve did not wait for an answer, which was a good job as he would have only learned that Lucy had been trying to reach him since 8:20 when the call came in. She had phoned his home, but he had already left and his mobile was switched off.

Steve was halfway down the corridor when he bumped into Lucy. 'What's going on Lucy?'

'It's a body, sir. They've found a woman's body in Wood

41

Lane in Moulton Bank. I tried to get hold of you, but your mobile's off.'

'Damn,' muttered Steve. 'I must have left it on the table at home.'

'The local bobby's on the scene,' Lucy continued. 'And Cooper's on his way too.'

'Where's Sergeant Watson?'

Lucy shrugged her shoulders. 'We couldn't raise him.'

'Okay, let's get down there right away,' said Steve. 'Here's my car keys, you drive. And I'll have your mobile.'

'I think Mr Hewitt wanted a word with you first,' replied Lucy.

'That's why we're taking my car and you're lending me your mobile,' was his only comment.

Within a couple of minutes the two officers sped off back in the direction of Moulton Bank. However, not before Steve had spoken to Wilkinson and told him that if Hewitt asked, he had not seen him that morning and when Watson arrived he was to call him immediately on Lucy Clark's mobile.

'Morning sir, Inspector Carmichael speaking,' said Steve. 'I just thought I'd better let you know that there has been an incident in Moulton Bank and that Lucy and I are on our way. Sorry sir, I didn't get the message. I haven't been in the office this morning. Lucy met me as I arrived and we left straight away. I'll speak to you when I get back, we'll be there in about ten minutes. Right you are sir, goodbye.' Steve pressed end on the mobile and smiled at the driver. 'Did you get that Lucy? You met me in the car park.'

'Yes sir,' replied the young DC.

They arrived at the crime scene at approximately 9:25 a.m. Steve had been impressed by the driving of his young companion, but could not help thinking that if he had been driving they would have been there five minutes sooner. The first thing that struck him was that Watson was already there. 'I thought you said you couldn't get hold of him?'

'I couldn't,' replied Lucy. 'I guess Cooper must have raised him when he was driving over.' Lucy stopped the car and the two officers got out.

At the scene were Cooper, Watson, a policeman in uniform who Steve assumed was the local bobby, a middle-aged man with a small dog, and two others. 'Morning sir,' said Watson. Steve didn't reply. He was too interested in having a look at the body and strode quickly past Watson.

Once he was out of sight, Watson turned to Lucy. 'What kept you Bamber? Did you stop off with the boss to help further your career?' Lucy ignored him and walked over to join Steve who was already crouching by the body. The dead woman was aged between 40 and 50, had short, cropped black hair and was smartly dressed in a dark blue dress.

'Do we know who she is?' asked Lucy.

'Her name's Linda Cartwright. She's a local woman,' replied Cooper.

'She's the village postmistress,' added Steve.

Cooper and Lucy exchanged a surprised glance. 'You know the woman, sir?, asked Cooper.

'I wouldn't go that far,' replied Steve. 'I know her because she attends our local church.'

At this point Watson joined his colleagues. 'The SOCOs would like to know if they can get started, sir?' he asked.

Up to that moment Steve had paid little attention to the two men in white trousers and coats. 'That's fine, but I don't want them to move the body until they've photographed the entire area. By the way, how did you get here?' Steve asked Watson.

'I was at my parent's house in the village when I picked up the news on my radio. They only live around the corner so I was here about 40 minutes ago.' replied Watson

'Well in future I want you to ensure that you let the station know where you are. They've been trying to raise you. I expect all my team's whereabouts during duty hours to be known at the station. Do you understand?'

'Yes sir,' replied Watson. 'Understood.' Lucy smiled to herself. She was pleased that her cocky colleague had been taken down a peg or two, even though the hypocrisy of Carmichael's comments was not lost on the young DC.

'OK, do any of you have any observations you would like to share?' Steve asked his three colleagues.

Cooper was the first to break the silence. 'I would only say that she doesn't appear to have put up much of a struggle. Her clothes are hardly creased and her hair looks as though she's just combed it.'

'Or at least it's *been* combed,' said Lucy.

'What do you mean?' asked Watson. 'She was murdered and then the murderer combed her hair for her?'

'So you are all sure she *was* murdered?' Steve asked. 'I don't doubt you are all right,' he continued, 'but we should await the postmortem before we make that assumption. My observation, for what it's worth, is that our victim does not appear to be wearing any shoes. Given that this is not the sort of area that you would expect people to be going barefoot I suspect that she died elsewhere and was dumped here.'

'Either that or we have a murderer on our hands with a shoe fetish,' Watson whispered to Lucy.

'OK, I'm sure that you all know that the first twenty-four hours in a murder hunt are the most crucial,' said Steve. 'Cooper, I want you to organise a detailed search of the surrounding area. Lucy, I want you to do a house to house on all the houses from the road junction to here. I want to know who was in this morning and what if anything they saw or heard. We'll meet back at the station for debriefing at four-thirty this afternoon. OK?'

'Yes, sir,' replied Lucy. Cooper nodded and the two officers marched off.

'What about me?' asked Watson, who was a little put out at being seemingly without a proper assignment.

'You're coming with me to the post office,' was the reply.

'If the postmistress isn't there, who has been managing the shop, and why have they not reported her missing? We'll take your car.'

'Right you are sir,' replied Watson, feeling pleased that he seemed to have secured himself the plum job. As he drove down the road they passed Lucy Clark, who was just about to walk up the drive of the first house.

'Slow down a bit Watson,' ordered Steve. Watson eased his foot off the accelerator.

'Lucy!' shouted Steve through the window. 'You take my car back to the office, I'll go back with Watson. If you need some assistance ask Wilkinson to send down a couple of PCs.'

'I will sir,' replied Lucy.

With that Steve wound up the window and the car sped away. 'We need to get to my house first Marc,' announced Steve 'I need to pick up my mobile. I left it this morning.'

*　*　*　*

It was about this time that Katie at The Railway Tavern opened the door to her visitor. 'What happened last night?' she asked. 'We did say ten o'clock didn't we? Where were you?' When no answer was forthcoming she ushered her visitor in. 'I hope nobody saw you,' she moaned. Her visitor checked furtively around before entering the building.

*　*　*　*

Penny was surprised to see Steve walking through the door. 'What are you doing here?' she asked. 'I didn't hear your car in the drive. Did you get the message from the station? They rang just as you drove off this morning.'

'Yes, I got the message,' replied Steve. 'Look, I'd like you to sit down a second. I've got some unpleasant news I'm afraid.'

45

Penny looked shocked. 'What's wrong,' she said nervously. 'It's not your mum is it?'

'No,' said Steve. 'It's nothing to do with the family. There's been a suspicious death. Earlier today Linda Cartwright's body was found at the end of Wood Lane.'

'Oh my God,' said Penny, and covered her mouth with her hand. 'Was she murdered?'

Steve nodded. 'It looks that way.' There was then a moment of silence before Steve spoke again. 'Look, I've got Watson in the car outside so I can't hang around. Can you tell me if she has any living relatives?'

'She has a brother who's a fair bit older than her,' replied Penny. 'But he left home when we were kids. I think he went abroad. Her mum passed away some time ago. I think her father's still alive, although I'm not sure and I guess that if he is he would be well into his eighties by now.'

'Look,' said Steve, 'I've got to go, I'm not sure what time I'll be home. I'll call you later.' At that he picked up his mobile kissed his wife and turned to leave. 'I see that bloody mate of yours has let us down again.'

'Actually he rang a couple of hours ago to say that he wouldn't be here until after lunch as he had to help someone out this morning,' said Penny.

'When I've finished with him he'll be the one needing help,' muttered Steve as he shut the door behind him.

It took Steve and Marc only a couple of minutes to get to the post office. To their surprise the door was open, and inside it looked as though it was business as usual. However, that was nothing compared to the surprise that confronted Steve when he saw who was serving behind the counter.

At first David Turner did not notice the two police officers. He was too preoccupied attending to the queue that had formed in the post office and in trying to make sense of the requests that were being mumbled at him through the tiny low opening of the glass partition. Steve and Watson waited

46

quietly by the door. When the last customer departed, Watson walked up to the counter and held up his warrant card, a theatrical gesture which Steve did not find necessary, given that David Turner was well aware of who they were.

'Good morning gentlemen,' said Turner.

'Good morning Mr Turner,' replied Steve. 'I didn't realise that you had two jobs.'

Turner smiled. 'I'm just helping out while Linda's away. Is there a problem, inspector?'

'Can we come through?' Steve asked. 'We'd like to ask you a few questions.'

'Of course,' replied Turner, who by now was becoming more than a little agitated.

'Watson, can you close the shop door, please?' said Steve. Marc nodded and dutifully obliged. Turner unlocked the door to the counter and ushered the two officers into the back room.

David Turner still retained the looks and physique of a man ten years his junior. In fact, he was considered quite handsome by many of the young mothers who collected their children from the village school. Indeed, it was a surprise to many of them that he had yet to marry.

Turner turned to face his visitors. 'Look inspector, I'm only doing a friend a favour. I don't get paid for this. I'm not moonlighting or anything.'

'We are not here about that,' interrupted the smiling Watson.

'No we're here about Linda Cartwright,' said Steve.

'Well, as I said before she's away for the morning, but I think she'll be back soon,' replied Turner.

'Does Linda Cartwright live here alone?' Steve asked.

'Yes, her father died a couple of years ago,' replied Turner. 'She's never married, so I and a couple of others help out if she has to go out. Is she in trouble?'

Carmichael pointed towards a comfortable-looking green

47

sofa. 'Please sit down David,' he said in a quiet but firm manner. 'I'm afraid I have some bad news for you.'

* * * *

Once Steve had left the house Penny made herself a strong cup of coffee. The news of Linda Cartwright's death had been a terrible shock to her. Linda had never been what she would have called a close friend, nevertheless Penny had always thought kindly of her. In Penny's eyes Linda was basically a sad but thoroughly good person. She tried hard to recall some happy memories of the girl she was in the same class with for the best part of 10 years, but in truth she could not remember having much to do with Linda at school. With her chin cupped in her hands Penny became overwhelmed with a feeling of guilt as she realised that the only recollection that she had of the dead woman was of her unfortunate involvement in the tragic death of little Gillian Pugh.

There was a loud knock at the door. Hoping that it was Steve returning once more she rushed down the hallway. 'Oh it's you,' she exclaimed when she saw Clive Penman standing on her doormat, tools in hand.

'Better late than never,' he replied with a broad smile.

* * * *

'So you're telling us that Clive Penman called you this morning and asked you to take over from him?' Steve asked the visibly shaken headteacher.

'Yes at about nine o'clock,' replied Turner. 'He said that he had to get a few bits and pieces for a job he was doing this afternoon, and that Linda would be back around noon.'

'So when did you get here?' asked Watson.

'At about ten-fifteen I guess,' replied Turner.

'And Clive was here?' asked Steve.

'Yes, he was here until about half an hour ago, then he went.'

'Do you know where this job is, sir?' asked Watson.

'No,' replied Turner. 'All I know is that it was some cash-in-hand deal he'd struck with someone in the village.'

Steve motioned to Watson to move into the next room. Once they were out of hearing of Turner, Steve whispered, 'Don't worry about Penman's whereabouts Marc. You stay here with Turner and take a full statement. Then get to the mortuary for the postmortem results. I'll find Mr Penman and then make my own way back to the station. I'll meet you there at four-thirty for the debriefing.'

'Right you are sir,' replied Watson, unaware that his boss knew exactly where to find Penman.

It took Steve no more than 10 minutes to walk to his house. When he arrived, Clive's red pickup van was parked outside, with both of its nearside tyres on the pavement. Steve couldn't help noticing that the tyres on that side were bald and that no tax disc was being displayed. He walked up the path and fumbled in his pockets for his front door key. As he struggled to do so he clearly heard his wife's voice from inside the hall. 'Oh Clive, just hold on to me,' he heard her say. Steve could hardly believe his ears. His search for his keys now became even more frantic.

At that moment Robbie appeared, walking down the path towards him.

'Hi dad,' his son shouted, 'what are you doing home?'

'Oh hello son,' Steve replied. 'I can't seem to find my key.'

'Don't worry I've got mine,' replied Robbie.

As soon as the boy produced his key Steve snatched it off him and opened the door. The sight that confronted the two of them was a surprise to say the least. At the end of the hall stood Clive, with Penny perched precariously on his shoulders fiddling with the ancient fuse box, which was

49

located just under the coving. 'I didn't realise you did circus tricks mum,' commented Robbie as he stomped up the stairs.

'What's going on?' Steve asked.

'Clive's not sure where the electric cables run in the wall,' replied his wife. 'I'm just switching off the power.'

'Why don't you use a ladder?' asked Steve.

'I left the ladder off the pickup this morning Mr Carmichael,' said the embarrassed builder. 'I've had a lot to do this morning.'

'Yes, I know you have,' snapped Steve. 'That's what I've come to talk to you about. Perhaps when you've managed to put my wife down you would be kind enough to spare me a couple of minutes to give me a more detailed explanation of your movements this morning.'

'Look Mr Carmichael,' replied Clive. 'I know that I said that I'd be here first thing, and I know that I've let you down before, but I had to help out a friend this morning. I only found out about it late last night.'

'I'm not talking about that,' continued Steve. 'I'm talking about Linda Cartwright.'

'Finished,' exclaimed Penny with an air of achievement, having managed to flick up the black switch on the fuse box. 'You can let me down now. Slowly mind.'

Up to that point Clive had only been able to catch a glimpse of Steve by straining his neck and peering over his left shoulder. Once Penny had safely reached the ground he turned full square to face Steve and in a concerned way asked, 'What about Linda?'

'I take it that you haven't told him then?' Steve said to his wife.

'Of course not,' replied Penny indignantly. 'I didn't know I could.'

Steve received this news with some relief. Perhaps his wife was not as close to Penman as he had feared. 'Look Clive,' said Steve in a controlled calm voice, 'go through into the back room. I'm afraid that I have some bad news for you.'

* * * *

At 4:30 p.m. Steve entered the main debriefing room. Cooper, Watson, Lucy Clarke and about a dozen uniformed officers had already assembled when the new inspector started the proceedings. 'So what have we got?' he asked the gathered assembly. 'Cooper,' he continued, 'did your search of the area come up with anything?'

'Sorry inspector,' replied Cooper. 'So far we've searched a radius of 250 yards around where the body was found and we've drawn a complete blank I'm afraid.'

'Any sign of her shoes?' interrupted Steve.

'No sign sir.'

'What about the house to house?' Steve asked Lucy.

'There are a total of fourteen houses down in Wood Lane, sir,' said Lucy. 'We managed to make contact with all but two of the occupants, the residents of number six and number eleven.'

'And with the ones you did speak to,' said Watson, 'did you discover anything that would help with the inquiry?'

Steve turned and fixed a disparaging gaze at the questioner. 'Thank you Marc,' he said. He then turned his attention back to the young DC. 'Carry on Lucy.'

'Yes sir,' said Lucy, who was starting to feel a little uncomfortable. 'Nobody has to pass the scene to get out of the road and onto the A59. However, a couple of people did indicate that they heard a car speed away from the lane between midnight and one this morning.'

'Did anyone see anything last night or this morning?'

'So far no, but as I said before, we still have a couple of householders to interview. According to the neighbours the occupants are both single men. One works in Manchester

51

and leaves quite early. The other is some sort of rep. His neighbour said that he left this morning and would not be back until Friday.'

'OK. Make sure that you get statements from them both. I'd like to read the statements that you've already taken at home so make sure that you get a copy of them to me before I go this evening.' Without waiting for an answer Steve turned to Watson. 'Did you attend the autopsy this afternoon?'

'Yes,' replied Watson. 'I don't have the full report yet. Dr Stock said he would have it on your desk tomorrow morning. He did tell me Linda Cartwright had been dead for at least nine hours and possibly anything up to twelve when she arrived at the morgue. She had been strangled, there was little evidence of a struggle, and in his opinion it was unlikely that she died where she was found.'

This observation was particularly interesting to Steve. 'What makes him believe that she didn't die at the scene?'

'Well, it had been raining for most of the night and as the clothes on the victim were only wet on the back, where she had made contact with the ground, Dr Stock concluded that she must have been dumped after it had stopped raining,' responded Watson. 'The doctor also asked whether we had found a small gold earring at the scene because she was only wearing one when she arrived at the lab.'

'Dr Stock sounds as though he's on the ball. Make sure you get that full report tomorrow Marc. I want to see it as soon as it comes through.'

'Right you are sir,' replied Watson.

'The body would have arrived at the morgue at around ten o'clock,' Steve announced. 'So that puts the time of her death at between ten-thirty and one.'

'What makes you say that?' asked Cooper.

'Because when I spoke to Clive Penman he informed me that he received a call from her at around ten-thirty last night to ask him to look after the post office this morning while she

52

was meeting a friend. Actually, Cooper, you can get onto the telephone company first thing in the morning and get a report on the calls made to and from the post office last night. That's the times and the numbers of all incoming and outgoing calls. Also get onto the local met office and find out exactly when it stopped raining in Moulton Bank last night. Assuming the good Dr Stock is correct we might be able to get a better idea of when she arrived at Wood Lane.'

'Right sir,' replied Cooper.

'Once you've done that I want you and Lucy to get over to the post office and collect all her shoes and bring them here. Also, while you're there, see if you can find her other earring.'

After a short pause Lucy asked, 'Who is Clive Penman?'

'To answer that maybe I need to brief you and Cooper on how Marc and I spent the day,' said Steve. 'Well this morning Watson and I went to Linda's post office. We met the headmaster of the local primary school who was minding the shop for Miss Cartwright. He informed us that he was covering for another local man and friend of Linda Cartwright called Clive Penman. I later met with Penman who informed me that he had received a call from Linda Cartwright at around ten-thirty last night. According to Penman she sounded in good spirits. She informed him that she was going to meet a close friend and was not sure if she would be back in time to sort out the marking of the newspapers and open the post office in the morning. She asked Penman if he would help out, and being a good friend he duly agreed. According to Penman he had often covered for Linda and had a set of keys to the post office. He had opened up the post office at about five-thirty, however when Linda had not returned by nine he phoned his friend David Turner, who he asked to take over from him while he went to do a part-time building job. Our account from David Turner supports his story. Isn't that right Marc?'

53

'Yes, Turner's statement says that he got a call from Penman at nine in the morning,' said Watson. 'According to Turner he had occasionally helped Linda in the past, but that was when she had a boyfriend.'

'So she hadn't a regular boyfriend?'

'According to Turner she had broken up with her long-time boyfriend about a year ago when he moved abroad with his job,' replied Watson, who by now was referring to his notes.

'See if you can get some more details on this boyfriend Marc,' said Steve. 'I want to know who he is and where he can be contacted'.

As soon as the debriefing had finished Steve strode out of the meeting room and headed up the stairs to update Hewitt. To Steve's surprise Hewitt's office door was open, and as soon as the chief inspector saw Carmichael approaching he ushered him into his office with a flamboyant sweep of his long wiry arm. Once inside Hewitt closed the door behind them and summoned Angela, on the intercom. 'No calls and no interruptions, Angela,' he instructed.

'Would you like some tea?' came back the reply.

'Yes that would be fabulous,' exclaimed the chief before he discontinued the call. 'Right inspector,' said Hewitt. 'what have we got on this morning's incident?'

'The body is that of a young women called Linda Cartwright,' replied Steve. 'She's the local postmistress. She was strangled and we are pretty sure that the murder took place elsewhere and that her body was dumped in Wood Lane early this morning. We have no major leads at the moment but we believe that she had an appointment with someone yesterday evening, which Marc is following up.'

'I want this one resolved quickly inspector. If you need more resources let me know. Murders are rare in this district and it's crucial that we are seen to be doing everything that's necessary.'

'Thank you sir. At the moment I think we have enough manpower to achieve an early result, but I appreciate your support.'

At that point Angela appeared at the door laden with tea and biscuits on a large silver tray. 'Ah tea,' commented Hewitt. 'Just lay it down here, Angela, and then you can get yourself off.' Angela set the tray down and then turned towards the door. 'Remember you have a meeting with Mr Prescott at nine tomorrow morning sir,' she said before departing.

Hewitt waited until Angela had closed the door before pouring them both a cup of tea and offering his guest a biscuit. 'That's the other thing I wanted to talk to you about,' he continued. 'Prescott is the super's man, he's coming to see me about the initiative we discussed when you first arrived.' Steve didn't comment although he was a little surprised that the chief seemed disinclined to find out more about the murder. 'He's here to discuss the appointment of a small task force from this station to investigate police corruption in the Lancashire force.'

'Corruption?' Steve said with astonishment. 'Is that a major problem?'

'I'm afraid so,' responded Hewitt. 'It's not a problem which is confined to the Met, I'm sad to say. We have bent coppers up north as well you know. And as I said before I would like you to head up the team. You have experience in these matters and a fresh face is preferable from my perspective. So you see we both need a rapid result on this murder.'

'Yes I see,' replied Steve.

'Anyway I've already put your name forward to the super so unless you've got some skeletons in the cupboard you can look forward to an interesting assignment during the coming months.'

'I'm flattered that you have such faith in me sir. I can assure you that I will give it a hundred per cent.'

'Good,' replied his boss. 'So let's get this crime solved quickly, then you and I can get our heads together to agree who should join you in your team.'

'I'd certainly like to have Lucy Clark.' said Steve. 'But I'm not sure who else.'

'Well let's wait until things are a bit more certain,' said Hewitt. 'You should use this investigation to take a closer look at all your officers, including Miss Clark.'

'Well sir, if that is all I'd like to get off now,' Steve announced as he rose from his chair.

'One last thing Steve,' Hewitt said in a quiet, almost hushed voice. 'I do expect all my inspectors to follow my instructions at all times.'

'Sir?'

'Yes, when I ask for a senior officer to report to me upon his arrival at the station I do not expect him to ignore the instruction. My window looks over the car park so it's not difficult to observe who comes and goes.'

Steve toyed with trying to bluff his way out of the allegation, however on reflection he decided that any attempt on his part would be pointless. 'I understand sir,' he replied.

'Capital,' replied the chief. 'Now get yourself home to your wife and family. You have a lot of detective work to do if we are to get that quick result which is so important to both of us.'

'Yes sir. Thank you again and have a good evening.' With that Steve left the office and returned to his own to collect his briefcase and coat.

When Steve arrived home Penny was waiting for him with his dinner in the oven. As he ate Steve gave his wife the lowdown on the day's events. As always he was impressed by her grasp of the case, and he couldn't help thinking how much more confident he would be if Penny was also in his team.

Chapter 6

When Steve had announced to his children that they were moving to Lancashire, their reaction was very much as he and Penny had expected it would be. At first Natalie was worried about leaving her school and her friends. However, it didn't take long for her to look upon the move as an adventure. Robbie took the news in his stride. For some unknown reason he had been an ardent Liverpool supporter since he was very small. His first, and probably his only consideration was that he would now have a greater opportunity to watch his team on a more regular basis than he had been able to do when he lived in Bushey. As soon as his father had agreed to the possibility of regular visits to Anfield he, like his younger sister, had become excited about the move. Jemma was always going to be the difficult one. From the first minute that she knew of the move right up to the day that they arrived in Moulton Bank her attitude never wavered. She thought it was totally unfair of her parents to make such a decision. The thought of changing school and being separated from her best friend Zoe was like the end of the world to the strong-minded 16-year-old.

On Tuesday Penny woke up early. She had already made a commitment to take Natalie and her new friend Charlotte to the seaside. Given what had happened the day before, her first thought was to phone Charlotte's mother to cancel the trip. However, after discussing it with Steve they agreed that a day by the sea was probably as good a tonic as she could get.

She decided to wait for Clive Penman to arrive before leaving for Southport. Steve wanted him to put in an additional power point by his desk in the attic and he had asked Penny to make sure that Clive did it that day.

Remarkably, and much to Penny's surprise, Clive arrived at nine o'clock on the dot. She gave the workman his instructions and within the space of 10 minutes was heading down the drive with her youngest daughter.

Amazingly her two eldest children had already left by the time Clive arrived. Robbie was spending the day at Andy's house and Jemma had told her mother that she was spending the day with Nicola, her new best friend. It would be some time later before Penny would learn that her daughter was actually meeting Jason.

It took them no more than 30 minutes to get to the pretty seaside town. Penny had always liked Southport. Some of her fondest memories from her childhood were of the times she and her father had spent on the beach and at the funfair. She parked the car on the seafront and walked with the two excited girls towards the pleasure beach.

Meanwhile Steve had finally managed to take a look at the file on Sarah McGuire's death. It took him over three hours to read through the thick file of reports, statements and notes, which started with a photocopy of Watson's hand-written notes and ended with a copy of the transcript of the report from the Preston coroner's court. Steve read every printed word in the file and by the time he had finished he quickly concluded that the similarities between the circumstances of the McGuire case with that of Linda Cartwright were too close to be coincidental. The body of Sarah McGuire had been found in the front seat of her bright red Vauxhall Frontera on the morning of 5 May. The vehicle had been parked off the road behind some bushes, well out of sight of passing motorists or pedestrians. She had been found at about 10:25 a.m. by some young boys who were taking a short cut to the village football pitch. The first officers at the scene were Watson and Moulton Bank's local bobby, PC Woods. The dead woman, who had been immediately recognised by Woods as Sarah McGuire, was smartly dressed except for her stack heeled shoes which she had kicked off in the front seat. In notes recorded by Watson on that day, he had described the shoes as 'tatty and dirty' and he had questioned whether they were the style of shoes that a woman would wear if she knew she was going to drive. The officers also found an empty bottle of vodka and an empty bottle of paracetamol tablets in the passenger footwell.

The very brief pathologist's report confirmed that she had died from a cocktail of sleeping tablets and alcohol. The last person who was known to have seen her alive was her husband. In his statement Ken McGuire stated that he had last seen his wife at breakfast on 4 May, when she seemed normal and had given him no reason to believe that she was planning to take her own life.

When he had finished reading the file Steve placed it in his desk drawer and, after spending a few seconds reflecting on all that he had just seen, he decided that it was about time he asked his wife about the two dead women.

*　*　*　*

Robbie had left the house very early that morning. His first act was to visit the village newsagents to find out whether there was a newspaper round available. Unfortunately for Robbie, they had no vacancies for paperboys at that time, although the newsagent assured the young boy that should a vacancy arise he would be at the top of the list.

Jemma didn't like having to lie to her mum, but she was not yet ready to tell the family about her latest boyfriend. Despite having only known Jason for a short time, she had already managed to ensure that her latest love was completely under her spell. Jason worked as an assistant in his mum's hair salon in the parade of shops in the centre of the village. Tuesday was one of Jason's days off and he had promised Jemma to take her to Blackpool for the day in his newly-acquired second-hand car. 'We have to be back by tea time,' Jemma told Jason as they sped north up the M6.

Back at the house, Clive Penman had followed his instructions to the letter and having completed the minor electrical job in Steve's study he decided to take a coffee break. As he sat back in Steve's amply proportioned red leather chair, he gazed around the room at the myriad of treasures that surrounded him. He was particularly intrigued by the array of certificates and photographs which festooned the walls and the various collections of medals and military memorabilia that Steve kept in a glass-fronted cabinet.

Next door, Mrs Applebaum opened a fresh can of pilchards for her beloved cat, before sitting back on her solitary kitchen chair to read the latest news in the *Moulton Bank Weekly Chronicle.*

In Wood Lane at about that time, a man out walking innocently stumbled upon a piece of evidence that the police had missed. He instantly knew what he had found and he immediately realised that his find could be used to his advantage.

*　*　*　*

'Blast it!' shouted Steve when he realised that he had left at home the statements that Lucy had gathered from the Wood Lane residents. He picked up the phone and called Angela. 'Hello Angela, it's Carmichael here. I've left some papers at home, which I need. I'm going to have to leave early this afternoon. If the chief wants me can you tell him he can reach me on Moulton Bank 423952.'

'Chief Inspector Hewitt's still in his meeting with Mr Prescott,' replied Angela, 'but I'll be sure to let him know when he's free.'

'Thank you. Can you also do me a favour and get hold of Cooper, Watson and Lucy Clarke? Tell each of them to call me at home if they have anything major to report on the Cartwright case, and can you also tell them that I want the four of us to have a team briefing in the meeting room tomorrow morning at eight-thirty.' Without waiting for a reply Steve put down the phone and made his way to his car.

It was almost 3:30 p.m. when Steve finally arrived home. Outside was Clive Penman's unmistakable van. As before it had been parked precariously, with its nearside wheels on the pavement. Steve walked briskly up the drive. He could hear the sound of a radio coming from inside the house, which was occasionally punctuated by the slow grinding drone of Clive's masonry drill. Steve opened the front door, walked up the narrow corridor and popped his head round the corner of the room from where the noise was emanating. Clive, who was kneeling in the corner, drill in hand, did not notice Steve arrive, and was startled when he heard Steve's voice. 'Hi Clive,' boomed Steve. 'You're making good progress.'

'Good heavens Mr Carmichael,' replied Clive. 'I wasn't expecting anyone home for another couple of hours. Penny said I'd have the place to myself until at least five-thirty'.

'Sorry if I surprised you. I'm going to have to work at home this afternoon,' replied Steve.

'Well actually I'm just about at the point I had planned on reaching today,' said Clive. 'What say I call it a day and let you have some peace and quiet?'

'Fine,' said Steve, who could not help smiling at Clive's choice of words. He found it amusing that Clive had the cheek to describe the way he worked as 'planned'.

'I'll be about ten minutes tidying up then you can have the place to yourself Mr Carmichael,' continued Clive.

'I've told you before,' interjected Steve, 'please call me Steve.'

Clive smiled. 'Right you are Steve,' he replied.

Steve went to leave the room when his thoughts returned to Linda Cartwright. 'Clive,' he said turning back once more to the builder. 'Tell me about Linda's boyfriend.'

'Well, I never met the latest one,' replied Clive. 'But I am pretty sure he was a local man.'

'Latest!' repeated Steve. 'Did she have many boyfriends then?'

'Not as far as I know,' said Clive. 'She had been dating Terry Mayhew for years. We all thought it would be wedding bells and everything. Then he gets this job in Hong Kong. I'm told he wanted her to go with him but she didn't want to leave the old man, and well that was that.'

'The old man?'

'Her old dad,' replied Clive. 'And the ironic thing was that her father died within a couple of months of Terry leaving, by which time he'd found himself a new girl out there.'

'So when was that?' asked Steve.

'My word Steve, you don't half ask a lot of questions,' replied Clive with an even broader smile. 'Should I revert back to calling you Mr Carmichael now until we've finished this particular round of interrogation?'

Now it was Steve's turn to produce a wry grin. 'I'm sorry,' he said. 'It's just that I need to get as much background as I can on Linda if we are to get the case solved.'

'That's OK,' Clive said as he started collecting his tools together. 'Linda and Terry were an item for years. Terry went overseas about a year ago, and to my knowledge Linda had no other boyfriends until quite recently.'

'But you don't know who he was?' probed Steve.

'To be honest I'm not certain that she had a new boyfriend, it's not that she ever introduced me to him, however I sensed that of late she was much happier in herself, and she had been seen a couple of Sundays ago walking hand in hand with a man down Wood Lane,' said Clive. 'I don't know all the new folk down Wood Lane but I thought it might be that Talbot bloke from number eleven. He's in advertising or something. He comes in The Railway now and then with some of the other successful set from Wood Lane. He's also a mate of Ken McGuire, I think.'

'Who saw them down Wood Lane?' asked Steve.

'I don't rightly remember,' replied Clive with a frown. 'You hear so many stories in a small place like this, it's often hard to recall who told you first.'

'And this Terry Mayhew,' continued Steve, 'does anyone have an address for him?'

'I think his brother might,' replied Clive. 'If you're lucky to catch him in a rare sober moment.'

'So Terry is Robin's brother?' said Steve, remembering his first and only meeting with the village drunk.

'Yes, Robin's the eldest and the black sheep and Terry's the successful one. Although to be honest I would rather spend an evening in Robin's company than ten minutes with that brother of his,' said the builder, picking up his tool bag.

'Thanks Clive,' said Steve. 'I appreciate your help.'

'No problem,' replied Clive as he exited the room.

'I'll see you tomorrow,' Steve shouted down the corridor.

'Ah!' replied Clive. 'It might be Thursday or Friday before I can get back, I've got a couple of other jobs that need finishing.' Clive didn't wait for an answer. He walked out of the front door and was away. In truth Steve was not that interested in Clive's final comments, he was still pondering over what he had said before.

Before Steve went up to his study he decided to make himself a cup of coffee. While the kettle was boiling the mobile rang. 'Carmichael,' Steve said as he clicked on the answer button.

'Hello sir, it's Cooper here. I've got some of the information you wanted sir. Miss Cartwright received three calls on the night before she was found. The first was at seven twenty-three, which lasted about fifteen seconds and was from a London number. I traced it and the person who made the call claimed to have dialled the wrong number.'

'What about the others?' asked Steve.

'Well the next was long distance from a callbox in America. It was received at nine forty-seven and lasted for twelve minutes.'

'Did you trace the call?' Steve asked.

'Yes. A callbox in the lobby of the Marriott Hotel in Harrisburg, Pennsylvania,' replied Cooper. 'I've asked the local police to send me a list of the residents that night, which they have said that they will do.'

'Make sure you get all their home addresses Cooper,' ordered Steve.

'Yes, I have already asked them sir,' replied Cooper.

'What about the last call?'

'That's the most interesting one. It was received at ten forty-seven from a public callbox but this time in Moulton Bank. It lasted five minutes'.

'Whereabouts in Moulton Bank is the box?'

'You won't believe it sir,' continued Cooper. 'It's at the end of Wood Lane.'

'Good work Cooper! Get the SOCOs down there PDQ. This could well be the last person to speak to Linda before she died. I need to know who he or she is.'

'Right you are sir.'

'Thanks for keeping me up to speed.'

'That's not everything sir. Two calls were made out on her phone that evening. The first was to Clive Penman's mobile, which was started at ten twenty-five and lasted three minutes. The second was to the vicar's house which started at ten thirty-five and lasted about two minutes.'

'The one to Penman will be the one to ask him to look after the post office, but I wonder why she wanted to speak to the vicar? Have you spoken to the vicar about the call?'

'Not yet sir.'

Steve thought for a moment then said, 'Leave the vicar. I'll speak to him tomorrow. You concentrate on finding as much as you can about that call from America and the one from the Wood Lane phonebox.'

'One last thing sir,' said Cooper. 'The local met office said that the rain started in Moulton Bank at about twelve-twenty and stopped at around four-thirty in the morning.'

'So we know for sure that she died after ten fifty-two and that her body was dumped in Wood Lane after four-thirty a.m. That's good detective work Cooper. Well done.'

After making himself his coffee Steve climbed the stairs to his study to read through the statements of the residents of Wood Lane. As Lucy had indicated the statements provided few clues. Mrs Collins at number eight thought that she had heard a car drive off at speed at around midnight and Mr and Mrs Spennymore at number nine were sure that they heard another car at around 1 a.m. Other than that Steve read nothing that was of any interest to him. He drained the last cold dregs from his coffee cup before picking up his mobile and calling Lucy's number.

'DC Clark.'

'Hello Lucy, it's Carmichael here.'

'Hello sir,' she replied.

'Have you made any progress with the two remaining residents of Wood Lane or in locating Linda's shoes?'

'A little sir. I have still to locate Mr Talbot at number eleven, but I have managed to speak to Mr Simpson at number six. He didn't see anything during the night, but he is sure he heard a car going down the lane at about five in the morning. He also thinks he heard it coming back about ten minutes later. He reckons that the car woke him up when it went down the lane and that when it came back it coincided with his alarm going off.'

'What about Linda's shoes?'

'I'm with Sergeant Watson now,' she replied. 'We have just left Linda's house with six pair of shoes.'

'Is that all of them?' Steve asked.

'I think so sir,' replied Lucy. 'It took us ages to find them. She had them locked in a downstairs cupboard. We had to break in to get them.'

'And the earring?'

'No sign of it I'm afraid.'

'OK. You've both done well today. Make sure you are at the debriefing in the morning, and bring those shoes. But try to get hold of Talbot. I have reason to believe that he might have been seeing Linda. If that is the case we need to talk to him before Friday.'

'Why do you think that sir?'

'I'll brief you on that tomorrow. You just concentrate on locating him. Try Ken McGuire and the landlord of The Railway Tavern. I understand that Talbot is a friend of McGuire and is a local in The Railway Tavern.'

'I'll pay them both a visit tonight,' she replied.

'On second thoughts, you concentrate on McGuire, I'll speak to the landlord this evening. I could do with a drink.'

'That's fine by me,' replied Lucy, who was pleased that she had only one task before calling it a day.

'One last thing Lucy. I read the case notes on Sarah McGuire's death. I think you were right. She was also probably murdered. And I have a nasty feeling she was killed by the same person as Linda Cartwright.' Lucy felt pleased that Carmichael seemed to confirm what she had known the moment she had seen the body of Linda Cartwright in Wood Lane. 'Be sure you take DC Cooper with you when you visit McGuire. And brief him fully on what I've just told you.' instructed Steve. 'It is important that neither of you make any mention of either murder. You are just trying to locate Talbot. Do you understand?'

'I understand,' replied Lucy. 'I'll see you in the morning sir.'

'Goodbye Lucy,' said Steve as he pressed the end button on his mobile.

* * * *

By 5:30 p.m. the entire Carmichael clan were gathered around the dinner table.

'Do you fancy a quick one in The Railway this evening Penny?' Steve asked.

'That would be great,' replied Penny. 'As long as you don't embarrass me again by interrogating my friends like you did last time.'

'What do you mean?' asked Steve, knowing full well that he would have to be more subtle than usual with his questioning that evening.

Following a brief silence Penny turned to Jemma and asked, 'Did you have a good day dear?'

'It was OK,' replied her daughter nervously.

'And how's Nicola?' continued Penny.

'Oh she's fine,' said Jemma, who by now was feeling very uncomfortable.

'What about you Robbie?' asked Steve, who sensed that his eldest child was disinclined to enter into a protracted dialogue with Penny, albeit that he didn't fully understand why she was so reticent.

'I went to the newspaper shop this morning to see if they had any jobs,' replied Robbie. 'But they haven't.'

'Don't worry Robbie,' said Penny. 'I'm sure if you keep asking they'll have one sooner or later. They're the sort of jobs that come up often and if you show them that you're keen I'm sure that you'll be OK. Don't you agree Steve?'

'Yes I'm sure you'll be OK. By the way, did any of you move my papers around this morning?'

'Not me,' replied Jemma.

'Me neither,' replied Penny.

'And not me. Although she went up there to get a pencil,' said Robbie, pointing his fork at his little sister.

'Mum!' shrieked Natalie. 'He's picking on me again.'

'I'm sure she didn't touch your papers,' interjected Penny. 'She was up there for two minutes and that was all. Nobody's the slightest bit interested in your papers Steve. You probably moved them yourself. You know what you're like.'

Chapter 7

It was a little after nine when Steve and Penny left home to take the short stroll to The Railway Tavern. The air was warm and dry and although the sun was already starting to set in the west behind Ambient Hill, it was still light enough for the swallows to swoop and dive high above in the sky, and for a group of youngsters to be out playing football in the park.

'Look at them,' Steve said, motioning in the direction of the young footballers. 'They're having the time of their lives.'

'You're right,' replied Penny. 'They look as though they haven't a care in the world.'

At that point the tranquil scene was shattered by one of the youngsters screaming and gesticulating vigorously. 'You cheating bastard!' he yelled at a small and decidedly rotund youth. 'That was fucking miles wide!' Without any warning a third tall, thin youth grabbed the first boy by the shirt and in one movement flipped him over on his back. Then with a thud that echoed into the street he kicked the now totally defenceless boy hard in the back. For a split second Steve contemplated intervening. However upon reflection he decided that it was just a harmless squabble. His decision was quickly vindicated when the foul-mouthed youngster got up, apparently no worse for his ordeal, and the game resumed. In fact he did not appear to be at all perturbed by the punishment that had been meted out to him.

'I wish I could do that,' Steve said.

'What, play football?' said Penny in mock jest. 'You're far too old and out of condition my dear.'

'No,' replied Steve. 'Deliver instant justice like that. It would make my job that much easier.'

Penny laughed. 'Isn't that what goes on behind closed doors when the the tape recorder's switched off?'

'Only on the TV *my dear*,' he replied. 'You've been watching too many old re-runs of *The Sweeney*. Real policing is much more civilised. Anyway, what do you mean out of condition. I'm still in my prime.'

'Of course you are dear,' replied Penny.

They crossed over Station Road hand in hand and within a couple of minutes had entered the pub. To their surprise the lounge bar was packed, a far cry from the only other time that they had visited Robbie Robertson's public house.

'What do you want to drink?' asked Steve.

'I'll have a half of lager please,' replied Penny.

Steve nudged his way through the throng that was standing by the bar and waited for an opportunity to catch the eye of any one of the three busy bartenders. After a couple of minutes Robbie noticed Steve. 'I'll be with you once I've finished serving this customer,' said Robbie.

As he waited Steve looked around to see if he could see anyone he knew. There was Robbie and his daughter Katie who were both behind the bar, Clive Penman and David Turner who were chatting with a couple of other men at a corner table and Robin Mayhew, who was in his usual spot at the end of the bar with a very large plaster over his right eye. Penny had managed to find a table and was waving to her husband so that he would be sure and find her once he had bought the drinks.

'What will it be?' asked Robbie.

'I'll have a pint of best bitter and a half of lager,' replied Steve.

'Oh, are you with Penny?' asked Robbie.

'Yes she's over there by the window,' replied Steve, pointing to his wife, who was still waving frantically from the table she had successfully captured.

'Let me bring them over to you,' said Robbie. 'I could do with a break, I'll join you if that's OK?'

'Of course,' said Steve. 'How much do I owe you?'

'On the house, inspector,' said Robbie in a loud voice.

At the sound of the word 'inspector' at least half the occupants of the lounge stopped their conversations and gazed towards Steve, much to his embarrassment. He made his way over to where Penny was sitting. 'We'll have to come here more often,' he said with a grin. 'Our host seems to be keen for us to keep our money in our pockets.'

'That must have pleased you,' responded Penny with a knowing look.

Robbie put the drinks on the table, including his own large pewter tankard. 'Well inspector,' said Robbie. 'How are you progressing in catching the bastard that killed poor Linda?'

His question took Steve by surprise, but he was glad that he didn't need to waste time on idle chit-chat. 'Well it's early days but I'm confident that we will be making an arrest soon.'

'Good,' said Robbie. 'She was a gentle lass, she didn't deserve to go like that.'

'What do you know about her Robbie?' Steve asked. 'Did she have any boyfriends?'

'Boyfriends! Not to my knowledge. Well, not since Robin's brother left for the Far East. No, she wasn't courting as far as I know. Why? Do you think she was killed by someone she knew?'

'I can't say,' replied Steve. 'But I'd heard that she was seeing someone from the village.'

'Who?' asked Penny.

'A man called Talbot.'

'Matthew Talbot!' exclaimed Robbie with a laugh. 'I don't

71

think so. He's not her type. He's a mate of Ken McGuire. In my experience those types aren't normally interested in plain and simple girls like Linda. No, they go for a different type if you get my drift.'

'But she was seen with him. And I was told that it was common knowledge in the village,' said Steve.

'Well it might be true but it's certainly news to me,' countered Robbie.

'Did Linda have any close girlfriends?' asked Steve.

'She had no real close friends,' said Robbie. 'She was quite friendly with the churchgoers like Clive and David, but I wouldn't say she was that close to anyone really. But I wouldn't really know, she wasn't a frequent visitor to The Railway. If you want to get more background you would be best advised to talk to Reverend Pugh. Outside of the shop she spent more time in church than anywhere else.'

'Come on you two,' interrupted Penny. 'Can we talk about something else please?'

'Of course,' replied Steve.

'It was my fault Penny,' said Robbie. 'It was me who started on the subject. Anyway, how are you and your family settling in?'

'Just great,' replied Penny. 'It's really great to be back. The kids seem to have settled in fine and, well, it's just great to be back.'

'Yes,' interjected Steve. 'Even Jemma's happy. She was the one who was least keen to move.'

'That's your eldest isn't it?' said Robbie. 'Katie tells me she's already got young Jason from the hair salon under her spell.'

'Pardon?' said Steve. 'She's got a boyfriend?'

'I think Katie must be mistaken,' said Penny.

'Oh, no, I'm sure of my facts on this one,' continued Robbie. 'Helen Parkes, who owns the salon, is Jason's mum. It was she who told Katie.'

Penny and Steve just looked at each other but said nothing. 'I thought we might have a barbecue on Saturday,' said Penny in a desperate attempt to change the subject. 'Why don't you come Robbie?'

'That would be great,' replied the publican. 'What time do you want me to arrive?'

'About noon,' replied Penny. 'And bring whoever you want. In fact the more the merrier.'

'That's great,' said Robbie. 'If I can find someone to help manage the bar I'll take you up on that.' With that the landlord emptied the contents of his tankard. 'I've got to be going, my ten-minute break's over. I'll see you on Saturday.'

'Thanks for the drinks,' said Steve.

Robbie returned to behind the bar. Penny and Steve finished their drinks and having decided that they would not have another, they left the pub and walked the short distance home in silence.

'Well, did you find out anything?' asked Penny once they reached the house. 'I assume that was the reason why we went to the pub. Am I right?'

'Apart from the fact that our daughter has a secret boyfriend, and that we are entertaining the village at a barbecue on Saturday, not much, to be honest,' replied Steve.

'So it was a wasted evening then?' said Penny.

'I wouldn't say that,' replied Steve. 'I've had a drink with my beautiful wife and I have a feeling that I did learn something that may be relevant this evening. I'm not sure what though.'

'So did I. But the difference is that I know what.'

'And what might that be?' asked Steve.

'That I'm due for a visit to the hairdressers very soon.'

*   *   *   *

73

Watson, Cooper and Lucy Clark were all ready in the incident room when Steve arrived. 'Good morning team,' said Steve, taking his place at the front. 'What progress are we making?'

'We didn't manage to speak to Ken McGuire last night sir,' responded Cooper. 'He's away at a conference in Leicestershire.'

'His housekeeper said he'll be back on Friday,' interjected Lucy.

'Housekeeper!' exclaimed Steve sarcastically. 'And did this housekeeper have the address or telephone number of the hotel?'

'Yes,' continued Lucy as she flicked through her pocket book. 'It's a place called Bedworth Hall.'

'OK,' said Steve. 'I'd like you to call the hotel and check that he has a reservation and also confirm when he is due to check out.'

'Yes sir,' replied Lucy.

'What about the autopsy report?' Steve asked.

'It's here,' replied Watson. 'But it's only just arrived so I've not had a chance to read it yet. However I have managed to find out a good deal about the ex-boyfriend. His name is Terry Mayhew. He and Linda had been dating since they were at school. He now works in Hong Kong. He has a brother who still lives locally and he's apparently coming back to Moulton Bank to attend the funeral.'

'Good work Marc,' replied Carmichael. 'Where did you get all that information from?'

'David Turner the primary school headmaster,' replied Watson. 'He contacted Mayhew yesterday morning about Linda's death. He says that Terry sounded absolutely devastated by the news.'

'Talking of the funeral,' interrupted Cooper, 'the vicar called this morning. He wanted to know when we will be releasing the body so that he can plan the funeral.'

'Now we have the autopsy report we have no need to hold on to the body,' replied Steve.

'Good. I'll call him and let him know.'

'No don't do that,' said Steve. 'I need a good excuse to meet the vicar. I'll pop over to see him later this morning. I'll tell him in person.'

'Did you speak to the landlord of The Railway Tavern about Mr Talbot?' asked Lucy.

'Yes I did. He confirmed that Talbot is a mate of McGuire but little else I'm afraid.'

'So what's the plan for today sir?' asked Cooper.

'Well first I'd like to recap on what we know so far. As I said before I would like to meet the Reverend Pugh. But first let's try and agree what we know, what we think we know and what we need to find out. I'll start but if I miss anything don't hesitate to interrupt me. This has to be a joint effort.' The rest of the team nodded in agreement. 'Lucy, I'd like you to take notes. Use the paper from the flip chart. Make a note of the key facts and assumptions that we come up with.'

'Shall I use a different colour depending upon whether it's a fact, hypothesis or unknown?' she replied eagerly.

'Good idea Lucy,' said Cooper. 'Let's use red for anything factual, blue if it's a hypothesis and green for the not yet known.'

Steve was impressed by the enthusiasm of his officers. For the first time since he had arrived he felt that they were working as a team. Within half an hour they had completed a summary of their progress in the first 48 hours of their investigation.

In red they had six clear statements. That Linda had been strangled between 10:52 on Sunday evening and 4:30 on Monday morning. That she had been dumped in Wood Lane after 4:30 on Monday morning. That she had called Clive Penman at 10:25 on Sunday evening. That she had called Reverend Pugh at 10:35. That she had received a call from

Harrisburg at 9:47 on Sunday evening and that she had received another call from an unknown source from the callbox in Wood Lane at 10:47 on Sunday evening.

In blue they had four items. That Linda was having a relationship with Matthew Talbot. That Talbot had made the call from the Wood Lane callbox. That Sarah McGuire had also been murdered, and that Sarah's killer was the same person who had killed Linda Cartwright.

In green they had seven unanswered questions. Who killed Linda Cartwright? Where was she killed? Why was she killed? Who called her from Harrisburg? Who called her from Wood Lane? Why did she need to speak to the vicar? And finally, why was she found without any shoes?

'We don't seem to have got very far,' said Watson despondently. 'We've no prime suspects and more questions than answers.'

'I agree,' said Lucy, who shared Watson's gloom. 'But my money's on Talbot.'

Steve shook his head. 'At this stage I think that we would be foolish to start speculating on suspects. Our focus over the next couple of days is to test our various hypotheses and to try and get more answers to the questions in green. Once we've spoken to McGuire, Talbot, Mr Pugh and the unknown caller from America we'll be in much better shape.'

'I agree,' said Cooper. 'So who is doing what?'

'Well I'd like you to follow up on the phonebox callers,' replied Steve. 'Make sure the SOCO people do a thorough job on the Wood Lane callbox. Also follow up with the hotel in Harrisburg. I want that list of residents this afternoon.'

'Understood,' said Cooper.

'Lucy, I want you to get hold of McGuire at his hotel. If need be go down there today and find out what he knows about Linda and her relationship with Talbot. Also find out if he knows where Talbot can be contacted.'

'Right sir,' replied Lucy.

'Marc, you concentrate on the autopsy report. Once you've done that, trawl through the Sarah McGuire case notes. I've read them but I'd like you to look and see if there are any similarities that we should be aware of. Also try to get your head around this issue of the shoes. That's really bugging me. I'm sure that it's important.'

'Fine,' replied Watson, although he felt that his tasks were somewhat less interesting than those of his colleagues.

'I'll pay a visit to Mr Pugh,' continued Steve. 'I'm sure he has some answers for us.'

Having agreed the plan for the day Steve requested that the team should reconvene the following morning for a further status report.

'Oh,' said Steve, 'my wife and I would like to invite you and your partners to a barbecue at our house on Saturday. It will be an opportunity for us to get to know each other a little better. I will be inviting some of the Moulton Bank locals too, so we should also have an opportunity to find out more about Linda Cartwight.'

A short time later a note was delivered by hand through the letterbox of one of the villagers.

Chapter 8

Moulton Bank had two churches, the Roman Catholic church, which was located in the centre of the village, and the C of E church, which stood midway up Ambient Hill on the main road to Preston. Both churches had been built in the early part of the nineteenth century. The Roman Catholic church had been built in 1846, financed by the Alcar family, the main landowners in the area. However, as was common in the mid 1800s the real wealth in this part of the country was in the hands of the new middle-class industrialists. It was one of these, a cotton mill owner called Matthew Dalton, who some five years later put up the money to build a new C of E church. To ensure that his patronage would outshine that of the Alcar family, he also financed a vicarage and a school for the children of his mill workers. Furthermore, his church had been deliberately built on higher ground than its neighbour and it was no mistake that it was also considerably larger than the Roman Catholic church.

Once Dalton's church had been built the old chapel, which had served the community since the Reformation, was demolished. On the site where it had stood Dalton had a large stone cross erected. He was a very practical man and as such he had instructed his workers to use the stone from the old chapel to construct the school building. The original school built by Dalton had been replaced by the larger, more modern and more accessible building in the late 1960s. The new building was erected much closer to the village and was the school that Penny had attended and that would be Natalie's school in September. Dalton's original school was now only used on Sunday mornings, when for about two hours it became the venue for the church Sunday school. For the rest of the week it remained empty and unused. The Reverend Pugh's vicarage however was the same one that had been built by Dalton 150 years earlier. It was situated next door to the church.

Steve had deliberately chosen to meet with the vicar alone. He felt sure that Mr Pugh would be able to help him with a number of unanswered questions and he was equally convinced that he would gain much more from the vicar if he were to meet him unaccompanied. Steve had already called the vicarage to make an appointment with Mr Pugh so he was sure that his journey was not going to be in vain.

As Steve pulled up the long gravel drive which led to the vicarage, he couldn't help feeling how lonely it must be for the vicar to live by himself in such a large, isolated and cold-looking building. Although in its prime the vicarage must have been a grand imposing house, the numerous years of neglect were clearly noticeable. The large gardens were overgrown with brambles and long brown grasses, the sandstone walls once bright red were now blackened and crumbling, and the paintwork around the windows and on the grand front door was cracked and peeling. There was no bell at the front door, only a large stiff brass knocker. After taking a deep breath Steve seized the knocker and pounded three times on the old oak door. Within seconds the door was opened by the stern-faced cleric.

'Good morning inspector,' said Pugh with a forced grin. 'Do come in.'

Steve followed Pugh down a long corridor and through into a large sitting room which faced the rear of the house. 'It's good of you to see me vicar,' he said as he made himself comfortable on a large old armchair.

'Not at all my boy,' replied the vicar. 'To be honest I expected you to call sooner.'

Steve was surprised by this comment, but chose not to pursue it further. ' I believe that you are keen for us to release Miss Cartwright's body?'

'Yes, we would like to arrange her funeral. Her brother, who should arrive tomorrow, has asked me to make the arrangements and given that he will not be able to stay too long, because of his business you understand, I was hoping that we could hold the funeral on Tuesday of next week.'

'I see. Well there is no reason for us to inconvenience you or Miss Cartwright's brother. We will be releasing her body to the undertakers today.'

'Oh good, Alan will be relieved.' After a short pause the vicar suddenly said, 'My word how rude of me. I have not offered you any refreshment. Would you like some tea inspector?'

Steve's initial thought was to decline but he decided that a short break while his host made a drink would give him an opportunity to gather his thoughts on how best to continue his interview. 'That would be wonderful,' he replied. Pugh smiled and left the room.

Steve studied his surroundings, which were as dowdy and unkempt as the outside of the house. He could not make his mind up whether he should ask the vicar about the telephone call Linda made to him on the night of her death or see if the vicar would freely offer up the information. He was still undecided on this point when Pugh returned.

'Here we are. I've brought some scones. Would you like one?'

'No, thank you,' replied Steve.

The vicar seemed a little put out by Steve's refusal. 'I hope you don't mind if I do,' he continued.

'Not at all.'

'The scones are shop-bought I'm afraid but the strawberry

jam is home-made. Made by the hand of Mrs Applebaum, my old cleaner. It's delicious. One lump or two?'

'Two please,' replied Steve whose gaze remained focused on the amount of jam the vicar had put on his scone.

'And how are you all settling in?' asked the vicar, picking up the scone. 'I understand that your eldest has already found herself a young man.'

'So I believe,' replied Steve, who was astounded that his daughter's love life was not only common knowledge in the pub but also known to the Church.

'She does remind me of Penny,' continued Mr Pugh as he bit deeply into the scone. 'She has that rebellious streak, just like her mother.'

'Yes, people often say she's like her mother,' said Steve. 'But enough of my family, I'd like to ask you some questions about Linda Cartwright if I may.'

'Fire away my boy.'

'First of all, what type of lady was she?' said Steve.

'In many people's eyes she would be quite ordinary I suppose,' said Pugh. 'But to those of us who knew her well she was remarkable.'

'In what way?'

'The only way I could describe it is that she was always putting duty before her own happiness. For example, there was the way she decided to stay in Moulton Bank, rather than go with her love to Hong Kong.'

'You are talking of Terry Mayhew now I suppose?'

'Ah!' said Pugh. 'I can see that you have already started to delve around into Linda's past. Yes, I do mean Terry Mayhew.'

'But surely it's not that unusual for a woman to choose to look after an ageing parent rather than go off with her boyfriend?' he asked.

'Of course you are right,' replied the vicar. 'But for the fact that Terry was everything to her, and had been since they were children. It took a lot of courage for her to forego her own happiness to follow her conscience in that way. I often felt that she should have been less charitable, but there you are.'

'I see.'

'And of course there was the way she befriended Sarah McGuire when she needed a shoulder to cry on, and of course Mary Robertson when she was ill with cancer.'

'So she was a friend of Sarah McGuire?'

'She was more recently,' replied the vicar. 'Though I could have forgiven her if she had chosen not to be; as both Sarah and Mary did make that poor girl's life a misery when they were at school. As girls do, you understand.'

'So she was at school with Mary and Sarah was she?'

'Not only at school with them but in the case of Sarah Mulholland, who became a McGuire, she was in the same class,' replied the vicar. 'As was a certain Penny Lathom, later to become Penny Carmichael.'

The link between the two dead women and Penny had not occurred to Steve up until that point. And from his expression, it was obvious to the vicar that this particular piece of information had given his interrogator something to think about. This amused Pugh, who couldn't help enjoying a wry, smug smile. Steve was irritated by this and decided that it was about the right time to ask the vicar some more pointed questions. 'How long have you been vicar in Moulton Bank?' he asked.

'Thirty-nine years,' replied Mr Pugh with an air of achievement.

'So you must have seen a lot of changes in the village?'

'Oh yes!' replied the vicar. 'And many for the better I'm pleased to say.'

'Like what?' asked Steve.

'Well, first of all there's the new school,' replied Pugh. 'I say "new" of course. It was built in the late sixties, so in reality it's hardly new I suppose. But you see it is a vast improvement on that relic over there.' As he spoke Mr Pugh pointed out of the window to the lonely Sunday-school building. 'The community spent years raising cash to get it built, but it was worth it.'

'Talking of the school I understand that David Turner's father was also once the headmaster?'

'Yes, Arthur was the first head of the new school,' replied Pugh.

'And I believe he died while he was the head?' asked Steve, hoping that the vicar would give him more information on the schoolmaster's death than his wife and Penman had been prepared to part with.

'I'm afraid that he did,' replied Pugh. 'I'm surprised that Penny has not told you. He took his own life you know. Shot himself.'

'Why?' asked Steve.

'Who knows?' replied the vicar. 'It shocked the whole village. In many ways even though it happened nearly thirty years ago we're still in shock over it. So much so that it's still something that the older people in the village feel uncomfortable talking about.'

Feeling more and more confident, Steve then tried to push for even more secrets from the past. 'I understand that you are also not a stranger to tragedy Mr Pugh?'

'You have been busy inspector,' replied Pugh. 'Yes, my only daughter Gillian was taken away from us when she was five years old. It happened about six months before poor Arthur's death.'

'If you don't mind me asking,' said Steve, who didn't mind at all. 'How did she die?'

'My wife and I went out for the afternoon to visit some sick eldery people in Preston,' said Pugh. 'We decided to leave Gillian with a couple of local teenagers from the village. Gillian was playing out the front with a ball. It ran into the road and, well, you can guess the rest.'

Steve could see that the vicar was now getting quite distressed. 'I'm sorry vicar,' he said with genuine concern. 'It's not relevant to this case and it's none of my business, so I'll not distress you any further.'

'That's OK inspector,' Pugh responded. 'People in the village don't usually mention Gillian. I think they don't want to hurt me. But since my wife departed I have had to bear the pain alone.'

'It must have tested your faith to the limit?'

'To breaking point my boy,' replied the vicar. 'But time is a healer and I soon managed to separate my grief from my anger at God.'

Steve decided that it would be better to get the conversation back on track. 'You mentioned a brother,' he said, referring to his notes. 'Mr Alan Cartwright. Where does Alan live?'

'Alan currently lives in America,' replied the vicar. 'He left Moulton Bank many years ago to travel the world. He is very much like his sister in looks and in his ways too, but unlike poor Linda he was always keen to see the world. A bit of a dreamer when he was young I suppose.'

'So when did he leave the village and where in the US does he live?' Steve asked with interest.

'He would have left Moulton Bank twenty or even twenty-five years ago, I suppose. Almost as soon as he left school he decided to travel and, well, he never came back. He always kept in touch with Linda though and I think for a good while with his old pals like Robin Mayhew, the McGuire boy and David Turner. But apart from attending his parents' funerals he's never been back.'

'But where exactly in the US does he live?' asked Steve again.

'He has a good job now in publishing. He's married and has two or it could be even three children, and lives in California,' replied the vicar. Steve's heart sank at the mention of California. For a brief moment he thought that he'd found Linda's mystery American caller. But he knew that California was hundreds if not thousands of miles away from Harrisburg, Pennsylvania.

'And when is Mr Cartwright arriving in Moulton Bank?' Steve asked

'On Saturday,' replied the vicar. 'Do you want his telephone number?'

'Yes that would be useful,' said Steve. The vicar fiddled around with some papers on his desk for a moment until he found a small scrap which contained a telephone number 13 digits long. He then proceeded to copy the number down on another even smaller scrap of paper, which he then handed to Steve.

'Thank you for your help vicar, there's just a couple of final questions that I'd like to ask you before I go,' said Steve.

'This is where Columbo asks the difficult ones,' chipped in the vicar with a now familiar grin.

'Quite. You said earlier that you last saw Linda in church on the Sunday morning.'

'Yes that's right,' replied Pugh. 'She read from John as I recall.'

'But we have reason to believe that she made a telephone call to you here at the vicarage that night,' continued Steve. He looked closely at the vicar as he asked this question hoping to see a crack in the chiselled smile that had been an almost permanent fixture on the cleric's face since the first moment Steve had stepped into the vicarage. But he was to be disappointed. Reverend Pugh remained quite calm.

'Yes she did call me,' he replied. 'She asked if she could come up to the vicarage to see me the following day.'

'What did she want to talk to you about?' asked Steve. 'And why did you not mention it before?'

'Well I didn't mention it because I didn't feel that it was important,' replied the vicar. 'And she would not say exactly what it was about, although she did seem excited. She said that she had found out something and she needed my advice.'

'And you didn't feel that that was important vicar?' Steve said in a raised but controlled voice. 'You didn't feel that this information was relevant to the investigating officers, when the woman who made this call to you was murdered within hours of making it.' For the first time the Pugh's smile disappeared. 'Is there anything else that I should know?' continued Steve.

'You're quite correct to chastise me,' replied Pugh. 'I should have told you about the call. I was wrong and I apologise. But I can assure you inspector that I have nothing else to tell you and I can also assure you that there is nobody more keen than I to see Linda's murderer caught.'

Steve felt sure that while the vicar was being honest when he said he wanted the killer caught, he was not being totally candid with him. He stood up and started for the door. 'Thanks for the tea vicar,' he said. 'I'm afraid I have to go but I would very much like to finish our conversation another time. In the meantime I would like you to pay a visit to the station and make a statement regarding the call you received from Linda on the night of her death.'

'Of course,' said Pugh. 'I'll drop in tomorrow morning. Should I ask for you in person inspector?'

'No,' said Steve, in a deliberate desire to be contrary. 'That will not be necessary. Any officer at the station will be able to help you.'

'Very well,' replied Pugh, 'let me show you out.' Steve followed the vicar down the corridor to the front door.

'There was one other thing,' said Steve as they stood on the doorstep. 'Did they ever catch the person who knocked down Gillian?'

'No, he was never caught,' replied Pugh. 'But I know that he will have been duly punished for his crime.'

86

'And how do you know that?' asked Steve.

'I have to believe it inspector,' replied Pugh, who by now was certainly not smiling. 'If I could not believe it then how could I carry on?' With that the vicar closed the door and Steve walked slowly to his car.

Chapter 9

'Good morning, Bedworth Hall Hotel.'

'Oh, good morning,' said Lucy, 'can you tell me whether you have a Mr Ken McGuire staying with you at the moment?'

'Let me check,' was the response. After a break of about 30 seconds the receptionist came back onto the line. 'Yes, he's with Mr Talbot's convention, is that correct?'

Lucy put her hand over the mouthpiece and shouted over to Cooper and Watson, 'McGuire and Talbot are together at the hotel in Bedworth.'

'Hello?' came the voice at the end of the line.

'Yes, that's correct,' replied Lucy. 'He's with Mr Talbot's party.'

'Would you like me to put you through to the York suite, where they are having their meeting?' asked the receptionist.

'Er, no, can you tell me when he's booked in until, please?'

'Can I ask who's calling?' said the voice, now suspicious.

'It's his sister speaking,' was the first thing that came into Lucy's head. 'I need to speak to him but I don't want to disturb his meeting.'

'Oh I see,' replied the receptionist. 'He's due to check out on Friday.'

'Thank you,' said Lucy. 'I'll ring him this evening when they've finished their meeting.' By the time Lucy put down the receiver Cooper and Watson had gathered around her.

'Talbot's with McGuire at the hotel,' announced Lucy excitedly. 'It's Talbot's meeting apparently. And they aren't due to check out until Friday.'

'Now that's a result,' said Watson. 'I think you two should get yourselves down there and interview them both.'

'I agree,' said Lucy, who was now visibly elated by her breakthrough.

'Where did you say the hotel was?' asked Cooper.

'Leicestershire,' replied Lucy. 'About two hours' drive away.'

'We better advise the local police first,' said Cooper.

'I'll do that,' said Watson. 'If you two go now you'll be there by mid-afternoon.'

*   *   *   *

It was a little after noon when Steve's car pulled away from the vicarage. He harboured no thoughts of going on to the office. Instead he pointed the car in the direction of The Railway Tavern. As Steve had expected, Robin Mayhew was at his usual station at the end of the bar. His head was bowed over his pint glass, which contained just a small splash of dark liquid. For the previous 10 minutes, Robin had been amusing himself by rolling the dregs of mild around the bottom of the vessel and was so engrossed that he did not noticed Steve join him at the bar.

'Hello Mr Carmichael,' said Katie. 'What can I get you?'

'I'll have a pint of bitter shandy and a steak and kidney pie please, Katie,' replied Steve. 'And get Robin a drink on me.'

'Are you sure?'

'Why? Don't you recommend the steak and kidney?' said Steve with a wink.

'Not the pies,' replied Katie. 'I mean buying him a drink.' Katie made no attempt to prevent Robin from overhearing, and to ensure that Steve knew exactly who she was talking about she moved her head in the direction of the recipient of her comments.

'Absolutely sure,' said Steve. 'Here's £10, I'd like the change. And can you bring our drinks over to us? We'll be over in the corner.' Steve pointed in the direction of a small table in the farthest corner of the room.

It had been some time since anyone had bought Robin a drink, so he was delighted when Steve asked him to join him. 'Robin, you once told me that you were the man to speak to about the goings-on in this village,' said Steve. 'Well I need some information. Will you help me?'

'Mr Policeman,' replied Robin. 'There's nothing I don't know about the goings-on in Moulton Bank, so fire away.'

'I'd like to know about a few things,' continued Steve. 'First of all I'd like to know how I can contact your brother Terry?'

'Terry?' said Robin. 'He's in Hong Kong making his millions.'

'But I need to speak to him,' continued Steve. 'Do you have a phone number for him?'

'I have it at home,' replied Robin. 'But he'll be over on Monday. He's coming back for Linda's funeral.'

'So he knows?' said Steve.

'Yes of course he does,' said Robin. 'I told him as soon as I knew. He and Linda were going out for ages.'

'But your brother's married to someone now I thought.'

'Yes, but he still cared for her,' said Robin as he emptied the last dregs from his glass.

'Didn't Linda have a new boyfriend though?' asked Steve.

'I believe so,' replied Robin. 'But I don't know who the bloke was. I heard that it was that flash bloke from Wood Lane, but I never saw her with him.'

'So who told you that she had a boyfriend?'

'I can't recall,' replied Robin. 'It could have been Robbie

or Clive or maybe it was David Turner.' Steve bit into his pie. He could not understand why in a village where everyone knew just about everything about anything that went on, nobody seemed to know for sure whether Linda had a boyfriend or not.

'I wouldn't say no to another drink,' said Robin.

'Of course,' said Steve. 'Katie? Can we have the same again please?' At first the barmaid didn't hear them. She had just received a call on her mobile. 'Katie?' repeated Steve loudly, 'can we have the same again please?'

Hearing Steve's cry, the barmaid smiled, nodded and began to pour the first pint, while continuing to discuss her plan of action with her accomplice at the end of the phone. 'That's great news,' she whispered, 'when can we meet up again?'

'Lovely girl that,' said Robin. 'She'll make someone a lovely mother-in-law one day.' Robin then let out a huge belly laugh.

'Robin, who do you think killed Linda?' asked Steve.

'Well I don't rightly know,' replied Robin. 'But I bet it's to do with that obsession that she had.'

'What obsession?' asked Steve.

'The great detective obsession,' replied Robin. 'To solve a murder that took place over twenty years ago.'

'What murder?' asked Steve.

'The vicar's daughter,' replied Robin. 'The hit and run.'

'But why would she be obsessed with finding the driver of the car after all these years?' asked Steve.

'Call yourself a detective,' snapped Robin. 'She was one of the vicar's babysitters when young Gillian was killed. She never forgave herself for taking her eyes off the young girl.'

'So how long has she been trying to find the driver?' asked Steve.

'It started about a year or so ago,' responded Robin. 'I don't know what prompted her to become so obsessed. But it was that which kept her trapped in this crap hole rather than go to Hong Kong with our Terry.'

Before Steve had a chance to ask his drinking partner any more they were interrupted by Robbie Robertson who appeared at their table with three pint pots. 'Your drinks gentlemen,' said the landlord, as he placed the drinks on the table. 'Can I join you?'

'Be my guest,' said Robin, who quickly picked up his pint and started gulping its contents.

'How goes the investigation?' asked Robbie.

'Fine,' replied Steve. 'We're making good progress.'

'Bollocks,' interjected Robin. 'I've more chance of solving Linda's murder than this guy.' With that he emptied his glass, stood up from the table and left.

'What have you said to him?' asked Robbie.

'I don't know,' replied Steve.

'Well it must have been serious. That's the first time in years that he's willingly left the bar before closing time.'

'I tend to have this effect on people,' said Steve with a forced smile.

'By the way,' continued Robbie, 'I've been asking around about this mystery boyfriend of Linda's and it would appear that there may have been someone.'

'Who?' Steve asked.

'That I don't know,' replied Robbie. 'But a few people have said that they thought Linda was seeing someone.'

*   *   *   *

Clark and Cooper had spent most of the journey to the hotel discussing how they should approach their questioning of Talbot and McGuire. In the end they had settled on a strategy, the cornerstone of which was to separate the two men before they had a chance to realise that they were both to be questioned. Cooper was to get the hotel to call McGuire first and to take him off for questioning prior to locating Talbot. Once he was safely closeted away Lucy would ask the hotel to find Talbot who she would question in a separate room.

They arrived at the grand eighteenth-century hall that was the Bedworth Hotel at 3:30 p.m. Although the receptionist was surprised when the two officers showed her their identity cards, she quickly located Ken McGuire and with the help of the duty manager Cooper and McGuire were found a vacant room for the purpose of a private conversation.

Once Cooper and McGuire were safely installed in their room, Lucy asked the duty manager to locate Talbot and within a few more minutes she and Talbot had also been found a convenient room to talk.

McGuire was a heavily built man in his mid- to late forties. He was smartly dressed in what looked like a designer suit and as Cooper soon discovered was a confident and articulate individual. Following the death of his wife, McGuire had been interviewed on a number of occasions by the Lancashire police. However, this was the first time he had met Cooper.

'I'm sorry to drag you away from your meeting Mr McGuire,' began Cooper, 'but I would appreciate your assistance in helping us with an inquiry which we are conducting.'

'Is this to do with Sarah?' asked McGuire, who was clearly frustrated at being dragged out of his meeting.

'No,' replied Cooper. 'This is in connection with a separate incident. However, I want to stress that you are *not* under arrest.'

'Must be serious though for you to come all this way?' remarked McGuire.

'It is a serious crime I'm investigating, sir,' replied Cooper. 'But as I said before you are in no way implicated but we felt that you might be able to help us with our enquiries.'

'Well I hope that it won't take too long,' continued

McGuire. 'This meeting is costing me a fortune. I've got forty sales guys out there. You've got fifteen minutes then I'm going to have to get back.'

Cooper remained calm. 'Fifteen minutes should be more than adequate,' he replied. 'First of all, can you tell me how long you have been at this hotel?'

'I got here on Monday, but surely you could have established that from the hotel?' snapped McGuire.

'Quite so sir,' continued Cooper. 'So what time did you leave Moulton Bank on Monday?'

'About six-thirty in the morning,' replied McGuire. 'I picked up Matt at his house and we drove down together in my car.'

'Matt? Would that be Mr Matthew Talbot?'

'Yes, that's right,' said McGuire, who was shocked that the policeman was aware of his friend. 'Is Matt in trouble?'

'Certainly not,' replied Cooper. 'And what connection do you have with Mr Talbot?'

'Look, if Matt's in trouble I want to know before I answer any more of your questions.'

'Mr McGuire,' said Cooper, 'I can assure you that neither you or Mr Talbot are in any trouble. There has been a major incident in Moulton Bank and we are keen to talk to you both to find out whether either of you have any information that may help us.'

'So are you going to be speaking to him also?' asked McGuire.

'Yes, he will also be spoken to today. So, how would you describe your relationship with Mr Talbot?'

'He's a business acquaintance, he runs a PR consultancy and helped organise this week's sales meeting for me.'

'Do you know Mr Talbot socially?'

'Well I wouldn't call us close friends but he lives in the same village and we do sometimes meet socially.'

'Is Mr Talbot married?' asked Cooper.

'Come on, what is this?' barked McGuire. 'I'm not answering any more of your questions until I know what's going on.'

Cooper reflected on the situation, and in an attempt to gain McGuire's cooperation he decided to give him some information about the murder. 'I do understand your concern. We are investigating a suspicious death which took place in Moulton Bank earlier this week. We are questioning everyone who was in the area at the time and we have reason to believe that you and Mr Talbot may have seen something that could help us.'

To Cooper's surprise, upon hearing this McGuire's attitude changed completely. 'Oh my God, I see. Who's died? And why do you want to know about Matt's marital status?'

'It really would help if you let me ask the questions and you supply the answers.'

'I'm sorry. Matt's single. He's never been married and to be honest I've never heard him mention a girlfriend. In fact I often pull his leg that he must be gay.' McGuire paused to see what response he got from Cooper. When he received none, he continued. 'He's not gay, but to my knowledge he isn't currently seeing anyone.'

'Thank you,' replied Cooper with a smile. 'The dead woman is Linda Cartwright. I understand that she was known to you?'

'Really,' replied McGuire, who appeared unfazed by the revelation. 'I've known Linda for years. I was at school with her. She was in my sister's class. And Sarah's for that matter.'

'You said that you travelled down here with Mr Talbot,' said Cooper.

'That's correct,' replied McGuire. 'We decided that it was stupid to take two cars. And we thought that we could go through the agenda while we drove down.'

'When you arrived at Mr Talbot's house, did you see or hear anything unusual?' asked Cooper.

'No,' replied McGuire. 'I arrived at about six twenty-five, parked the car and as Matt was ready we left almost straight away.'

'Did you enter Mr Talbot's house?'

'No. He was ready. I was only there about two minutes. When I knocked on the door he was already packed and he just came straight out. I can't remember seeing anyone. It was dead quiet.'

'When was the last time you saw Miss Cartwright?' Cooper asked.

'I can't remember,' replied McGuire. 'Although I've known her for years, I didn't really *know* her, if you see what I mean. She was always around but I can't recall ever having a conversation with her.'

After a brief pause Cooper looked McGuire in the eye and said, 'Thank you Mr McGuire, you've been a great help. I'm sorry to have interrupted your meeting.'

'That's it?' asked McGuire.

'Yes,' responded Cooper. 'You're free to go.'

McGuire sprang up from his chair, shook Cooper's hand and then made his exit.

Talbot was a different animal from McGuire. He was less confident than his friend and was certainly more nervous about the prospect of being interviewed by the police. As a result of this and her inexperience of interviewing, Lucy's interview with him was very different from the way Cooper had questioned McGuire. Once they were comfortably seated, Lucy started her interview. 'I'm sorry to interrupt your meeting Mr Talbot, but I am investigating a murder which took place earlier this week, and in the course of our investigation we have been led to believe that the dead woman was known to you.'

'Really?' replied Talbot. 'Who?'

'A lady by the name of Linda Cartwright.' As she answered she looked closely at Talbot's facial expression. To her dismay he showed no signs of emotion. In fact as he heard the name of the dead woman he shook his head, which Lucy took to mean that he did not recognise the name.

'I'm sorry officer,' he replied. 'I think you are mistaken. I've never heard of Linda Cartwright.'

'Are you quite sure?' asked Lucy. 'She was the postmistress in Moulton Bank.'

'I'm quite sure,' replied Talbot. 'I have never met this lady. Why did you think I had?'

'Mr Talbot,' continued Lucy, 'I put it to you that you did know Miss Cartwright, and what's more you were having a relationship with her.'

Talbot shook his head. 'This is ludicrous,' he replied. 'I'm telling you that I have never met or heard of Linda Cartwright. And I can assure you that I was certainly not having a relationship with her.'

This threw Lucy, who had convinced herself that she would get a totally different response. 'Can you tell me what you were doing on the night of Sunday the seventh?'

'I played cricket on Sunday afternoon and went home at about seven-thirty' replied Talbot. 'I then made myself some supper, packed my stuff for the morning, watched some TV and went to bed at about eleven-thirty.'

'Can anyone corroborate your story?' Lucy asked.

'Well the whole of the Moulton Bank Cricket Club will vouch for me in the afternoon, but apart from a ten-minute conversation that I had with a builder who had called round to collect some money I owed him I spent the night alone.'

'So apart from this builder you were alone from about seven-thirty on Sunday evening until you left for the meeting the following morning?'

'That's right.'

'And what time did you leave on the Monday morning?'

'Ken arrived at about six-thirty,' replied Talbot.

It was at this point in the interview that Cooper joined

them. 'Mr Talbot, can I introduce you to DC Cooper,' said Lucy.

Talbot stood up and shook Cooper's hand. 'Can you please tell this woman that I am not a murderer and that I have never met this person called Lisa Cartwright?'

Cooper looked at Lucy who by now was feeling very frustrated with her lack of success with Talbot. 'As I am sure my colleague has told you,' commented Cooper, 'you are not under arrest and we are only here to see if you can help us with our enquiries.'

'And it's *Linda* Cartwright,' interjected Lucy.

'Lisa, Lucy, Linda, whatever her name is *I don't know her*,' snapped Talbot, who by now was totally exasperated by the whole experience. 'If I'm not under arrest I'd like to go.'

'Of course,' replied Cooper. 'But if you can recall anything that happened last Sunday evening or early Monday morning, would you please let us know?'

Talbot rose quickly from his chair and without another word left the room.

'Bugger,' said Lucy. 'I made a right mess of that.'

Chapter 10

After leaving The Railway Tavern, Steve's first action was to call into the station to find out how Watson, Clark and Cooper had progressed.

'Hello Marc. It's Carmichael. Have there been any major developments today?'

'Hello sir,' replied Watson. 'Lucy and Clive have travelled down to McGuire's hotel. It appears that Talbot is also there.'

'Really,' Steve said. 'Well, we should at least find out whether Talbot was seeing Linda. That's still a mystery. I met with the vicar this morning, he was certain that Linda was not seeing anyone, but the local publican reckons that she *did* have a boyfriend.'

'I've been going through the autopsy report,' interjected Watson. 'Dr Stock has now narrowed the time of death to between eleven-thirty and one-thirty. Her last meal was eaten at about six that evening and was pasta and chicken, and apart from the bruising around her neck there were no other obvious marks on the body.'

'Any other clues?' asked Steve.

'Well there is one other thing. According to Dr Stock she was strangled from behind. And he is pretty sure that she was seated or kneeling at the time.'

'How does he come to that conclusion?'

'Well it's to do with the bruising on her neck. It would appear that the bruises show that the thumbs of the killer were close together on the back of her neck. This suggests that he was standing behind her as he strangled her. Also the prints were very high up on her neck which suggests that he was standing over her.'

'Right,' replied Steve. 'That's good information.'

'Did you learn anything from the vicar?'

'Not much,' replied Steve. 'Although I'm sure that he knows more than he's telling me.'

'Why did Linda call him?' asked Watson.

'He reckons he didn't know, although I think that it could have been to do with information about the death of his daughter in the early seventies.'

'Gillian,' interrupted Watson. 'But that was years ago.'

'You know about the death of the vicar's daughter?'

'Oh yes,' replied Watson. 'My dad was the local bobby in Moulton Bank at the time.'

'Of course,' said Carmichael. 'What do you know about that case?'

'I don't know much I'm afraid. I was only young at the time and dad never discussed it with me.'

'Your dad still lives in the village doesn't he?'

'Yes that's right.'

'Would he be free to see us this afternoon?'

'I expect so,' replied Watson. 'Do you want me to call him?'

'Yes, if he's free he might be able to help fill us in on the link with Gillian's death.'

'OK. I'll call him now and then phone you back.' Within 10 minutes Watson was back on the phone to confirm that he had spoken to his father and that he was willing to meet with them both later that afternoon. Watson gave his boss the address and they agreed to meet outside his father's house an hour later. Steve decided to dash home to see Penny. His aim was to see if she could provide him with any further information about the hit and run on Gillian Pugh, before he met with Watson's father.

After his meeting with Pugh earlier in the day, Steve had become convinced that the death of Gillian Pugh was in some way linked to the murder of Linda Cartwright and the death of Sarah McGuire. He was nervous about the prospect of having to question his own wife on the subject, but he was certain that Penny could provide him with more information.

For once Steve's timing was perfect. Penny had spent most of the morning thinking about her schooldays and to help her remember she had brought out her old school reports and class photographs. So when Steve arrived at the house he found his wife at the kitchen table with a pile of photos and papers scattered around her.

'Hello,' said Penny. 'You're home early.'

'Yes,' replied Steve. 'I met with the vicar this morning and I'm meeting Marc later so I thought I'd pop home to see how you were.'

'That's nice,' commented Penny. 'Have you had any lunch?'

'Yes, I grabbed a pie in the pub,' replied Steve. He then noticed the contents of the cluttered table. 'What's all this?'

'Oh, it's some old school stuff,' replied Penny. 'Look, here's my old school reports and class photos.'

'You've never shown me these before,' said Steve as he picked up a school report for Penny Lathom, dated Summer 1974. He read out loud the final comments from the headmaster, Arthur Turner. 'Penny is a capable student, she has a sound understanding of numbers and has progressed well in science this term. She reads well and has performed well in English. She tries hard in games and her swimming is improving. She is a confident girl who is always ready to contribute in class discussions.'

'Here's my final year school photo,' said Penny, handing Steve a slightly faded and crumpled print. 'Which one do you think I am?'

Steve looked closely at the picture. To his surprise he had

no idea which was his wife. 'This one?' he said, pointing to a rather plump child sitting in the front row.

'Thanks,' responded Penny sarcastically. 'That's Lisa McGuire.'

'Well, that one at the back with the plaits.'

'Wrong again Sherlock.'

'Give me a clue,' begged Steve with a smile.

'I'm in the back row.'

'Ah, I should have guessed,' sniggered Steve, 'the one in between the two boys.'

'Correct. That's me. That's Clive on my left and David Turner's on my right.'

'Which one is Linda Cartwright?' asked Steve.

'She's in the front row at the end and next to her is Sarah Mulholland and a girl called Frankie Leeman,' replied Penny. 'This was our final year photo before we went to secondary school.'

'So who are the adults in the photo?' Steve asked.

'The bald thin man is Mr Turner, the headmaster. The lady at the other end is Miss Barber who taught us in our final year, and that's Mr Pugh at the end of the back row. He got in every photo. I don't know why!'

'My God, so it is,' exclaimed Steve. 'He looks quite fierce in this photo.'

'He was,' replied Penny with great emphasis. 'Although not as fierce as Mr Turner; he was really frightening when we were small.'

'Penny, tell me about Gillian Pugh,' asked Steve.

'Gillian? Why do you want to know about Gillian?'

'I don't really know for sure,' replied Steve. 'I met with Mr Pugh this morning and he confirmed to me that Linda had phoned him before she died. Apparently she arranged to meet him the following day. I've also found out that she was one of the babysitters who was supposed to be looking after Gillian when she was killed.'

'Yes, she was,' responded Penny. 'It was her and Terry Mayhew.'

'What's more, Robin Mayhew maintains that Linda was doing some investigating into Gillian's death. According to him she had been obsessed with the death of the vicar's daughter for the last year.'

'That would make sense I suppose,' said Penny. She paused thoughtfully before continuing. 'Linda always blamed herself for Gillian's death. You see, Linda was supposed to be helping Mary Turner look after Gillian. Mary was a couple of years older than us and to be honest it was her who the vicar left the child with. But for some reason Mary went off and left Linda and Terry Mayhew to look after her. Anyway, Linda and Terry must have taken their eyes off her and she must have run into the road. They never caught the driver.'

'So where was Mary Turner?' Steve asked.

Penny shook her head. 'I don't know. She was probably with her boyfriend.'

'And who was that?' asked Steve. 'Robbie Robertson?'

'No,' replied Penny. 'Robbie came along a lot later. She was dating Robin Mayhew at the time.'

'Oh really?'

'Yes, they were an inseparable couple for ages,' said Penny. 'Then Robin dumped her and McGuire took up with Sarah Mulholland, who Robbie had been dating. Sarah married McGuire and then shortly after that Robbie married Mary.'

'So who was your boyfriend, while all this was going on?'

Penny shook her head slowly. 'I had a couple of short romances. But there was nobody special, certainly not when I was that age.'

'What about Clive?' said Steve.

'Clive!' exclaimed Penny. 'He was always a good friend, but there was no romance between us. He was just a good pal really. Talking of Clive, I've not heard from him today.'

'Oh, I forgot to tell you,' said Steve. 'He told me yesterday that he wouldn't be able to come back until tomorrow or Friday.'

'If he's coming tomorrow he'd better arrive early,' said Penny. 'I've got a hair appointment at nine.'

'I'll call him tonight and make sure he arrives before you leave,' replied Steve. 'I assume that the hairdresser is the one where this boy's mother works?'

'Jemma's young man you mean,' replied Penny with a smile. 'Do you know, I think it is.'

'Does Jemma know that you're going?' Steve asked.

'No, not yet,' said Penny. 'I'll slip it into the conversation over dinner.'

Steve shook his head. He knew that Penny's announcement would almost certainly cause sparks to fly. It was at that point that he decided that it was time that he left to keep his appointment with the Watsons.

* * * *

Wally Watson was in his late eighties. He and his wife, Doreen, lived in a chocolate-box bungalow on the edge of town. He had retired from the police as soon as he reached 65, after 37 years' service. Although he now struggled to get around, his mind was still agile and fortunately for Steve his memory was still very much in full working order. Marc was the youngest child of Wally and Doreen, whose eldest offspring (a daughter called Elisabeth) had married and now lived in Yorkshire with her husband and three teenage children.

Marc met Steve outside his parents' house, where they spent a couple of minutes updating each other on the day's developments. Once inside Marc's mother disappeared into the kitchen to make her guests a cup of tea. Marc showed Steve into the living room where his father was waiting.

'Dad,' said Marc. 'Can I introduce you to Inspector Carmichael.'

'Good to meet you inspector,' replied Watson senior. 'You will excuse me for not getting up, my pins are not as strong as they used to be.'

'Not at all Mr Watson,' replied Steve. 'It's nice to meet you and very good of you to see us at such short notice.' Steve and Marc sat down opposite the retired village constable. 'I'd like to pick your brains about a couple of cases that occurred in Moulton Bank in the seventies.'

'There were *only* two significant cases in the seventies,' retorted Watson. 'The hit and run on Gillian Pugh and the suicide of Arthur Turner. I suspect that these are the cases that you are referring to inspector. Am I right?'

Steve smiled. 'Yes, sir, you are quite correct.'

'I'd like to ask *you* a question, inspector,' said Watson senior.

'Of course,' replied Steve, who had already warmed to the old gentleman.

'Why do you think that these cases are linked to the murder of Linda Cartwright?'

'Well,' said Steve. 'We have reason to believe that Linda was doing some detective work of her own relating to the death of Gillian. And although I've no reason to link the suicide of the headmaster to our current inquiry, I have a hunch that his death is also somehow linked.'

'You modern policemen still have hunches then,' teased Watson. 'I thought that was a relic from my time.'

'Dad,' interrupted Marc, who was very agitated at the tack his father was taking. 'This is serious. I'm sure that the inspector would appreciate you answering the questions rather than asking them.'

Watson senior smiled. 'You're right lad. I'm sorry inspector, but when you get to my age you'll realise that the art of asking questions doesn't disappear as soon as you retire from the force. Anyway, what do you want to know?'

It was Steve's turn to smile. 'Thank you sir. As I said before your help with these cases would help us enormously.'

Wally Watson leaned back in his chair and fixed his gaze at the light shade above Steve's head. 'She was a delightful little girl, full of life and always smiling. She was his pride and joy. The vicar and his wife had been trying to have a child for years, and when Gillian came along they were overjoyed. When she died they put on a brave face but I don't think I'm being too over-dramatic when I say that it killed them both. It certainly killed their marriage.'

'In what way?' asked Steve.

'Well, for the first couple of years they tried to keep their problems hidden, but after a while they didn't even seem to try and hide the fact that there were problems.'

'What sort of problems?'

'Well I think that Jane, that's the vicar's wife, always blamed her husband for Gillian's death. When Gillian was born she'd never leave the child but on that particular day I understand that the vicar was adamant that his wife should join him, and although she didn't want to she reluctantly agreed. The whole village was shocked when she left him, but really I suppose nobody was too surprised.'

'The vicar's wife's not dead then!' said Steve, who had assumed from his conversation with the vicar that she had died.

'Oh no, she's not dead; well as far as I know she's not. She left him about three years after the child had died.'

'So where is she now?' asked Steve.

The retired policeman shrugged his shoulders. 'That I don't know. To my knowledge nobody has heard from her in over twenty years. Some said she went to live abroad, but I really don't know.'

'So what happened on the day that Gillian died?' Steve asked.

'The vicar and his wife had left the child with the daughter of the headmaster. They had planned to be away for no more than a couple of hours and they knew Mary well so I guess that they thought that the little girl would be safe.'

'But she wasn't,' interrupted Marc.

'No,' replied his father. 'They got delayed in traffic. There had been some roadworks and they were late returning back. Mary had planned to meet her boyfriend and, well, she got Linda and Terry, who were much younger kids, to come up to the vicarage to look after the child for a short time while she went to see her boyfriend. Anyway, Linda and Terry must have taken their eyes off the child and before Mary got back she'd run into the road and been hit by a car.'

'So Mary was intending to return?' Steve asked.

'Oh yes,' replied Watson. 'She was only planning to be away for thirty minutes, which was about the length of time it would take to get back to her house to meet her boyfriend and walk back.'

'And how long was she away?' asked Steve.

'Well it was a little longer,' replied Watson. 'By the time she got back it had all happened. It must have been forty or fifty minutes.'

'And did you ever find out who the driver was?' Steve asked.

'No,' replied Watson. 'We never caught the driver.' For the first time Watson dropped his stare from the ceiling to his interrogator. 'I always felt that it was a local man. No evidence to prove that, but that was always my hunch.'

'Why did you think that dad?' asked Marc.

'I don't know really,' replied his father. 'Just a gut feeling I suppose.'

After a brief pause Steve decided to move his questioning on to the suicide of Arthur Turner. 'Tell me about Mr Turner's death,' he said.

Again the ex-policeman fixed his gaze above the head of the questioner. 'That was another big shock,' he replied. 'He died about six months after the little girl. Shot himself with his own rifle in his bedroom. There was no suicide note as such but there was a note left on the front door telling David not to come in and to fetch me. He'd obviously planned his suicide carefully even down to realising that he might be found by his boy, who was at a cricket match that day, so he'd written a note and stuck it to the front door.'

'What did the note say?' asked Steve.

'It said, don't come in. Get the police,' replied Watson. 'So the boy came to me and I went into the house by myself.' Watson senior took a deep breath. 'You never forget a sight like that, never.'

Steve could see that the old man was getting quite disturbed by re-living the events of that day. 'So you have no idea why he took his own life?' he asked.

'None at all,' replied Watson.

Doreen had been listening to the conversation for some time. However, she chose this moment to enter the room with a tray laden with tea and biscuits. 'Let me help mum,' said her son as he pulled up a small table for her to rest the tray.

For the next ten minutes the conversation moved away to more trivial matters before the retired policeman brought them back on track. 'So you think that Linda's death is linked to the death of the little girl?'

'She was certainly doing some of her own detective work and one of her last calls before she died was to the vicar,' replied Steve. 'Apparently she wanted to meet with him the next day with some urgent news. So I'm assuming it was something to do with the little girl's death.'

'And that Linda's killer didn't want her to pass on the news,' said Watson senior.

'That's my theory,' replied Steve.

'Well if you're right then you should also look at Arthur Turner's suicide,' said Doreen Watson. 'He killed himself because of that little girl, I'm certain of it. Whether it was the guilt of his daughter leaving her I don't know. But what I do know is that a man like Mr Turner would not take his own life unless there was something he couldn't cope with. And it's always been my belief that it was the guilt at the part Mary played in the child's death that made him shoot himself.'

' We don't know that Doreen,' snapped her husband. 'And I guess we'll never know.'

'She knows,' responded Doreen. 'Beth Turner knows. And if you ask me, Mary always knew and so does David.'

'That'll be Mr Turner's widow and children?' asked Steve

'Yes,' replied Doreen. 'The black widow, her precious daughter, the son; and I wouldn't be surprised if the vicar himself doesn't know.' Marc stared at his mother with his mouth wide open. He could not remember her ever being so animated about anything before. She continued, 'They knew more about what went on than they've ever said. They never told you the truth, did they Wally? If I were you inspector, I'd speak to Beth Turner, she'll have all the answers.' Her husband nodded. 'But I doubt whether she'll tell you any more than she told Wally thirty years ago,' she continued. 'Not if it detracts from the memory of her husband. But mark my words inspector, she knows!'

Chapter 11

It was just before 8:30 a.m. when Steve entered the incident room for his early morning review with the team. He was pleasantly surprised to see that Cooper, Watson and Lucy were already assembled. 'Morning sir,' said Lucy, with a bright smile.

'Morning team. I'm pleased to see that you've already made a start.' The three junior officers had already been in the room for 20 minutes, and they had wasted no time in updating the charts that they had worked on the previous day. 'So what progress did we make yesterday?' Steve asked.

'As for our facts we have just about the same as we had yesterday,' replied Watson. 'But we've amended our list of theories.'

'So run through the changes you've made to the list,' Steve instructed.

'Well, we are no longer convinced that Talbot was seeing Linda,' said Lucy.

'Why do you say that Lucy?' Steve asked.

'When I spoke to him yesterday he maintained that he didn't know her and to be honest I believed him,' replied Lucy.

'He could be lying.'

'Yes he could,' agreed Lucy. 'But that would be a dangerous ploy. Surely, if he was seeing her then someone must have seen them together so he would be taking a big risk in making such a strong denial if it wasn't true.'

'I take your point,' replied Steve. 'What do the rest of you think?'

'I think that Lucy's probably right,' said Watson.

'I also felt that he was telling the truth about Linda,' interjected Cooper.

'OK, let's assume that Talbot is telling the truth, but I want him to remain on the list. Until we're certain we're wrong we must keep anything that's written on the list intact.' The team nodded their approval. 'So what new hypotheses are you adding?' Steve asked.

'Well we would also like to add the following,' continued Lucy, holding up a new sheet of paper from the chart.

Steve read out the three sentences that made up the latest contributions of his officers. Number one stated that Ken McGuire murdered Linda Cartwright and Sarah McGuire. The second stated that whoever made the call to Linda from the phonebox at the end of Wood Lane was the murderer. The final addition stated that Linda's murder was linked to the death of Gillian Pugh in the early 1970s.

'Whose is the Ken McGuire theory?' he asked.

'Mine,' replied Lucy proudly. 'He never had a strong alibi for his wife's death, he never seemed to be too concerned either, and he had the opportunity to dump Linda's body down Wood Lane before he collected Talbot on Monday.'

'OK,' said Steve. 'It can be your job to investigate that theory Lucy. But keep an open mind on it. We've no evidence at all to support it as yet.'

'Yes sir,' replied Lucy, who was excited at having this line of investigation as her brief.

'Who came up with the phonebox theory?' continued Steve.

'That's mine,' replied Cooper. 'With me travelling to Leicester with Lucy yesterday, I've not managed to find out what the SOCOs came up with on the box.'

'OK,' replied Steve. 'You get on to that. And while you're

at it chase up on the names of the guests at that hotel in Harrisburg. I want you to find the mystery caller.'

'Yes sir.'

'Who came up with the last theory?'

'That was me,' replied Watson.

'I agree,' said Steve. 'After our meeting with your parents yesterday and my meeting with the vicar, I'm convinced that there's a link. We should also add to the list that Linda was doing some detective work herself.'

'Do you want me to follow it up?' asked Watson.

Steve thought for a moment before answering. 'No Marc,' he replied, 'I'll do that. I want you to spend today going through Linda's possessions. I want her house searched from top to bottom. I want you to see if she had a diary, I want that earring found and I want you to spend some time on why she was not wearing any shoes. Also we need to know who it was she knew in the US. See if you can find an address book and if she has any photos that might help us identify this mystery boyfriend.'

Marc's reaction could not disguise his disappointment at being given this particular assignment. 'It's important Marc!' snapped Steve. 'I want you to take your time on this one. I don't want anything missed. My guess is that if you do a thorough job, by this time tomorrow you will have made more progress than the rest of us put together.'

'Right you are sir,' replied Watson, although he was still not very impressed with his assignment.

'We'll get together at the same time tomorrow,' continued Steve. 'Good hunting team.' With that the three officers left the room leaving Steve to glance with a great deal of concern at the limited results of their efforts during the last three days.

Shortly afterwards he was joined by Hewitt. Steve was starting to understand his new boss and was therefore neither surprised nor disappointed when the chief appeared to lose interest in the details of their efforts after about five minutes.

'Remember Steve,' Hewitt said as he made his exit from the room. 'We need a quick resolution to this one.' Steve had no chance to respond as his superior was already well out of earshot.

* * * *

When Steve arrived home that evening the rest of the family had already started their evening meal.

'Hi dad,' shouted Robbie. 'Guess what?'

'I don't know,' replied Steve.

'I've got a paper round,' exclaimed his son.

'Only for two weeks while someone else is on holiday,' announced Natalie.

'I know,' replied Robbie, who was clearly irritated by his little sister's put-down.

'That's great news,' replied Steve. 'I told you that you'd get a chance.' Penny looked sternly at her husband, for as usual he was taking the credit for her efforts of encouragement. One of his most annoying habits she thought.

Steve sat down at the table. 'What's for tea then?' he asked.

'Sausages, eggs and beans,' said Penny. 'One egg or two?'

'Two please,' replied Steve. After a brief pause he said, 'You look different today Penny. Is that a new jumper you're wearing?'

'Dad!' exclaimed his exasperated eldest daughter. 'She's had her hair cut.'

'Oh yes,' commented Steve. 'It suits you.'

'Thanks Sherlock,' replied Penny. ' I hope you're more observant at work than you are at home, that's all I can say.'

'Where did you get it done?' he asked, although he knew full well where she had been.

'In the village,' replied Penny. 'A nice lady called Mrs Parkes cut it for me.'

Steve glanced in the direction of Jemma expecting to see some reaction to the announcement. He was to be disappointed. His daughter remained totally unaffected by the news. 'Well she's done a nice job,' he said.

'And how was your day dad?' asked Robbie. 'Have you apprehended the murderer yet?'

'No,' replied Steve. 'But I'm starting to believe that this quiet little village is not so quiet after all. And I'm coming to the conclusion that its inhabitants are full of secrets and surprises.'

'Tell me more?' said Penny. 'It sounds as though you've had an interesting day.'

'Later,' replied Steve.

He always made it a rule not to talk about important cases in front of the children. He felt that this case should not be an exception. For the remainder of the meal the discussion migrated through a number of topics. These included the not so unexpected absence of their builder, Jemma's desire to go to the village disco on the following evening (and her need for her father to drop her off), and the expected attendees at their barbecue on Saturday.

'I'll give Clive a call and make sure he's coming tomorrow,' said Steve at the end of the meal. He allowed the phone to ring for about three minutes before replacing the handset. 'No answer,' he shouted through to Penny. 'I'll try again later.'

Steve had been keen to talk to Penny about the day's events, but he had to wait until ten o'clock, before he could talk freely and without interruptions, as it took until then for all the children to depart to their rooms. Penny was very interested in hearing about the new theories that the team were investigating and even more keen to know the details of his meeting with Beth Turner earlier that day.

However, Linda's missing shoes and Steve's preoccupation with them was totally lost on her.

*   *   *   *

As soon as the morning's briefing had finished, Steve had decided he would pay a visit to Beth Turner. It was almost lunchtime when his car pulled up outside the pretty detached house in Applegate Lane. As he waited at the door, the comments of Doreen Watson rang through his head. 'She'll have all the answers,' she had said, 'Mark my words she knows.' When the door finally opened, Steve smiled at Mrs Turner and introduced himself. He had seen her at church, but until that morning they had never spoken.

They made their way into the lounge. The room was quite small with a noisy geometric-design fitted carpet. The wallpaper design was more subtle made up of two shades of pink in vertical regency stripes. Against one wall was a gas fire with a disproportionately large surround. On the wall above the fire hung a large black and white family portrait with Beth and Arthur (or so Steve thought) with two young happy smiling children on their knees. On every possible flat surface were photographs of the Turner family in various sizes and differing frames. On the sideboard there were at least a dozen smaller photographs of David and Mary, which were obviously taken when they were at either primary school or slightly older.

'Mrs Turner, I'd like to ask you a couple of questions about Linda Cartwright.'

'Of course. How can I help?'

'I expect that you must have known Linda quite well? I was wondering if you could tell me what sort of woman she was.'

'I've known Linda since she was a young girl,' she replied. 'She was a quiet woman, kept herself to herself. I liked her very much. It was such a shame that she died so cruelly.'

'Do you know any reason why anyone would kill her?' Steve asked.

'No,' replied Mrs Turner. 'That's what's made the news such a shock. She had no enemies at all.'

'One of our lines of enquiry suggests that Linda was investigating the death of Gillian Pugh. Did she ever discuss that with you?'

'No. I didn't know that.'

'And in the course of my investigation it has been suggested that the death of your husband was also linked with Gillian's death. I realise that it might be painful to talk about it, but was there a link?'

On hearing this Mrs Turner's expression changed. 'You have children don't you inspector?' she said.

'Yes,' replied Steve, 'we have three.'

'And what length would you go to protect your children?' she asked.

Steve's thoughts went back to Jemma and those difficult times when she was ill and badly needed an operation. 'Just about anything.'

'And Arthur was just the same inspector,' she replied. 'When he died I made a promise to myself that I would not discuss the reason he took his life and I'm not about to change my mind.'

'Not even if it will help the police solve the murder of Linda Cartwright?' responded Steve.

'Inspector, if you can prove to me that Linda's death is connected with Arthur's, I'll reconsider. But until then, no,' she said.

* * * *

'To me that sounds like there is certainly a link between Arthur Turner's death and the death of Gillian Pugh,' said Penny.

116

'Yes,' replied Steve. 'She almost confirmed that. But it was her comment about the lengths we go to protect our children that I find most interesting.'

'But which child does she mean?' replied Penny. 'Mary or David?'

After a short pause Steve said, 'It's late, I'm going to bed.'

'Oh!' exclaimed Penny, 'I almost forgot. Mrs Applebaum from next door accosted me when I was coming home. She wants to talk to you.'

'What about?' asked Steve.

'She wouldn't say. But she said it was important that she speak to you.'

'The mind boggles,' said Steve. 'I'll pop round tomorrow before I go into the station.'

'Try to get through to Clive again won't you Steve? I could do with him getting it finished soon. I'm really fed up with the mess.'

Steve picked up the phone and dialled Clive's number. He could not get through.

'Try him on his mobile,' said Penny. 'I've got his number somewhere.' Penny fumbled through her handbag until she found a crumpled piece of paper with Clive Penman's mobile number, which Clive had given her earlier in the week. To Steve's relief Clive answered his mobile after only two rings.

Chapter 12

Although she was now in her late eighties, Clara Applebaum was still very active. Apart from being partially deaf in one ear she was very much in control of her faculties. With the exception of her ageing cat, she lived alone. Her husband Raimund had died 20 years previously and she rarely saw any of her three children, her eight grandchildren or her ten great-grandchildren. Of course she received the usual cards on her birthday and at Christmas, and although she occasionally received phone calls from Alexandra and Christina, her daughters, and from her daughter-in-law Doreen, it was only Alice, the youngest of her grand-daughters who ever took the trouble to visit her.

Not that Mrs Applebaum minded, she was pleased that her offspring and their children were all happy and healthy. In her eyes they were all successful in their chosen lives. To most women of her age the lonely life she led would have been a constant source of complaint. Mrs Applebaum was different. She had long since come to acknowledge that every extra day she woke up was a bonus.

To most of the people who lived in Moulton Bank Clara was just a tiny old lady with a German accent. However, hers had been an interesting life. As a young and newly-married couple she and her husband had arrived in Coventry from Germany in the late 1930s, when Kraft Machine Tools, Raimund's employer, opened its first overseas branch. They quickly came to love the people and way of life in England,

and within a year of their arrival Clara discovered that she was pregnant with their first child. In 1938, Raimund and Clara Applebaum became the proud parents of a baby boy, who they named Albert. For the next 12 months they lived blissfully in Coventry and their family grew further with the arrival of Alexandra in 1940. It was shortly after Alexandra's birth that their lives changed.

Despite them both being Jewish, Clara and Raimund were German citizens and this was enough for them to be interned with thousands of other Germans who were domiciled in Britain at the outbreak of the war. For nearly five years Clara and Raimund were separated. Clara and her children were interned in a camp on the Lancashire plain midway between Southport and Wigan, while Raimund had been placed in a camp 200 miles away on the west coast of Scotland. Although Clara and her children were well treated, life was not easy for her during this time. After the war, the Applebaums settled in Moulton Bank. Raimund found himself a job with a local engineering firm while Clara supplemented her husband's wage by taking up a job as a cleaner at a number of large houses, including the village vicarage.

Since moving to the village, Steve had never had a full conversation with Mrs Applebaum. They had exchanged the odd pleasantry, either when he left in the morning or upon his return in the evening, and he had regularly had the pleasure of listening to her television through the wall, which she normally had on full volume. So Steve was intrigued to find out why his aged neighbour wanted to speak to him. He was also interested to find out what sort of lady she was.

As Steve closed the front door, Clive pulled up in his van. As usual he parked it half on and half off the pavement. 'Morning Steve,' he shouted as he slammed the van door.

'Morning Clive,' Steve replied. 'Nice of you to turn up.' Clive either didn't hear or more likely chose to ignore the comment. He marched up the path, nodded to Steve and banged hard on the Carmichaels' front door. By the time Penny opened the door Steve had already reached Mrs Applebaum's front door and had rung her bell.

Despite being only a couple of inches over five feet tall, Clara Applebaum made a striking impression on Steve. Once he had introduced himself, he was ushered into the lounge where he took a seat in a large armchair opposite his neighbour. It was no shock to find that the TV in the corner of the room was on and fairly loud, but he was surprised when Mrs Applebaum did not switch it off when he sat down. She lowered the sound a little, much to Steve's relief, but it remained on throughout their discussions.

' I understand that you have something that you would like to tell me?' Steve enquired.

'Actually a couple of somethings,' replied Clara. 'But first let me make you some tea, inspector.'

'If you don't mind I'll skip the tea, Mrs Applebaum,' replied Steve. 'I've just had a cup and I'm in a bit of a hurry.'

Clara nodded although she was disappointed that her offer had been rebuffed. 'Then I'll get to the point,' she said. 'I've been reading about the murder of that poor girl Linda. I am right in thinking that you are investigating her death?'

'Yes I am,' replied Steve.

'And I also understand that you too believe that her death was linked to the death of Arthur Turner and Gillian Pugh.'

'Why do you think that?' asked Steve, who was stunned by her knowledge and by her bluntness.

'Inspector, I may sound like I have only recently arrived from Germany, but I've lived in Moulton Bank for over sixty years. This is a small place and when I heard that you had visited the vicar and Sergeant Watson, it did not take me long to realise that you too think that there is a connection.'

'You said me too,' repeated Steve. 'So *you* think that the deaths are connected?'

'Inspector Carmichael, I *know* they are and I know that the other two are also linked.'

'Which other two?' Steve asked with surprise.

'Sarah McGuire and the other boy,' she replied.

'But Sarah's death was suicide.'

'Inspector, inspector,' retorted the old lady, 'if you believe that you need to look again. I knew that girl since she was a baby. She was not happy with her husband that is true, but she would not have taken her life, believe me.'

'Even if you are correct, how do you know that there is a link to Linda Cartwright's death?' Steve asked. 'And who is the other boy you mention?'

'The other boy is Gary Leeman. He lived here in the seventies with his mother and father and his young sister Frankie. His father was an American seviceman, his mother was English. He was a rascal when he was young, always in trouble with Sergeant Watson. Anyway, the family moved back to America about twenty years ago.'

'But he's been murdered?' said Steve.

Clara rose from her chair and walked over to her sideboard. She carefully opened the top drawer and extracted a folded copy of the *North Carolina Herald* and handed it to Steve. Steve opened the paper and read out loud the first line of an article he immediately spotted on page two that had been ringed in pen.

'Policeman drowns at local beauty spot. In the early hours of Monday morning officer Gary Leeman, aged forty-seven, was found dead at a popular picnic area ten miles north of Winston Salem.' Steve finished reading the article with interest but in silence. Once he had finished he looked at Mrs Applebaum and said, 'But this does not suggest that his death was anything other than a tragic accident and there is nothing that links it to the other deaths, other than the fact that he lived in the village twenty years before.'

'Inspector,' responded Clara, 'Linda was convinced that

121

Leeman was involved in the death of Arthur Turner. She was obsessed with his death and the death of Gillian Pugh. About six months ago she asked me if I had the address of the Leemans in the USA. She knew that I had kept in touch with Gary's mother, Brenda and I understand that through Brenda she had made contact with Gary. Then he dies.'

'Mrs Applebaum, there is nothing that you have told me that links any of the deaths. Gillian Pugh was run over thirty years ago, Arthur Turner committed suicide at around the same time, Gary Leeman was drowned in North Carolina, Sarah McGuire committed suicide and Linda Cartwright was murdered. I admit that this village has more than its fair share of suspicious deaths but there is no *evidence* of a link between any of them.'

'Maybe not, but the only person I showed the newspaper article to was Sarah McGuire, and within a week of that she is dead.'

For the first time since they had met, there then followed a pause. It was Steve who broke the silence. 'You mentioned that you had two things to tell me. I assume the death of Gary Leeman was the first; what was the second?'

'Her accomplice,' replied Clara. 'That queer one who was helping her.' It was at that point that there was a loud knock at the door. 'I wonder who that could be,' said Clara. She rose and disappeared through the door into the hall, closing the door behind her.

As he waited, Steve smiled to himself. He had come to like Clara Applebaum. He admired her intellect and directness. He was intrigued by the information she had given him about the death of Gary Leeman. He would certainly check out this latest development. He wondered what else Clara would be able to tell him. Did she know who Linda's boyfriend was? How ironic it would be if the little old lady next door was the person who provided him with the breakthrough he needed. His own Miss Marple, he mused.

Steve's attention was drawn to the TV, which was showing a programme about the rise in house prices in the North-West. This amused Steve, as the difference in pricing between Moulton Bank and Watford had been something he still found hard to comprehend.

After about ten minutes had elapsed Steve started to wonder what was keeping his host. When a further couple of minutes passed without any sign of Mrs Applebaum he decided to investigate.

He gingerly opened the lounge door and peered out into the hall. The front door was ajar, but to Steve's surprise neither Clara nor her visitor were in view. Steve was starting to wonder where she could be when he heard a groan. On the floor behind the front door in a pool of blood lay the limp body of Clara Applebaum.

As Steve rushed towards her, he could see splashes of blood on the wallpaper just above where Clara's body lay. She was still alive but her condition looked serious. As he reached her she groaned once more, but this time very weakly. She was slipping into a state of silent unconsciousness.

Steve was very concerned. He knew that Clara needed help urgently. He pulled out his mobile phone and dialled for an ambulance. Having made the call he then squeezed between the open door and its frame. He dared not force the door open as that would have disturbed Clara and he was scared of moving her.

The partition wall between Clara's house and his own was too high to climb over so he had to run down and out of the gate before he was able to get into his own driveway. He glanced up and down the road. Neither a pedestrian nor a car was in sight. Steve banged hard on his front door. It seemed to take ages before Penny opened it.

'Mrs Applebaum's been attacked,' Steve bellowed.

Having heard the commotion, Clive appeared at the top of the stairs. 'What's happened?' he shouted at Steve. Clive received no answer as Steve was already on his way back to where Mrs Applebaum was lying.

In no more than a minute Steve was joined first by Penny and then, a few seconds later, by Clive.

'What on earth's happened?' asked Clive for a second time.

'I don't know,' replied Steve. 'We were chatting, then she went to answer the door. She must have been attacked by whoever called.'

'That's a nasty blow she's received,' said Penny. 'We should try and stem the flow of blood.'

'I'll find something that we can use as a bandage,' replied Clive as he made his way up the staircase.

After a good deal of searching, Clive managed to find a cotton tea towel in Mrs Applebaum's airing cupboard. Penny used it as best she could to prevent the patient from losing even more blood.

It was about 15 minutes before the ambulance arrived and took Clara away to hospital.

Steve called into the station. He instructed Lucy to get to the hospital and to make sure that she spoke to Clara as soon as she regained consciousness. 'Clara had something important to tell me which related to the death of Linda Cartwright,' he told Lucy. 'She told me that she had an accomplice. If she comes round try and find out who it was.' Steve also asked Lucy to tell the rest of the team that their debrief would have to be delayed until four o'clock that afternoon.

Clara Applebaum never regained consciousness. She died in the ambulance.

* * * *

Steve had already been informed about the death of Clara Applebaum by the time he and the other officers gathered in the meeting room. The news had hit Steve hard. This was the first time in his career that he had actually known a victim of one of his murder inquiries. Even though he had only met the old woman that morning, he was surprised how deeply he was affected by her death.

'We've got to catch this vicious killer,' said Steve angrily. 'I don't want any more victims of this maniac.'

For a couple of seconds the team remained quiet. It was Cooper who broke the silence. 'I think I've had a bit of breakthrough with the call from Harrisburg,' he said.

'What's that?' said Steve.

'The hotel was hosting a sales convention for a North Carolina cigarette company. I managed to contact the human resources manager from the company who checked with his employees to see if anyone had called Linda Cartwright.'

'And?'

'Well, one of their employees did make the call,' replied Cooper.

'Who was it?' asked Steve. 'Have you spoken to them?'

'Her name's Frances Leeman,' replied Cooper. 'Unfortunately I wasn't able to speak to her as she's on leave at the moment and is not expected back until next Wednesday.'

Steve was amazed. 'Frankie Leeman. She used to live in Moulton Bank. She was one of the gang who hung around with Sarah McGuire.'

'There's more,' said Lucy. 'Tell him about her brother.'

'What's this?' asked Steve.

'Well, according to the HR manager, she had taken leave from her home in Winston-Salem to go backpacking in the mountains. When I questioned him more he said that she'd taken the leave to be by herself. She had been under a great deal of stress since the death of her brother. Apparently, a few months ago her brother drowned.'

Steve paused for a moment. 'When is she due back did you say?' he asked.

'Next Wednesday,' replied Cooper.

'Then we should be there to meet her,' said Steve. 'Lucy, I want you to come with me to the US. It might help us to have a woman officer present. Make contact with the local police and see if they can help us. I'd also like to see the file on the death of the brother.'

Neither Lucy nor Steve noticed the knowing look that was exchanged between Cooper and Watson.

'I'll have to get this approved first,' continued Steve. Then turning to Cooper he nodded with appreciation, 'Good work Cooper. Let's hope this is the breakthrough we've all been waiting for.'

Chapter 13

On the morning of the barbecue, Steve had woken up at a little after nine. For him this was very late, even for a Saturday. He had spent most of the previous evening in his study going over the deaths of Linda Cartwright and Clara Applebaum.

Steve's first thought was to check on the weather. He clambered out of bed, made his way to the window and peered gingerly through the curtains. It was a bright and sunny morning, so at least there was a good chance of it staying dry for the barbecue, he thought. However, the last thing he really wanted to do that day was to play host to half the village, particularly if one of his guests was a murderer. Before him the garden lay silent and still, save the presence of a couple of magpies who he watched with some amusement as they bullied and harassed any other bird that dared to trespass into their territory.

By the time Steve arrived at the breakfast table Robbie and Natalie were already well embedded into their bacon and eggs. 'Morning,' said Penny cheerfully. 'What time did you come to bed last night?'

'I don't know,' replied Steve. 'Late.'

'Dad,' interrupted Natalie. 'Can I have some money to buy a magazine?'

'What?'

'It's pardon actually dad,' commented Jemma loftily as she swept into the kitchen.

'What magazine's this?' asked Penny.

'My horse magazine,' responded Natalie.

'I gave you money only yesterday for that music magazine,' said Penny. 'Don't pester your father, he's got a lot to do this morning to get ready for the barbecue.'

'Have I?' asked Steve with a frown.

'Yes you have,' replied Penny. 'You've got to go to the butchers to get the meat. Then you've got to get the wine and beer. And then you need to get back here to light the barbecue.'

'And there was me thinking that I was going to have a nice quiet morning,' retorted Steve under his breath.

The first guests to arrive were Robbie and Katie Robertson, David Turner and Clive Penman. 'Nice day for it,' said Robbie as he handed over a crate of bottled beer to his host. 'As you can see we managed to get cover for the pub.'

'Thanks Robbie,' replied Steve. 'I think we've got plenty of beer but every little helps.'

Robbie, David and Clive headed straight for the buffet table, which Penny and Jemma had spent the last half hour loading with bread rolls, salad, cakes, crackers and a multitude of cheeses and jars of sauces and relishes.

Katie did not follow her father. Instead she hovered close to Steve until she was sure that the others were out of earshot. Since the death of Linda Cartwright she had been concerned that she might know the identity of the killer. She could not help thinking that the failure of Adrian Hope to meet her on the night of Linda's death was in some way connected with the murder. When she had challenged him about this, he had apologised and explained that he had not been able to get away from home that night because his wife had been late home from her Spanish evening class, so he had nobody to mind the children. Although this seemed a plausible excuse and at first had satisfied Katie's curiosity, she had later found out from Mrs Henderson, who ran the classes, that on the night of Linda's murder Lisa Hope had not attended. In fact, according to Mrs Henderson, Lisa had not attended any of the Sunday classes for some time, although she had paid her fees for the entire 12-week session.

'Inspector,' she began. 'I need to talk to you about something.'

'Oh yes?' replied Steve, as he removed the cap from a bottle of American lager. 'It's about Linda Cartwright,' continued Katie hesitantly 'On the night she died …'

At that moment from the corner of her eye she noticed David Turner making his way back to where they were standing.

'Do you have any information?' Steve asked.

'Er, no,' she replied, 'I was just wondering if you had anyone specifically in the frame,' she babbled without too much thought.

'Just about everyone,' replied Steve.' But don't worry, we'll catch the killer.'

It was out of character for Katie to lose her nerve like this, however she could not see Adrian Hope as a murderer and as such she decided that her suspicions were almost certainly wrong, and that she would keep them to herself.

By this time Steve had opened three bottles of lager and had met David and handed over the bottles to him for distribution to each of his three male guests.

Steve returned to the barbecue and the serious business of preventing the sausages and chicken portions from total cremation. If the truth was known he was a terrible cook. For Steve it was impossible to have a barbecue without at least some of the food being burnt to a crisp or for some of his own body hair to be consumed by the inferno. However, he was persistent and so far on that particular day by his own standards he was doing OK. He'd lit the barbecue in plenty of time, he'd waited for the coals to go white before starting to cook the food, and as a result he felt reasonably confident that he had everything under control.

After a couple of minutes Marc Watson and his wife Susan arrived. Then, steadily, the rest of the guests. Within about 20 minutes the party was complete and the garden air was full of gossip, jokes and small talk. When the guests had all had an opportunity to sample a morsel of chef Carmichael's cuisine, Steve decided to remind his troops to mingle with selected suspects. Handing over the tongs to Jemma, he left his post at the barbecue and strolled over to where Lucy and Marc Watson were standing. 'Great chicken sir,' said Watson.

'Thanks Marc,' replied Steve with genuine pride. 'Have either of you had a chance to speak to any of our guests yet?'

At that moment they were joined by Marc's wife.

'Inspector,' said Watson, 'can I introduce you to my wife, Susan.'

'Pleased to meet you,' said Steve, as he shook her hand.

'How are you settling in inspector?' asked Susan.

'Fine,' he replied. 'But please call me Steve.'

During the next couple of minutes Steve discovered that Susan was also from London. He also discovered that she had moved to Moulton Bank 10 years earlier when she had taken up a job as a journalist on the *Manchester Evening News* and that she had met Marc Watson about three months after arriving in the village. 'He came to my rescue when I reported a break-in at my flat,' she explained to Steve and Lucy.

'Was the culprit found?' asked Steve.

'No,' replied Susan. ' I lost my stereo, my video-player, my record collection and ultimately my job, and in exchange I got myself a husband and two children.' She laughed loudly.

Steve immediately took to Susan. She was attractive, bright and bubbly and he could not help wondering what she saw in Marc. However, she was obviously happy and showed no signs of any regret at her lot.

'Sorry to talk shop Susan,' said Steve, 'but I'd like ten minutes with Marc and Lucy if that's possible.'

Susan smiled. 'No problem Steve,' she said. 'I'll make myself scarce shall I?' With that she turned and walked over towards a group of people who she obviously knew, who were gathered near the buffet table.

Once she was safely out of earshot Steve turned his attention to Marc and Lucy. 'Where's Cooper?' he asked.

'He's here somewhere,' replied Lucy. 'I saw him talking to the vicar.'

'That's good,' replied Steve. 'I'm pleased he's already getting down to it. Now I want you both to get among the guests and do a bit of covert questioning,' he continued. 'Lucy, you concentrate on the Turners and Mr Pugh. Marc, you concentrate on the crowd from The Railway Tavern. Let's see if the good people of Moulton Bank will be a bit more forthcoming in a more relaxed environment.' The two officers nodded before heading off to complete their various challenges.

It was then that Steve caught sight of Cooper, who was in deep conversation with Robbie Robertson and a lady who Steve assumed was Mrs Cooper.

'Good afternoon Mr Carmichael,' came a voice from behind him. Steve turned to be greeted by the now familiar face of Mr Pugh. 'I don't believe that you've met Terry Mayhew,' continued the vicar, who gestured towards a tall younger man standing a couple of paces behind him.

'I hope that you don't mind me gate-crashing your party, inspector,' said Mayhew. 'I'd like to spend some time with you regarding Linda's murder, when it's convenient.'

'Of course,' replied Steve. 'And there are a number of questions that I'd like to ask about Linda if that's all right with you?'

'Yes, of course,' replied Mayhew. 'And I suppose that you will want to discuss the death of poor Mrs Applebaum also?'

'You knew Mrs Applebaum?' asked Steve with some surprise.

'Indeed I did,' replied Mayhew. 'She was my mother's cleaner for many years, as she was for Mr Pugh.'

'Really?' said Steve. 'Then we must talk soon.'

'How about Monday?' Mayhew asked. 'I'm staying at the Oddfellows Arms, in the village. If you can spare the time, Monday would be good for me.'

'Monday it is then,' replied Steve. 'What time would be convenient?'

'Shall we say two o'clock?'

'Fine,' said Steve. 'I look forward to it.' After a slight pause he continued, 'Can I get either of you a drink and maybe something to eat?'

'Nothing to eat for me thank you,' replied the vicar. 'I'll just have a glass of orange juice.'

'And I'll have a glass of beer,' said Terry. 'And maybe some chicken.'

Steve left and to his delight when he returned with their food and refreshments he found that Mrs Turner had joined the two men and that Lucy was already well advanced in fulfilling her chosen assignment. He handed over the food and drink, smiled at Mrs Turner, and left to find Cooper.

Cooper and his wife were engaged in deep conversation with Penny and Susan Watson in the kitchen. 'Marc has many talents, but an appreciation of the English language is not one of them I'm afraid,' said Susan. 'Only the other day we had a discussion during which he was adamant that "Ethos" was one of the three musketeers.' With that she let out a hearty roar.

'Am I interrupting something?' asked Steve as he joined them.

'Steve,' said Penny, 'have you met Susan and Julia?'

'I've met Susan,' said Steve, smiling at her as he spoke, 'but I have not yet had the pleasure of meeting Mrs Cooper.'

'Allow me then,' said Penny with a grin. 'Julia Cooper, this is Steve, my husband and the *chef de maison*.' At this Susan and Penny both roared with laughter.

'Pleased to meet you Julia,' said Steve. 'I'm glad you could come.'

'We were just comparing notes about the various skills of our highly distinguished detective husbands,' said Penny.

'Sounds ominous,' said Steve. 'I heard that Marc is no Shakespeare, but what of Paul and I?'

'Well we were just about to get the full lowdown on Paul from Julia,' replied Penny. 'And as for you, that's our secret I'm afraid.'

Steve realised that his wife may well have had quite a few glasses of wine already.

'Well Cooper,' he said turning to his fellow officer. 'I think we should leave these good ladies to their investigations. I need a word with you in private regarding our own, albeit less important, investigation.' Cooper was relieved to be drawn away from the female gaggle and quickly followed Steve into the hall.

As soon as the two officers were out of earshot Steve grabbed Cooper by the arm. 'Paul, I'd like you to mingle with the guests and see if you can find out anything that could shed light on any of the murders.'

'Of course. Anybody in particular?'

'I've asked Lucy to concentrate on the good reverend, David Turner and his mother. Marc's speaking to Robbie Robertson and Clive Penman, so I'd like you to spend a little time with Robin Mayhew. I think you've already met him, he's the drunk scruffy one at the buffet table. Try to find out anything you can about Clara Applebaum. And see if you can find out if he knows who Linda's accomplice was. Mrs Applebaum mentioned to me that she had a sidekick and I'm certain that this person, whoever they may be, is the key to all this.'

'That reminds me,' said Cooper. 'The pathologist's report on Mrs Applebaum arrived late last night after you'd left the station.'

'Anything in it that I should know?' asked Steve.

'Yes, something very interesting. It would appear that she was killed by a single blow to the back of her head. They believe the weapon was probably a hammer.'

'So?'

'So,' replied Cooper, 'she either turned her back on the killer at the doorstep or whoever killed her was already in the house.' With that Cooper departed for the garden leaving his superior to mull over this new piece of news.

Carmichael, Cooper, Watson and Clark spent the next few hours trying hard to probe and prod the guests in an attempt to find more clues to the deaths of Linda and Mrs Applebaum. In truth they had little success.

Penny and Susan got on like a house on fire. Penny learned that Susan was thinking of returning to journalism in the next 12 months, but had not managed to find anything that she could do that would not conflict too much with her family commitments.

'Wouldn't it be easier if you lived in London?' Penny asked.

'Yes it would,' replied Susan, 'but Marc wouldn't leave his parents and he doesn't seem keen to leave his current role either. So I'm going to have to keep looking round here.'

Susan for her part discovered more about the Carmichael family, particularly Jemma and the operation that she needed when she was small.

'What was wrong with her?' she asked.

'She had a weak valve in her heart,' replied Penny. 'It's quite common I believe.'

'So what did you do?' Susan enquired.

'Well we hadn't much money at the time so it was really hard. We were told we might have to wait for several months to have it done on the NHS. So we enquired about going private. They could do it within weeks, but that cost a fortune.'

'That must have been a real worry for you both,' said Susan with genuine concern.

'Yes it was,' Penny replied. 'But Steve managed to borrow the money and she had the operation done really quickly.'

'And has she fully recovered?' asked Susan.

'Oh yes,' replied Penny. 'She was under regular observation for about five years, and she still gets checked out every year, but she's absolutely fine now.'

The two women also discussed Lucy Clark. It was Susan who brought her up in the conversation. 'So what do you think about little miss perfect?' she had said while at the same time sending a laser-beam glance in Lucy's direction.

'Lucy, you mean,' replied Penny, trying to sound neutral about her.

'I don't trust her,' said Susan. 'Marc reckons she was part of the reason Inspector Rowe moved to another station.'

Penny was desperate to find out more, but she didn't want to appear to be too interested. 'Inspector Rowe?' she said slowly. 'He was Steve's predecessor wasn't he?'

'That's right,' replied Susan in a whisper. 'Well, the story goes that Inspector Pearson and he fell out over her in some way. Not sure what it was, but Marc seems to think Pearson wanted Lucy in his team and Rowe objected.'

'I don't see why that would be her fault,' Penny asked. 'If she's good and two stupid guys start fighting over her then it's their problem isn't it?'

'Only she made it clear to Hewitt that she would prefer to be with Pearson,' Susan continued. 'And it was at that point that Hewitt realised that one of the inspectors had to move on.'

'I see,' said Penny. 'But why did Lucy ask to work under Pearson rather than Rowe?'

'Well it's common knowledge that Hewitt is being lined up to head up some special team,' said Susan in a hushed tone. 'Pearson had been promised a part in this team and he was using it to lure Lucy away from Rowe.'

Penny just nodded to get Susan to continue. However she fully realised that the secret special team that Hewitt had talked to Steve about was not only not so secret, but Steve was not the only person to have been offered the job of heading it up.

'Well, Pearson thinks he's a bit of a ladies' man,' continued Susan. 'For his age he's not too bad I don't suppose, but he's so obvious and shallow that any idiot can see through him. Actually, he tried it on with me once, but I put him straight I can tell you.'

'Go on,' prompted Penny eagerly.

'Anyway,' continued Susan, who was now in full flow. 'Whatever you think of Lucy, she's nobody's fool. So for her to go to Hewitt it's clear she'd been promised something by Pearson.'

'I suppose so,' replied Penny. 'But Rowe was moved to another station and Lucy's working for Steve now, not Pearson.'

'Just goes to show that Hewitt's not as daft as he looks,' said Susan knowingly. 'I suspect he judged Pearson to be the better man, which is why Rowe went. But I suspect he thinks Steve is an even better choice for the special assignment and I suspect that Lucy has twigged that too.'

'I see,' replied Penny. I'll have to keep my eye on her, she thought.

It was well after eight, when the last guests left. 'Well I think that was a success,' said Penny, as she sat beside her husband on the sofa.

'Yes,' replied Steve. 'Although I'm surprised you remember. You'd had a few before two o'clock.'

'What do you mean? I was just being sociable. Anyway, talking of having a few, *who* invited Robin Mayhew?'

Steve shrugged his shoulders. 'I have no idea, maybe he came with his brother?'

Penny who was now becoming abruptly serious, shook her

head in a slow and deliberate way. 'I am not sure Mrs Turner or the vicar were that impressed when he decided to urinate in the flower bed.'

'I don't think the marigolds were that impressed either,' chortled Steve. 'But no real harm was done. I think the great and good of Moulton Bank are all too familiar with Robin's little foibles.'

'Maybe so,' replied Penny firmly. 'But I would have preferred that the children were not exposed to such a sight in their own back garden.'

'I suppose you've got a point. But I'm sure they won't be too damaged by the experience. Anyway, I thought Clive Penman played a blinder by taking him home in the back of his van.' Wishing to end this particular train of conversation Steve decided to change the subject. 'What do you think of the team then?' he asked.

'Well, they seem very nice,' observed Penny. 'And I did like Susan Watson. She's a really good laugh.'

'Yes,' said Steve. 'But not at all the sort of person I'd expect to be married to Marc.'

'Why do you say that?' asked Penny with obvious surprise.

'Well, she seems so energetic,' responded Steve. 'She's intellectual and she's obviously well educated. Marc's a good guy, don't get me wrong, but he's not what you'd call energetic, in fact he's quite lazy. He never went to university and he's not yet demonstrated that he's got anything like her intellect.'

'So you think that it's essential that couples have equal intellects and educational backgrounds, do you?' teased Penny.

'No of course I don't mean that,' said Steve. 'All I'm saying is that they are an unlikely match.'

'They *are* different I suppose,' said Penny. 'And she was saying that she wanted to move to London to help get back into journalism, but he was not happy moving away.'

'Exactly,' responded Steve. 'He's become fat and lazy here, that's what it is. I'll have to keep an eye on him.'

Penny yawned. 'Well I like them both, and the Coopers.'

'What about Lucy Clark?' Steve asked.

'I only spoke to her for a short while,' replied Penny. 'But I can't say I was that struck on her.'

This shocked Steve. 'What was it that made you form that opinion?'

'Nothing really,' replied Penny. 'I just got the impression that she was a bit secretive.'

'You're wrong,' Steve assured her. 'She's young and a bit shy that's all, but she's OK. In fact I think that she's a darn sight better than Marc. In my opinion she'll make a first-class officer and I wouldn't be surprised if Watson and Cooper don't find themselves reporting to her within the next four or five years.'

'Maybe,' said Penny. 'That's even more reason for people to be a little wary of her.'

'You're jealous of her ambition,' said Steve with a grin.

'That's rubbish,' said Penny as she elbowed her husband in the kidneys. 'I only met her for a couple of minutes, so I may be doing the poor girl a gross injustice. I'm sure she's a capable officer and destined for great things. But she did nothing for me I'm afraid. Give me Susan or Julia any day. At least they know how to let their hair down.'

Penny elected not to inform Steve about the conversation she'd had with Susan about Lucy. She saw little value in sharing this at that moment.

*   *   *   *

Steve normally slept well, but that night he could not settle. He could not help thinking about what Cooper had said earlier in the day; and as hard as he tried to maintain an open mind on whether the killer was inside or outside the house,

Steve couldn't help feeling that Clara Applebaum's killer was inside the house all the time. The fact that he had knocked at the door, when there was a perfectly good bell, in Steve's mind supported this theory. He further believed that Clara had been killed to prevent her from telling him something.

But there were still a couple of questions that Steve could not answer. Firstly, how did the killer gain entry to the house, and secondly, how did the killer know that Clara was talking to him in the first place. He decided that he would go back to the murder scene the following morning before the family went to church. He was certain that the answers to these questions lay in the house next door.

Chapter 14

The phone rang three times before Susan Watson had a chance to grab the receiver. 'Hello, the Watson residence,' she said in a chirpy voice.

'Oh hello,' said Steve, who had expected Marc to pick up the phone. 'It's Steve Carmichael here. I'm sorry to disturb you so early on a Sunday morning but can I speak to Marc?'

'Of course,' she replied. 'I'll get him for you. By the way, I did enjoy the barbecue yesterday. It was nice to meet you and Penny.'

'Thank you,' replied Steve. 'We thought it went well.'

A couple of seconds later Marc arrived on the other end of the phone. 'Morning Sir.'

'Marc, I'm sorry to have to call you so early but I need your help.'

'Of course,' replied Watson. 'What do you want me to do?'

'I want to have a look at the pathologist's report on Clara Applebaum, and I would like to have another look around her house. Could you collect the report and the house keys from the station and bring them over?'

'Of course,' replied Watson. 'But could I bring them over a little later. I've promised to take my eldest to the swimming baths this morning.'

Normally Steve would have been a little more demanding, however considering the fact that Marc had spent most of the

140

previous day at the barbeque, and having just been so warmly thanked by his charming wife, he didn't have the heart to push Marc on the matter.

'That's fine Marc,' he replied. 'What time do you expect to be able to get over?'

'About eleven? Is that OK?'

'We won't be back from church by then,' said Steve. 'So why don't you come round early this afternoon? Let's say one o'clock?'

'That's fine. I'll see you then.'

Marc put down the receiver and rolled back over to face his wife. 'Now where were we before we were so rudely interrupted?' he whispered.

Susan wrapped her arms around her husband's bare body. 'What's all this nonsense about swimming?' she said with a grin. 'The kids won't come back from your mum and dad until lunchtime, as well you know.'

'If Carmichael thinks he can rob me of the opportunity to spend the morning in bed with my beautiful wife then he's got another think coming,' replied Marc.

*   *   *   *

That Sunday the Carmichaels arrived at church with more than a couple of minutes to spare before the service was due to start. To Steve's amazement and delight, Jemma had managed to get ready without any need to be nagged. What Steve did not realise was that her enthusiasm was a direct result of her romance with Jason, rather than a sudden Road to Damascus experience. Jemma had arranged to meet Jason at the church before the service, a fact that only became apparent to Steve when he saw the young man standing at the end of the path from the car park to the church. Before Steve had an opportunity to meet Jemma's young man his attention was suddenly distracted by the headlines on the front of the *News of the World*, which he caught sight of through the window of the car parked next to him.

'**Vice squad chief suspended amid bribery claims**' he read.

As he strained to read the copy through the window, his heart started to beat faster and faster. He pushed his face hard against the window to see if he could make out the name of the officer involved, even though he knew full well that it would be Butler. If it was Butler, who else would be implicated, he thought.

All through the service all he could think of was the £5,000 he had borrowed from Butler all those years ago, and he re-lived again and again that sickening feeling he had experienced when he realised that the loan was financed from one of many backhanders from the local criminal gangs.

When the service was over Steve ushered the family out of the church and into the car, much to Jemma's disgust. She had planned to use that moment to introduce Jason to her parents. On the way home Steve stopped at the local newsagents and purchased a copy of the *News of the World*, and when the family eventually arrived home he dashed up to his study and read the article about the arrest of Chief Inspector Nick Butler.

It was exactly one o'clock when the doorbell rang. 'That'll be him now,' Steve announced to Penny from the top of the stairs. 'I'll only be an hour or so.'

'OK,' replied Penny. 'Take a key, I might quickly nip to the supermarket while you're out.'

* * * *

'Good afternoon sir,' Marc said as his boss appeared.

'Hello Marc,' replied Steve. 'Thanks for coming out like this. I didn't want to wait until tomorrow to go over the pathologist's report and after what Cooper told me yesterday

I felt that we needed to have another good look at the crime scene.'

'What did Paul say?' asked Marc who was now quite curious.

'He reckons that the report suggests that Mrs Applebaum was struck from behind. Which means that the killer was in the house,' said Steve as they walked up the path towards Mrs Applebaum's door.

'But that's impossible because you were the only other person in the house,' remarked Marc.

'Yes,' responded Steve. 'So either it was me who killed her or there was someone else inside the house.' After a slight pause Steve continued. 'I can assure you I didn't kill her, so that leaves us to assume that the killer was already there.'

'But surely if Mrs Applebaum had a visitor when you arrived she would have mentioned that to you?' queried Marc.

'I've been mulling that over too,' said Steve. 'I have only two alternative answers. Either she already had a visitor who she didn't think was connected to Linda's death or the intruder managed to get in without her knowing.'

'There is a third option,' said Marc.

'And that is?'

'That she let the intruder in and as she closed the door he hit her. He'd be behind her then wouldn't he?'

'I don't think so,' replied Steve. 'If that was the case why didn't he ring the bell? I heard a knock. The doorbell is working perfectly well. And even if he had come in through the door, the way Mrs Applebaum fell would have made it almost impossible for him to leave by the front door. When I found her she was slumped against the door. I'm convinced that the killer could not have left through the front door.'

'I see. So the killer probably broke in and almost definitely broke out of the house while you were there.'

'I think so,' said Steve. 'But if he did I didn't hear him. It's

143

possible though as she had the TV on quite loud when I was there, but I don't remember hearing anything that sounded like a break-in.' By this time the two officers had reached the front door of Mrs Applebaum's house. 'Have you the key Marc?' said Steve, with his hand stretched out.

'Of course,' replied Marc, and he handed over a small bronze Yale key.

As Steve turned the key in the lock, Marc pressed the doorbell three times. The sound of the chimes reverberated down the hallway. 'I see what you mean,' said Marc. 'There's nothing wrong with that.' When they were both safely inside the house Steve closed the door behind them. 'What shall we do first?' asked Marc.

'First of all let's look for any signs of forced entry,' replied Steve. 'You go upstairs, I'll stay down here.'

'Fine,' said Marc as he climbed up the stairs.

'But for God's sake don't disturb anything. We will need to get SOCO here today and I don't want them just getting your prints,' Steve shouted up at him.

Mrs Applebaum's house was a mirror image of his own, but to Steve it somehow seemed much smaller. This was probably due to the fact that in every room there were a myriad of cupboards and shelves, all of which were covered with ornaments and photographs. Steve couldn't help wondering how the old lady could have kept everything so tidy and clean. At the back of the house were two rooms, the kitchen and a small back room. It was the kitchen that Steve entered first.

In one corner was a walk-in cupboard, with strong wooden shelves covered in old wallpaper. In the opposite corner was a small wooden table with two chairs. Apart from an intricately embroidered lace doily, the table was bare. Facing out to the back garden was a heavy wooden door and a wide metal-framed window over a deep enamel sink. Steve checked the door. It was locked. He also inspected the windows. They were shut fast. Unless the intruder had a key there was no way that he could have gained entry through the kitchen. Steve then made his way to the back room. This was in keeping with the rest of Mrs Applebaum's house. It was neat and tidy with a long ancient oak sideboard running the length of one wall and opposite an even older Welsh dresser. Both were crammed with tiny ornaments, china cups and saucers, and everywhere there were small portraits in ornate picture frames. Facing the back garden was an old rickety French window. With two fingers, Steve gently tried the handle. It was open.

At that moment Marc arrived. 'There's no sign of forced entry upstairs,' he said.

'I think that this is how the intruder got in,' replied Steve, opening the door to demonstrate.

'Shall I get SOCO over now?' asked Marc.

'Yes,' replied Steve. 'They need to dust here for prints and I want them to check outside for footprints. If we're lucky he may have left us a clue or two.' Marc left the room and made the call from the hall.

It was after three o'clock before the scene of crime team arrived. Steve showed them through to the back room and once they had started their search, he and Watson left the scene. 'We've done enough today,' said Steve. 'Get yourself home.'

'I'll see you tomorrow,' replied Marc.

'Yes,' Steve mumbled as he turned up his path, his thoughts having returned to the revelations in the *News of the World.*

Chapter 15

The following morning Steve made it to Kirkwood station in a new record of 29 minutes and 30 seconds. Even though he had a lot on his mind that day he was still able to allow himself a modest amount of smug satisfaction in achieving a new personal best time.

He had spent most of the previous evening pondering the implications of the newspaper headlines. However, before he had gone to bed he had convinced himself that it was a waste of his time and energy to worry about Butler. It was so long ago that the chances of the Butler investigation having any repercussions on him were almost zero. He also kept telling himself that as he had accepted the loan in good faith and paid it back in full, any case against him would be very thin indeed. He had gone to bed feeling pretty much at ease, although there was still a part of him that remained a little anxious that his association with Butler would yet return to haunt him.

'Morning team,' Steve barked as he entered the room. 'Let's get cracking, I can smell a result in the air.'

He made his way to the front of the incident room in confident mood. He was convinced that the SOCOs would discover something concrete at Clara Applebaum's house for the team to pursue. For the first time in the week since Linda Cartwright's body had been found he started to feel that they were getting close to identifying the killer.

Watson, Clark and Cooper had not seen the boss like this

before, and at first they weren't sure how they should react. 'First of all we need to update our charts,' said Steve, pointing to the three lists that were neatly written out in red, blue or green marker pen. 'Lucy, can you please act as scribe? We'll start with the facts.'

Lucy picked up a red marker.

'Shall we go through the ones we already have first?' asked Cooper.

'Yes,' replied Steve. ' I think that would be a good place to start.'

Within the hour the team of four had completed the review. Not only had they revisited all the previous entries, but they had also added many new ones. The known list (in red) now had 10 items, which Lucy had written in chronological order. They read as follows:

1 Linda Cartwright had started investigating the deaths of Gillian Pugh and Arthur Turner about a year ago.

2 Linda had an accomplice who was helping her with her investigation.

3 Linda had received a telephone call at 9:47 p.m. on the evening of her death from Frankie Leeman in Harrisburg.

4 Linda had telephoned Clive Penman at 10:25 p.m. asking him to mind the post office the following day.

5 Linda then phoned Mr Pugh at 10:35 p.m. requesting a meeting for the following day.

6 Linda received a call at 10:47 p.m. (from an unknown person) from the callbox at the end of Wood Lane.

7 Linda was strangled between 11:30 p.m. and 1:30 a.m.

8 Linda's body was dumped in Wood Lane after 4:30 a.m.

9 Clara Applebaum had been killed by someone who was inside the house.

10 The murderer of Clara entered and left the house through the French window in the back room.

The hypothesis list (in blue) also had 10 entries, which were as follows:

1   Linda's murder was linked to the deaths of Gillian Pugh and Arthur Turner.
2   Sarah McGuire was murdered.
3   Sarah McGuire was murdered by the same person, or persons, who had killed Linda.
4   Linda had a relationship with Matthew Talbot.
5   Linda was murdered by the unknown caller from the Wood Lane phonebox.
6   Linda was killed because of her delving into the deaths of Gillian Pugh and Arthur Turner.
7   Ken McGuire murdered Sarah McGuire.
8   Clara Applebaum was murdered to prevent her from informing Carmichael about something to do with Linda's death.
9   The death of Gary Leeman was linked to Linda's death.
10   Reverend Pugh murdered Linda.

Item 10 on the list had been Steve's only addition. He was still very suspicious of the cleric, although even he was not convinced that the vicar was really murderer material. Depressingly for the team, the third list (in green) was the longest of them all. This was titled 'unknowns'. It read as follows:

1   Who killed Linda Cartwright?
2   Where was Linda killed?
3   Why was Linda killed?
4   Why did Frankie Leeman call her from Harrisburg?
5   Who called her from Wood Lane?
6   Why was she found without shoes?
7   Where is her other earring?
8   Was Sarah McGuire murdered?

9 Was Sarah's death linked to Linda's murder?
10   Who killed Gary Leeman?
11 Was Leeman's death linked to Linda's?
12 Who killed Clara Applebaum?
13 Why was Clara killed?
14 What prompted Linda to start looking into the deaths of Gillian Pugh and Arthur Turner?
15 What had she found out about the deaths?
16 Did Linda have a boyfriend?
17 Who was she meeting on the night she died?
18 Who was Linda's accomplice?

When the lists were all completed the four officers surveyed the 38 items before them. It was Cooper who broke the silence first. 'I wouldn't be surprised if items 16, 17 and 18 on the green list were all the same person.'

'If they are you can bet he's our man,' interjected Marc.

'Yes, I think that you would be right,' said Steve. 'We should make that hypothesis number eleven.'

Lucy grabbed the blue marker and scribbled this at the bottom of the list. There was a further short pause before Steve said, 'I think we are ready to add one more list.'

'What's that?' asked Lucy.

'Our suspects list,' replied Steve.

'I'll have to use black for that one,' enthused Lucy. 'We've run out of colours.'

When they had finished this list it had just three names on it. These were:

1 Ken McGuire.
2 Matthew Talbot.
3 Reverend Pugh.

'It's a bit like Cluedo isn't it,' Watson whispered to Cooper. Fortunately for him, Steve didn't hear this comment, which had made Cooper turn away to hide a broad grin.

'So what now?' said Lucy.

'We should divide up between us some of the statements in either blue or green,' said Steve. 'And then painstakingly try to see if we can either make them red or delete them.'

'Good idea,' said Cooper, who had regained his composure.

'So who is taking what?' asked Marc, who fully expected to get the least interesting of the various hypotheses or unknowns.

'Lucy and I can address the Leeman theories when we go to Winston-Salem, later in the week,' said Steve. 'And I'm seeing Terry Mayhew this afternoon. Hopefully he'll be able to give me some more information about Linda.'

'What do you want me to do?' asked Lucy.

'Did you get the police report from the US on Gary Leeman's death?'

Lucy nodded. 'It was here this morning when I arrived.'

'I'd like you to spend the day going through it so that we are up to speed when we meet his sister,' Steve said. Then turning to the other two officers he continued, 'I want you, Cooper, to go through the four SOCO reports associated with these murders.'

'Four?' replied Cooper in surprise.

'Yes,' said Steve. 'The report from where Sarah McGuire was found, the report from where Linda Cartwright was found, the report from the Wood Lane phonebox and the report from Mrs Applebaum's that they did yesterday.'

'OK,' said Cooper forlornly.

'See if there's anything that links the three murders,' Steve ordered, before turning to address Watson. 'I'd like you to go back over Linda's personal possessions. I'm convinced that we've overlooked something. Remember we need to find her shoes and the earring. I'd also like you to try again to find a diary and her passport.'

Marc smiled to himself. This time he'd not done so badly, he thought.

Steve spent the rest of the morning with Chief Inspector Hewitt. Even by his own high standards, Hewitt was in a particularly pompous mood. 'We need an early result, inspector,' he said on at least three occasions during their discussion. As usual Hewitt's lack of interest in the detail of the case was clearly evident to Steve. However, to Steve's surprise he did make one suggestion which Steve took on board, which was that he should meet with Ken McGuire and Matthew Talbot himself. 'Don't take this the wrong way,' said Hewitt. 'But Cooper's not the brightest officer in the station and Lucy Clark's very inexperienced. I'd interview those two personally if I were you.'

'I'll do that,' replied Steve.

Hewitt suddenly asked 'Did you read the papers yesterday?'

'I read a little,' Steve said, knowing full well what was coming next.

'Did you read about Butler?' asked Hewitt.

'Yes,' responded Steve, 'terrible business.'

'Indeed,' said Hewitt. ' I suspect that there's a lot more to come out from this one.'

'I'm sure you're right,' replied Steve, who was starting to feel small beads of perspiration appearing from the hairline above his ears.

'Police corruption's a nasty cancer in the force,' continued Hewitt. 'I'm glad I haven't any corrupt officers in my team.' Steve said nothing, although he could not help thinking that Hewitt was suspicious that he might somehow be linked to Butler's corrupt activities.

'If that's all sir,' he said, 'I need to get on.'

'Of course,' responded his superior. 'Remember we need a quick result on this one inspector.'

With that Hewitt turned his gaze to some papers on his desk and Steve departed.

* * * *

At lunch Steve saw that Inspector Alan Pearson was seated alone in the canteen. He hadn't seen Pearson for a while, so he decided to join him.

'Hello Steve,' said Pearson. 'Long-time no see.'

'This looks interesting,' Steve said as he studied the stir-fry on his plate.

'Actually it's not so bad,' replied Pearson.

Steve gingerly prodded his meal with his fork.

'So how's the case going?' asked Pearson. 'How many murders are you up to so far?'

Steve smiled. 'It's an interesting one, that's for sure,' he replied. 'We have two definite murders and two that are possibles.'

'Also, what's all this about you and the lovely Lucy going to the US?'

'My God you *are* well informed,' Steve replied.

'Hey, it's the talk of the station,' commented Pearson. 'I even understand that there's a book being run on how quickly she makes sergeant once you get back.'

This remark stung Steve a little. Until now he had not heard any adverse comments about the planned trip with Lucy. He tried to stay calm. 'You're only jealous.'

'Too bloody right I am,' responded Pearson. 'If you fancy a swap I'd happily oblige. I'd much rather have a couple of nights away in America with Lucy than chasing after burglars and lowlife drug pushers any day.'

'I hadn't realised that you had a soft spot for Lucy,' Steve said calmly.

'Soft spot?' exclaimed Pearson. 'I fall asleep at night thinking of Lucy, and I won't tell you what my dreams are like.'

Pearson's comments shocked Steve. Up until that moment he had not considered Pearson to be the sort of officer to

152

make such sexist remarks about a fellow officer. He tried to move the conversation onto a different subject. 'I'm sorry you couldn't make the barbecue,' he said.

'Yes, me too,' replied Pearson. 'The wife's father has been ill for some time and we had to go back home to Bristol on Saturday. I believe you had a good turnout.'

'We sure did,' said Steve. 'Plus we had the pleasure of most of our suspects, so we were able to do a bit of work as well.'

'Well, I'm through,' announced Pearson, pushing his plate away from him. 'I've got to rush.'

'Me too,' said Steve. 'My soft southern stomach can't manage any more of this.'

The two officers rose from the table and headed for the door. As they chatted, little did Steve realise that this would be the last friendly conversation that the two men would have for a long time.

*　*　*　*

Steve arrived at the Oddfellows Arms at precisely 2 p.m. Terry Mayhew was waiting for him in the lounge of the pub and when he saw Steve approaching he rose and stretched out his long thin arm to greet his visitor. 'Good afternoon inspector.'

'Good afternoon Mr Mayhew,' Steve replied.

Although Mayhew was younger than Steve by three years, his appearance and demeanour suggested that he was much older and it did not take Steve long to realise that Terry was a serious, impassive creature, the complete opposite to his elder brother. After a few minutes of pleasant niceties, the two men made themselves comfortable and got down to business. 'I suppose that you are aware that Linda and I were an item?' Mayhew said, as he peered from behind his thick black spectacles.

'Yes sir,' replied Steve. 'However, I understand that your

relationship ended when you moved to Hong Kong? And I also understand that you have since married.'

'Quite so,' responded Mayhew, who was impressed and somewhat surprised by Carmichael's knowledge. 'I moved to Hong Kong last August, to take up a position with our Asian division. And I am married, to a local girl called Li Lan, much to the astonishment of my friends and family.' As he uttered those last words, he smiled faintly, which Steve took to be a smile of satisfaction. It's probably the only time he's ever done anything unpredictable in his life, Steve thought to himself. 'But you are wrong to link the move with the ending of our relationship,' continued Mayhew.

'Oh?' Steve said, looking puzzled. 'So, what did cause you and Linda to split up?'

'Probably the same thing that brought about her death,' responded Mayhew.

'Which was?' Steve prompted.

'Which was, inspector, her complete and utter pre-occupation with discovering why Arthur Turner took his life,' Mayhew said with sharpness hardening his voice.

'Why was she so obsessed with the deaths of Mr Turner and Gillian Pugh?'

'I thought that would be obvious,' remarked Mayhew.

'I'm sorry, Mr Mayhew,' replied Steve. ' But it's not obvious.'

'So, you've not been told,' said Mayhew. 'Then let me fill you in on a few things. I think you'll find they're central to Linda's murder.' Steve said nothing, as he realised that at last he was going to get the breakthrough that he had so yearned for. 'It all started when Mary Robertson died. She had lung cancer and just before the end she called for me and Linda and a few others to visit her.' At this point he bowed his head and his gaze moved away from Carmichael. 'I wish she hadn't. If we hadn't gone to her I'm certain that none of this would ever have happened. But Mary needed to clear her conscience I suppose.'

Steve remained silent. He knew that he did not need to prompt the witness at this stage. 'Anyway, Mary announced to us all that she had killed the child all those years ago,' said Mayhew.

'You're talking about Gillian Pugh I take it?' Steve asked.

'Yes. You see, we had all assumed it was Mr Turner not Mary. Nobody ever talked about it, but it was sort of understood that he'd done it not Mary.'

'So how did it happen?' Steve asked.

'Mary was supposed to be babysitting. Because she was the daughter of the headmaster, they knew her well. She was sensible and I suppose Mr and Mrs Pugh trusted her. They'd never have left Gillian with just anyone. Mary was going out with Robin at the time and I was seeing Linda. He was supposed to meet her at the vicarage, but he was held up and he asked me to go up and tell her. Linda and I went up there, but when we told Mary she went berserk. He'd messed her about before and she thought he was with another girl. Anyway, she asked us to stay and look after Gillian while she went to find him. She said she'd be about half an hour.'

'And when did she return?' asked Steve.

'Not until after the child had been killed,' he whispered nervously. 'Nobody knew who the killer was. But then when Mr Turner shot himself, rumours spread that he had been the hit and run driver. When Mary announced that she was the killer we were shocked. For almost thirty years Linda and I had carried the guilt for our part in the girl's death. We'd only taken our eyes off her for five minutes, but that was enough.'

Steve could feel his mouth drop. 'So what did Mary say?' he asked.

'She said that she was sorry and that she had regretted not coming clean at the time,' said Mayhew. 'But that once she had found Robin, who was drunk as usual, she'd realised that she would be late getting back to the vicarage. Foolishly she agreed with Robin's stupid suggestion to use her dad's car.'

'But she would have only been seventeen at the time,' Steve reminded him.

'Yes. She had started having lessons but she hadn't passed her test. Her mum and dad were out somewhere, so they just took the keys and drove off up the hill to the vicarage. I suppose they thought they could get there before the vicar got back, hide the car somewhere and then, after the vicar had returned, drive it back. But of course that didn't happen. The child apparently saw her as she turned into the drive and ran to meet her. Mary didn't see the child and being an inexperienced driver she panicked when the child ran out. Instead of braking she accelerated and hit Gillian.'

'But wasn't the child found further down the road?' Steve asked.

'Yes that's right,' replied Mayhew. 'Linda and I were in the house, so we heard nothing. Apparently Robin and Mary picked up the child and put her in the car. She said that their intention was to take her to the hospital, but as soon as they realised she was dead they panicked and they left the body on the grass verge down the lane. Naturally people thought Gillian had run into the road and had been hit by a hit and run driver.'

Steve could not believe his ears. 'But if she knew the facts of the child's death why did Linda become so obsessed with her investigation,' Steve asked. 'What was she trying to find?'

'She wanted to find out why the headmaster had died,' replied Mayhew. 'You see, Mary also revealed that he was being blackmailed.'

'Blackmailed?' exclaimed Steve with surprise. 'By who and what about?'

'That was what we were trying to discover,' said Mayhew. 'But after eight or nine months we'd found out nothing and to be frank I'd lost my appetite for it.'

'So you left her for a job in Asia?' Steve said.

'Yes,' replied Mayhew quietly. 'I suppose I did. Mind you, I wanted her to come with me but she wouldn't.'

' Was that because of her father?' Steve asked.

'Partly. But we knew he was dying and if she'd agreed we could have delayed our plans for a couple of months. My start date in Hong Kong was very flexible. But she wasn't interested. She said she could manage better without me and that was that really.'

'I see.'

There then followed an uncomfortable pause in the conversation. Steve broke the silence by asking, 'Did you have any help with your investigations?'

'No,' replied Mayhew. 'It was just Linda and I.'

'What about after you'd left?' Steve asked.

'She may have. But I really couldn't say.'

'Could she have had a new boyfriend?'

'Possibly. You'd have to ask someone who was here and close to her.'

'Like who?' Steve asked.

'Like the vicar, David Turner, or Clive Penman,' replied Mayhew. 'Outside of them, there were few people that she could call close friends. If she was going to confide in anyone it would be one of them.'

'Thank you Mr Mayhew,' said Steve. 'I've just one last question. You said that Mary summoned a number of you to her when she confided that she'd killed Gillian Pugh. Who were the others?'

'I thought you'd ask that. I took the liberty of writing their names down for you.' With that he handed Steve a neatly folded piece of paper upon which he had written five names, two of which were Linda Cartwright and Terry Mayhew.

Steve quickly looked at the names before placing the paper in his pocket. 'Thank you Mr Mayhew,' he said as he rose from his chair. 'You have been most candid with me and the information you have given me this afternoon has been most helpful.'

'Catch him quickly inspector,' said Mayhew. 'Linda was a dear friend. She never hurt anyone in her life, she didn't deserve to die.' Steve nodded in agreement. At last he knew he was making progress.

When he emerged from the Oddfellows Arms Steve was almost blinded by the brightness of the sun, which shone down from a cloudless blue sky. On such a gorgeous summer's day it would have been a crime to go back to the office. He decided that he would take the short drive to Wood Lane.

His car drew to a halt near to where Linda's body had been found. Was it really only a week since he had first been summoned to this quiet little country lane? With this in mind his first impulse was to congratulate himself on the progress that he had made with the case, but then as he looked around him he became struck by the simple beauty of the place. Gone were the dozens of people who had scuttled around the week before, and gone were the scores of cars which had been parked up on the grass verge that lined the tiny lane. In their place was pure silence, broken only by the gentle rustle of the trees and the low whistling sound of the breeze as it caught the long brown grass. The spot seemed so peaceful to him now, with its unspoilt landscape stretching out like a green carpet as far as the eye could see.

The only object to break the tranquil vista was the imposing church on Ambient Hill, where eight days earlier he had listened to a quietly spoken spinster read the lesson. Even that somehow only added to the view. His thoughts lingered on that vision of Linda in church that Sunday. Little had he known then that within such a short space of time such a plain and ordinary woman would be murdered, and in an attempt to trace her killer he would have discovered so much about her.

Steve remained motionless in that spot for about 20 minutes contemplating what Terry Mayhew had just told him. 'You need to speak to Robin again,' he mumbled to himself, not knowing that such a conversation was now out of the question.

When he walked back to the car, he did not notice the body of Robin Mayhew, which had been carefully concealed under a large mound of brambles. It would be a couple more days before the killer's latest victim would be found.

* * * *

When Steve's BMW reached number 11, he stopped suddenly. There in Talbot's drive was a bright red Audi. 'I wonder,' Steve said out loud to himself, as he recalled Hewitt's advice. 'I wonder,' he said again, before climbing out of the car and striding purposefully up Matthew Talbot's drive.

When Talbot answered the door, Steve was surprised at the diminutive size of the man that confronted him. For some reason the picture Steve had built up in his mind of Talbot was of a taller and more physically attractive person than the one that stood in front of him. 'Mr Matthew Talbot?' Steve asked.

'Yes,' replied Talbot, hesitantly.

'Good afternoon,' continued Steve. 'My name is Inspector Carmichael. I understand that you met with a couple of my officers the other day?'

Talbot's expression became sullen. 'They belong to you do they?' he growled. 'Well you could do with sending them on some courses. They accused me of all sorts of rubbish, including being the boyfriend of the woman that was found dead down the lane.'

Talbot's anger took Steve by surprise. 'I'm sorry if my officers offended you Mr Talbot,' he said. 'However, this is a

159

murder inquiry and we think that you may be able to help us with our enquiries.' Steve paused before asking, 'Can I come in?'

Talbot moved to one side and beckoned Steve through. Once inside he was shown into the lounge, which was quite clearly undergoing some major building work.

'I see you're in the process of renovation, Mr Talbot,' Steve said. 'I'm having some work done on my house at the moment.'

'Well I only hope that your builders are more reliable than mine,' snapped Talbot. 'Two bloody months this has been going on. He's never bloody here.'

Steve smiled. 'I can empathise with you completely, Mr Talbot,' he said. 'I think that you'll find that they're all the same in that respect.'

'Anyway,' continued Talbot. ' You didn't come here to talk about my building alterations.'

'No,' replied Steve. 'It's about the evening of the murder and the following morning that I'd like to talk to you.'

'Well on the Sunday evening I was at home, but I can assure you inspector that I neither saw or heard anything,' replied Talbot. 'And as I told your colleagues, I left here early on the Monday morning with Ken to go to Leicestershire. Once again I can't recall seeing or hearing anything that was unusual.'

'What time did you leave on the Monday morning?' Steve asked.

'About six-thirty. The same time I told that little girl you sent to interview me last week. And before you ask, I was all alone the night before,' replied Talbot curtly. 'Well apart from about twenty minutes when the builder from hell came round to collect some money from me.'

'This builder,' Steve asked. 'Do you know where I can contact him?'

'I've got his card somewhere,' replied Talbot. 'The

company is local, called CAP Building Contractors.' With that Talbot opened a drawer in his lounge cabinet and rummaged through to find the builder's business card. After a short while he turned to face Steve. 'I'm sorry,' he said, 'I appear to have mislaid it.'

'Not to worry,' said Steve. 'I can find them, if they're based in Moulton Bank.'

'Is that all?'

'I think so.' Steve rose from the armchair and made his way to the door. 'Actually there was one other thing,' he said as he reached the door. 'You say that you were not having a relationship with Linda Cartwright?'

'That's correct,' replied Talbot.

'Are you in a relationship with anyone at the moment?'

Talbot laughed. 'Inspector,' he said, 'I am in a relationship. Not that it's anyone's business but mine.' Talbot stared into Steve's eyes as if to gauge his reaction. 'I'm sure she was a perfectly nice, respectable lady Mr Carmichael, but you see she's not my type,' he continued. 'For reasons I can't explain, I seem to be attracted to more unobtainable women.'

'What do you mean?' Steve asked.

'My relationships for the last ten years or so have been almost exclusively with married women,' continued Talbot, who by now was taking great delight in seeing the expression on Steve's face change to obvious bemusement. 'Ken thinks I'm gay,' he said with a smile.

'You mean Mr McGuire?' Steve asked.

'Yes inspector, Mr McGuire.'

'But why is that so amusing?' enquired Steve.

'Because, inspector, the latest focus of my affections has been his little sister, Lisa Hope,' announced Talbot.

'I see,' replied Steve. 'And am I to take it that she was with you on the evening Ms Cartwright was killed?'

'For a good part of it,' replied Talbot. 'She has a key and was here when I got in from playing cricket. Apart from the twenty minutes or so when she hid out the back when the builder came she was with me until about eleven-thirty.'

'Will she be prepared to vouch for you?' Steve asked.

'Yes, I'm sure she will,' replied Talbot. 'But for God's sake be discreet. That prat of a husband has no idea what's going on. He thinks that she's attending evening classes to learn Spanish.'

'And her brother thinks you're gay,' Steve said.

'That's right,' confirmed Talbot with a wry smile.

*   *   *   *

'Hey, you're home early,' exclaimed Penny as Steve appeared in the hallway. 'What sort of day have you had?'

Steve smiled. 'An interesting one,' he replied, before heading up the stairs to his study. As soon as he reached his sanctuary he picked up the phone and quickly dialled Cooper's number.

'Hello Cooper. What have you found out today?'

'Well the main revelation was in the report from the SOCOs,' replied the excited officer. 'It confirmed that the fingerprints found at the telephone box at Wood Lane and on a fifty-pence piece in the coin box matched prints that were found on the patio door at Clara Applebaum's house.'

'That's very interesting,' Steve replied. 'All we need to do now is find out who owns them.'

'Yes,' continued Cooper. 'Only problem is there's no match on the police computer. So whoever it is hasn't got a record.'

'Not to worry,' said Steve. 'The net is certainly closing. It won't be long before we find the owner, I feel sure of that.'

'I agree,' said Cooper. 'And we also know what size feet our man has.'

'Oh yes?' said Steve.

'They also found size eleven footprints in the soil in one of the flowerbeds in Mrs Applebaum's back garden.'

'That's really great news Cooper,' Steve said.

Steve's next call was to Watson. 'Any joy at Linda's house?' he asked.

'A little,' replied his decidedly subdued colleague. 'I found her passport, but it had no US immigration stamps in it.'

'Anything else?'

'No,' replied Watson. 'I'm still drawing a blank with the earring and her shoes and there's no sign of a diary.'

'Don't worry Marc,' said Steve, trying hard to get Watson to feel his efforts had not been wasted. 'At least we now know that Linda didn't visit Gary Leeman. It must have been her accomplice.'

'I suppose you're right,' replied Watson.

Steve's final call was to Lucy.

'What did you find in the police report on Leeman's death?' he asked.

'It does look suspicious,' she announced. 'He drowned in the local lake, even though he was known to be an excellent swimmer. The coroner's report gave an open verdict, but reading between the lines the likelihood is that his death was not an accident.'

'Great work Lucy,' said Steve. 'I'll see you tomorrow at the funeral service.'

It would be a further three hours before Steve descended from his attic retreat. He had spent this time sitting quietly at his desk, going over and over in his head the day's revelations. On the desk in front of him he had laid the small piece of paper given to him by Terry Mayhew, containing the five names of those present when Mary Robertson made her confession.

Having eliminated Mayhew, he was left with just four

names. Two were the victims whose deaths he was investigating, which left him with just two. He felt sure that one of these would be the killer.

Chapter 16

From the bedroom window Steve could see the steady rain thumping down on the cherry trees that lined Tan House Row. 'Why does it always rain when there's a funeral?' he mumbled. Penny didn't answer. Having reclaimed her share of the duvet, she was fast asleep and oblivious to Steve's early morning weather report.

The funeral service was not due to start until 10:30 a.m., so Steve had decided to stay at home and continue to mull over the case some more. He also planned to use this as a chance to gain some brownie points with Penny, who had not been overly impressed by his unsociable mood the evening before.

'Tea darling,' he exclaimed about 10 minutes later when he re-entered the bedroom.

'Oh that's lovely,' muttered Penny, as her tired limp torso rose gingerly from its reclined position. 'What time is it?'

'About seven I think,' he replied, although he knew full well it was 20 minutes earlier.

'You're up early,' she groaned. 'I thought you didn't have to be at the church until ten-thirty? Are you going into the station first?'

'No,' replied Steve firmly. 'I thought I'd take the opportunity to spend some quality time with you and the kids this morning.'

'Great,' replied Penny. 'You can wash Natalie's hair for her and then if you still feel virtuous you can iron Robbie a couple of T-shirts.'

165

This was not what Steve had intended. He decided to change the subject. 'Tell me about Clive, David and Robbie?' he asked.

'What about them?' replied Penny, as she gulped her first mouthful of hot and over-sugared tea.

'What were they like when they were kids?'

'Well Robbie is a couple of years older than us three, so he didn't spend much time with us when we were young kids,' she began. 'It was only later that we all seemed to become, er, become ...' She struggled for the word to end her sentence.

'Friends?'

'Well not exactly,' replied Penny. 'More like acquaintances really.' She paused to have another gulp of tea before she continued. 'Well that's not strictly true either. Clive and David have always been close. Robbie and David only became friends once Robbie turned sixteen or so.'

'And you and Clive were once an item,' Steve said in a half questioning half-teasing manner.

'No,' exclaimed Penny. 'We never dated. I told you that. We were like brother and sister. Soulmates rather than a couple.'

A long pause dissected the conversation. 'Well I hope your soulmate gets his arse around here tomorrow to finish off this building work,' Steve suddenly announced.

Penny laughed. 'I'll call him this morning,' she replied. 'That's if you trust me to talk to him.'

Steve scowled. 'Don't worry yourself, I'll see him at the funeral I guess.'

'Well just in case you don't see him, take his mobile number, it's in the telephone book,' said Penny. 'I wrote it in there yesterday. Don't bother with his landline. He told me the other day that it had been out of order for weeks and that he was still waiting for BT to fix it.'

Steve was still a little sensitive about the friendship between his wife and Clive. He was sure that she was telling

166

him the truth about the absence of romance between them, nevertheless he still felt suspicious and a little jealous about their seemingly close relationship.

There was a larger turnout at Linda Cartwright's funeral than Steve had expected. In addition to Lucy Clark, Cooper and Carmichael, there must have been about 60 other people at the service. The only obvious absentees were Robin Mayhew, who Steve assumed would be still recovering from the excesses of the day before, and Matthew Talbot. Other than them just about all the possible suspects that the team had considered as their serial killer were in attendance.

With the exception of his notable use of clichés such as, 'a tower of strength' and 'an example to us all', Mr Pugh did a fine job in conveying Linda's life and her values. Consequently there was a great deal of sniffing and sobbing to be heard within the church. It had been Linda's wish to be buried next to her father and mother. However, what she couldn't have realised when she made that request was that it would be raining so heavily. So when the congregation had all trooped out to the graveside the ground was already saturated. As her coffin was lowered into her grave, water could clearly be seen creeping up the side of the pine box. And when the coffin finally came to rest on the bottom of the trench, a small trickle of water, light brown from the clay soil, ran across the width of the casket, stopping only when it reached the raised lip of the brass plaque, which carried the simple words:

LINDA SUSAN CARTWRIGHT
1960–2005

The Reverend Pugh made his final pronouncements before the gathering dispersed and headed away towards the gates that led to the car park.

Steve conveyed his sympathy to Terry Mayhew and Alan Cartwright before turning his attention to Ken McGuire, who throughout the service had remained motionless at the rear of the church.

'Mr McGuire,' said Steve, with his right arm stretched out to receive a handshake. 'My name's Carmichael, I wonder if you would be kind enough to spare me a few moments of your time?' McGuire agreed and the two men walked slowly until they were out of earshot of the rest of the funeral party.

'How can I help you?' McGuire asked.

'I'm heading up the murder inquiry into Linda's death, and I would like a brief chat with you about your relationship with her.'

'What relationship?' enquired McGuire. 'I can assure you inspector, that I was not giving Linda one.'

The directness and base way that these words were delivered unnerved Steve. He took an instant dislike to McGuire, but he tried hard to keep his feelings to himself. 'I see you've been talking to Mr Talbot,' he commented.

'There's no law against that, I hope,' snapped McGuire.

If Ken McGuire's name had been on the list that Terry Mayhew had given Steve on the previous day, Steve would have made him his prime suspect without any question. But McGuire was not on the list. Steve bit his lip and continued regardless of all his negative thoughts. 'Mr McGuire,' he said in a forced controlled manner, 'I am not suggesting for one moment that you were on intimate terms with Miss Cartwright. I am simply trying to understand from you what you thought of her and what sort of relationship you had with her.'

'I was at a business conference recently,' announced McGuire pompously. 'The speaker was a famous athletics coach, who basically believed that you can divide people into two groups.'

168

'Really?' replied Steve, who was wondering where all this was leading.

'There's the successful types that always seem to win at whatever they do and then there's the rest, that always seem to miss out. The losers,' continued McGuire, oblivious to the inspector's building frustration.

'And which was Linda?' Steve asked.

'She was what he called a valley person,' said McGuire. 'That was his term for a loser.'

Steve was again stunned by the blunt and direct way that McGuire spoke about the woman whose funeral they had just attended.

'I guess,' McGuire continued, 'that I had known her for over forty years. And in all that time I can honestly say that she consistently remained a complete non-entity. I would not be surprised to discover that she had never achieved anything that could be classed as even average by the standards of others.'

Steve could not contain his frustration any longer. 'Maybe her achievements were not obvious to you, Mr McGuire, but I am sure that she had them, just as we all do. Perhaps she just did not flaunt them as much as others.'

'I see that my honesty has upset you inspector,' observed McGuire. 'Don't think I am picking on the poor old girl. In my opinion valley people like her are in the majority in this village. Just look around you, we are surrounded by them.'

Steve turned to look in the direction that McGuire was pointing. 'So who else in Moulton Bank lives in this valley of yours Mr McGuire?' he asked.

'It would be quicker to pick out the winners,' responded McGuire 'However, let me help you.' McGuire then put his hand to his chin as if to look as though he was thinking. 'Well there's that wimp of a brother-in-law of mine. Adrian Hope the hopeless house-seller. Then there's my dear sister, for marrying him.' The mention of his sister in this way amused

Steve. Clearly McGuire had no inclination of her relationship with Talbot. 'Then there's that drunk Robin Mayhew. Now he's a big-time loser. Then there's Penman. He's got about ten different jobs and is crap at all of them. Then there's that mummy's boy schoolmaster, and then finally and quite clearly the worst is Robertson the publican.'

'A comprehensive list,' observed Steve.

'Oh yes,' replied McGuire, oblivious to the tone of Steve's mockery. 'Moulton Bank is full of failures.'

'So who are the winners then?' Steve asked. 'Apart from your good self of course.'

'Inspector,' McGuire said, 'I've no problems with modesty. I'm proud of all I've got out of life. You'll never find me embarrassed in reflecting on the rewards of my achievements.'

'I can see that,' Steve said. 'But who else has ascended from the valley?'

'Not many is the truth,' replied McGuire. 'I'd include Matt in my list, but after him I'm struggling.'

'And how would you have described your late wife Sarah?' Steve asked.

Without any hesitation McGuire responded: 'She was an insecure, feeble drunk, inspector. That's a valley person as far as I'm concerned.'

Steve could hardly believe his ears. Even by McGuire's own standards this latest remark was particularly insensitive. He had had enough of this particular conversation and decided that maybe it was time to finish his dialogue with McGuire. However, before he did he could not help asking one last question. 'So if the losers are valley people, what are the winners called?' he asked.

'Mountain people,' replied McGuire with great pride.

'Well,' Steve commented, 'I hope the loneliness on your mountain is not too unbearable for you Mr McGuire. And I hope that the air is not too thin for you.' With that Steve turned and walked away from the odious Ken McGuire.

Based upon what he knew of Linda, Steve did not agree with the damning condemnation that McGuire had given her. In fact he was amused by the irony of the fact that she was almost certainly killed because she had been successful where all before her had failed. In his view her death was almost certainly caused by her getting close to understanding the truth about the death of Arthur Turner, Gary Leeman and Sarah McGuire. In that respect she was a true 'mountaineer' he concluded. However, albeit with some reluctance, Steve did agree with McGuire's less than flattering synopsis of Adrian Hope, who was to be the next recipient of the inspector's questioning.

Steve had first met Adrian Hope back in May when Penny and he had come up to the village to find a suitable home. Given a choice, the Carmichaels would not have stuck with Mullion and Thorpe. They were very unreliable but were the only estate agent in the village, and it was quite apparent that the lack of competition had somewhat influenced the way that Hope and his colleagues performed. Hope, in particular, was a cause of much frustration to the Carmichaels. His vague understanding of just about every property that the Carmichaels enquired about would never have been tolerated had an alternative agency been available. However, once they had resigned themselves to the fact that they had no chance of changing the culture and attitude of the village estate agent, Hope slowly became a figure of amusement to Steve and Penny. So much so that until he had seen Hope with his wife and family at church, Steve had been fairly sure that Hope was certain to be one of those middle-aged men who still lived at home with mummy.

When Steve arrived where Adrian Hope and his wife were standing he shook the estate agent's hand and introduced himself to Lisa Hope. 'Did you know Linda Cartwright well?' Steve asked the couple.

It was Mrs Hope who answered. 'Linda and I were at school together,' she said. 'We weren't close, but I felt that it was only proper for us to pay our last respects.'

If it had not been for his conversation with Talbot the evening before, it was unlikely that Steve would have noticed Lisa Hope at all. However, with her having an adulterous affair with Matthew Talbot, Steve made a quick but thorough analysis of Mrs Hope. Although she was in her forties and to Steve's knowledge had mothered at least three children, she had clearly kept a good figure. She had a fairly plain but attractive face, her hair was neatly arranged and she was dressed simply but with a reasonable amount of style. In short, for her age she looked pretty good with only the odd wrinkle around her eyes and a sort of tired look on her face to betray her years.

'I understand that you are the officer in charge of the murder inquiry?' Adrian asked.

'Yes that's correct,' Steve said. 'Is there any way that you can help me?'

'I'm sorry,' said Lisa. 'As I said, Linda was more of an old acquaintance than anything else. The truth is that although I've known her for years and although we attended church together every Sunday, I can't honestly say I knew her well at all.'

Steve smiled. This was starting to become a standard response that he was all too familiar of hearing. 'Not to worry,' he said. 'But it would help our enquiries if you could come down to the station and give us some insight into Ms Cartwright, as an acquaintance.'

'Is that really necessary?' asked Adrian, with an air of indignation in his voice.

'No problem,' interrupted his wife. 'I would be pleased to help.' Steve could tell that she knew full well what he needed her for. She had clearly already been primed by Talbot to corroborate his alibi. 'I'll come in tomorrow,' she added.

172

'That would be fine,' replied Steve. 'If you ask for DC Cooper or Sergeant Watson, they'll be pleased to take your statement.' With that Steve decided to depart from the Hopes and link up with Cooper and Lucy, who were engrossed in deep conversation. As he went to make a move, Adrian Hope said. 'How are you settling into your new home?'

'Very nicely,' replied Steve, without bothering to look back. 'It's all that we had expected. We are very happy with our new home thank you.'

Lucy and Cooper had spent the time that had lapsed between the end of the burial service and Steve's arrival comparing notes. Although they both agreed that Matthew Talbot was now out of the frame, Lucy still had a hunch that Ken McGuire was involved. Cooper wasn't so sure.

'My money's staying in my pocket for the time being,' he said to her. Secretly though he was sure that the Robertson, Turner and Penman trio had not been as forthcoming as they could have been, and he felt equally the same about Mr Pugh.

'Okay team,' said Steve. 'I saw you both in conference. What's the verdict?'

Lucy laughed. 'We are certain that Matt Talbot's out of the reckoning, but that's about as far as it goes.'

'What do you think boss?' asked Cooper.

'I've asked Lisa Hope to come into the station to give a statement. Assuming she does confirm that Talbot was with her the evening Linda Cartwright died, I think we can cross him off the list,' he replied. 'And if that's the case I'm pretty sure that the killer is one of the surviving people that Mary Turner confided in on her deathbed, but even that's not a certainty.'

With that he put his hand in his pocket and withdrew the folded sheet of paper that Terry Mayhew had given him. 'I think that it's one of these two,' he said, pointing to the last two names on the list.

'Well hopefully we'll be wiser after we meet Frankie Leeman,' said Lucy, with excitement.

'Yeah,' responded Steve. 'I've got a warm feeling about this trip.'

Chapter 17

Angela organised the flights for Steve and Lucy. However at such short notice she was unable to find any available economy flights that flew from Manchester to America and she could not find any airport in the UK which had services direct to Greensboro in North Carolina. As a result, for their outward journey Steve and Lucy had to set off early and would be taking three separate flights before they arrived at their destination. The first of these was a one-hour flight from Manchester to Heathrow. They then had to wait two hours before catching their flight from Heathrow to Washington. Fortunately there were no delays on their flight into Heathrow and Steve was very relieved when the United Airlines 767, bound for Washington Dulles Airport, departed on time from Terminal 4. For the first hour of flight UA958, Steve hardly spoke. He was far too preoccupied with running through the details of the case in his head. It was only when the stewardess placed a large plastic tray on the fold-down table in front of him that he decided to engage Lucy in conversation.

'So, what do you make of the case so far?' he asked.

'I feel there is a link between Linda's death and the deaths of all the others,' she replied.

'Why do you think that?' probed Steve.

'I think that it's clear Linda and Clara Applebaum were murdered by the same person,' said Lucy.

'I agree,' replied Steve. 'But what about the others?'

'I also think that Linda almost certainly found out something that linked her killer with the murder of Sarah McGuire or the death of Gary Leeman. And if that's so there's then a fair chance that the schoolmaster and Gillian Pugh are somehow linked. I also believe that the killer was known to Linda.'

'I can't fault your logic so far,' said Steve as he took a bite of his bread roll.

'The most likely suspect for me is either Ken McGuire or one of her school chums,' continued Lucy.

'I certainly don't like McGuire,' Steve replied. 'But I don't see why he's your prime suspect.'

'It's just a feeling I have,' replied Lucy. 'It's quite clear from what he said to you at the funeral that he had no great love for his wife and he would have been an acquaintance of Gary Leeman. So he could easily have concocted a reason to visit Leeman here, and then kill him.'

'I think that we will need a little more to go on before we make an arrest,' said Steve with a broad smile. Lucy smiled and nodded her concurrence before tucking into her chicken dinner.

'So why did you want to become a police officer?' asked Steve.

'Rather than an air hostess or hairdresser?' came back Lucy's swift reply.

'I touched a bit of a nerve there, I see,' said Steve.

'I'm sorry,' said Lucy, realising that her response had been a little more aggressive than she had meant. 'I don't really know. I suppose I wanted to join the force to prove to myself that I could survive in a male-dominated environment.'

'Really? Is that so important to you?'

'Yes, I think it is,' responded Lucy. 'I don't expect you to understand. But for me to excel in such a male stronghold would be such a major achievement.'

'And I'm sure you'll reach your goal,' Steve remarked.

176

'Thank you sir,' said Lucy.

Steve liked his companion. He found her willing, intelligent and he enjoyed her company. He also found her very attractive.

'I couldn't help but notice that you came to the barbecue alone,' continued Steve. 'Is there nobody special in your life at the moment?'

'Not at the moment,' replied Lucy with a wry smile. 'But I'm always on the lookout.'

Steve laughed and raising his glass of wine said, 'Good hunting.'

'Thank you sir,' replied Lucy.

During the next six hours Steve discovered much more about his young companion. She was born and raised in Gateshead, the youngest of three children. Her father had been an insurance broker, her mother a primary-school teacher, and they had both retired to a small seaside town some 10 miles south of Berwick-upon-Tweed. Lucy had attended the local comprehensive school in Gateshead, which she left with three A levels and nine GCSEs. After leaving school she had spent a year touring Europe and then Australia, before returning to take up a place at university where she received an upper second degree in sociology. Lucy had applied to three forces and was accepted by all three. She decided upon the Lancashire police as this allowed her to live not too far from her native north-east but far enough away to require her to live away from her parent's house. She had a wide range of interests including cycling, walking and swimming, and she was widely read. She had split up from her long-time boyfriend about four months earlier, but she insisted that the two were still very much good friends.

For her part, Lucy had already developed a healthy respect for her boss. She felt sure that under his guidance her career would flourish. She also thought that he was in remarkably good condition in spite of his age, and being a little over-weight. Not her type of course, she kept telling herself, but not altogether unattractive.

When the aircraft finally touched down at Washington the local time was 13:35.

'Our connecting flight is scheduled to depart at fourteen-thirty,' Steve said as they walked towards the terminal building. 'We should have plenty of time.'

What Steve had not realised until he got into the terminal was that the departure lounge for the connecting flight to Greensboro was situated just about as far away from where they had landed as was possible at Washington airport. This coupled with the fact that they also needed to be processed by US immigration at Washington before making their connection made Steve a little anxious about their chances of making the flight. However they were fortunate. The queue that they chose turned out to be the quickest and as a result they managed to arrive at their gate with ten minutes to spare.

The connecting flight to Greensboro was quite different from the journey from London. The tiny Jetstream aircraft only seated about 30 people, a massive contrast to the aeroplane that had left Heathrow earlier that day. Furthermore, the seats were a good deal smaller than the business class seats which they had occupied during their flight to Washington. The sudden movements of the plane as it fought its way through the strong turbulence over the Appalachians made the two officers feel a little uncomfortable on more than one occasion. For almost the entire journey the plane seemed to pitch and roll. They could feel every thermal they encountered and every slight turn the pilot made, and one such jerk was so violent and unexpected that Lucy unintentionally grasped Steve's arm. When she realised what she was doing she released her grip quickly, much to Steve's amusement.

Another major difference between the two flights was the noise level. Having experienced seven hours of relative peace and quiet, to have to listen to the constant drone of the aircraft's engines did little to enhance their enjoyment.

'Thank God that's over,' said Steve as his feet landed safely on the concrete runway. Lucy smiled, trying hard to make her boss believe that she had not been troubled by the experience.

'I didn't expect it to be so warm,' she said once they had entered the tiny terminal building.

'Yeah,' responded Steve. 'It must be ninety degrees.'

'What's that in centigrade?' asked Lucy with an impudent grin.

'I have no idea,' responded Steve. 'But your dig about my age has been noted and will be recalled at your next performance appraisal.'

They were met at the airport by a police officer from Winston-Salem, who introduced himself as Sergeant Usselmann. Once in the back of Usselmann's car it took them no more than 20 minutes to arrive at the Marriott Hotel, where they were booked in for the next two nights. Steve was impressed with his room, which was located on the fourth floor. Out of his window he could see an array of expensive-looking shops and a myriad of restaurants and diners, with names like McCartney's, Sam's Plaice, Rob Ryan's and Ed's Diner, none of which were familiar to him.

Once Steve had got into his room he called Penny. By now the local time was 6:15 p.m., 11:15 p.m. at home, so he expected that Penny would still be awake. He was correct.

'Hello darling. Did you have a good flight?' she enquired.

'Yeah,' replied Steve. 'It was OK.' In all the years they had been married, they had been apart at night on only a handful of occasions. So it was a strange experience for both of them to endure, although neither of them was prepared to give the other the slightest indication that they were missing their partner.

'So how's the hotel?' Penny asked.

'It's fine,' he replied. 'Actually it's more than fine, it's very plush. You know, air conditioning and all that.'

'So what's the temperature like over there?'

'I don't know,' said Steve. 'I guess it's around ninety degrees or maybe more. I don't know what that is in centigrade.'

'It's about thirty something degrees, I think,' replied Penny.

For the next few minutes Steve gave his wife a summary of his day. Penny's update, which followed, focused mainly on their offspring's activities. This included Jemma bringing home her new boyfriend, the fact that Robbie's bike had been stolen and the latest on Natalie's fashion demands (three dresses, two pairs of shoes and a selection of new tops and accessories). 'You'll have to hide that bloody catalogue from her,' Steve said.

'Never mind about her,' said Penny. 'What about Jemma and this boy?'

'Well all I can say is it's about time she came clean. We've known for over a week now.'

'I know,' replied Penny. 'I think she was a little worried about what you would think of him. That's why she chose the day you went away to invite him over.'

'Look, I'll have to go,' said Steve. 'I'm supposed to be down for dinner at seven, and I'm desperate to unpack, shower and change.'

'OK,' replied Penny, trying hard not to sound disappointed. 'I'll see you on Friday.'

'Yes, on Friday,' Steve replied. 'Goodnight.'

As soon as Steve put the phone down he realised that he had forgotten to ask if Clive had finished the work. He toyed with calling again, but after a quick glance at his watch he realised that he needed to get a move on if he wanted to meet Lucy at seven.

*   *   *   *

Although she knew he was only going to be away for a couple of days, Penny was still apprehensive about being apart from Steve. She had put on a brave face that morning, maintaining her composure, and only allowed herself a few tears once Steve had departed for the airport.

Then, having successfully despatched Jemma and Robbie to their respective friends' houses, she settled down with Natalie to play a game of cards. Gin rummy was Natalie's favourite and whenever the youngest of the siblings had the opportunity to get either of her parents to herself she would use all her guile to attain their participation in a game.

Clive had arrived at about 10:30 a.m. Although at first his demeanour appeared normal enough, within a few moments it became quite clear to Penny that he was not in the best of moods that morning. Whatever had brought on this mood swing remained a mystery to Penny, who had hardly spoken to him from the moment he had arrived. She figured that it might be due to the fact that he had discovered from her that Steve was away for a few days. Having not been party to the financial arrangements between the two men, she assumed that Clive was expecting some more money from Steve to assist him with the work. To avoid the incessant noise of banging and drilling she decided to take Natalie out for a while.

'Clive?' she shouted down the hall. 'I'm going out. If the kids come back while I'm out tell them that I've taken Natalie for a walk.'

When Clive did not answer, she walked down to the doorway of the back room and repeated her announcement. Clive just nodded and then carried on working.

'Are you all right?' Penny asked.

'I'm fine,' he replied. 'I've just got a lot on my plate at the moment, that's all.'

'If it's about Steve not being here to give you some more money,' she said. 'then I'm sure he'll settle up with you on Friday when he's back.'

Clive looked surprised at this. 'Well, it's all well and good agreeing a cash in hand job, but the deal was that I'd get a steady flow of cash each week. I need it for materials.'

Penny could not help thinking that his bad mood was totally disproportionate to the magnitude of the issue. Also she could not imagine that Clive's total outlay for materials at that time would have amounted to much. A few screws, some light fittings and the odd couple of dozen nails could not have amounted to a major financial undertaking. She wisely decided not to pursue the conversation any further, as she could see that Clive was in no mood for a debate on the issue.

Having spent the remainder of the morning and most of the afternoon in the countryside around the village, mother and daughter returned to their home to find that Clive had almost finished the job, with the exception of a couple of the electrical fittings. Clive however was nowhere to be found.

It was at that moment that Jemma made her entrance with Jason in tow. 'Mum?' she shouted down the hall. 'Is it OK if a friend stays for tea?'

It was no coincidence that Jemma had brought Jason home for the first time when she knew her father would be away. Ever since she could remember she had always felt that her father was difficult to please, and as her mother had correctly observed, she had decided that her best strategy would be to gain her mother's approval for her new boyfriend before exposing the poor lad to dad. Jemma's gut feeling about her mum's impression of Jason was spot on. By the time he left the Carmichael household he had clearly gained her approval. She was both pleased and relieved that her plan appeared to be working.

*   *   *   *

Penny had been waiting for Steve to call her, even though she could think of little to say when he did. It was only when she put the phone down that she realised that she had not mentioned that Clive had almost finished the work. 'Never mind,' she thought to herself. 'It will be a pleasant surprise for him when he gets home.'

Chapter 18

When Steve arrived in the hotel lounge, Lucy had yet to come down, so he made his way to the bar and sat down on a tall stool. 'Can I get you anything?' asked the barman.

'A beer would be great,' replied Steve.

'We've got Sam Adams, Coors, Bud and Labatts on draft or there's bottled beer,' replied the barman.

'A Bud would be fine,' Steve said.

Lucy arrived as the barman placed the cold glass on the small circular napkin in front of him. 'Hi,' she said as she slipped onto the stool next to him.

'Hi,' replied Steve as he caught his first taste of her perfume. 'Would you like a drink?'

'Yeah,' she replied with gusto. 'I'll have what you're having.'

'Another Bud coming up,' said the barman without Steve saying a word.

Lucy looked totally different in her tight white trousers and baggy grey top. 'You smell nice,' said Steve.

'Thank you,' replied Lucy with a broad smile.

The barman laid the second cool glass of beer next to Steve's. Without hesitation Lucy picked up her glass and motioning it towards Steve said, 'Cheers.' Steve reciprocated and they both took a deep swallow of cold amber liquid.

'That's just what I needed,' said Steve as he set his glass back down on the bar.

'Me too,' replied Lucy.

After they had finished their drinks they decided to try one of the diners across the street. 'We seem to be spoilt for choice,' remarked Steve.

'Yes,' said Lucy. 'Which one do you fancy?'

'Oh I'm easy.'

'OK, I'll choose. Let me see, it's either Ed's Diner or Rob Ryan's restaurant. Einee meenie minie mo.'

'Good God,' exclaimed Steve. ' I hope you're more methodical in identifying criminals.'

Lucy smiled broadly. 'Ed's,' she announced.

'Ed's it is,' agreed Steve.

Ed's Diner was a typically American diner. In the centre of the room was a large rectangular bar surrounded by chrome barstools. In the middle of the bar, high up on the wall, was a television, which blasted out a baseball game. Around the walls were photos and mementos dedicated to baseball legends, past and present. Not that it made any impression on either Steve or Lucy, neither of whom knew anything about baseball. The diner was badly lit, but could boast at having an extremely efficient air conditioning system.

'Table for two?' asked the young waitress.

'Yes please,' replied Steve.

The waitress showed the couple to a circular table, which was covered in a large red and white checked tablecloth. Before they were seated they had been presented with a menu with a large pig's head on the front. The pig was smiling broadly with the words, 'Ed's Diner … Eat Mo Pig' embossed above his head. Surprisingly the logo looked familiar to Steve, but he thought little of it. Lucy laughed. 'It looks like Cooper.'

'That's hardly a nice thing to say about one of your colleagues,' said Steve with a grin. 'However, I have to admit there's more than just a passing resemblance.'

They spent the next two hours in the diner. Steve had buffalo wings and a steak, Lucy skipped the starter and had the Cajun chicken. She made up for her lack of a starter by ordering the most sickly-looking chocolate pudding that Steve had ever seen for her sweet. When they finally decided it was time to go and Steve had paid the bill, they were each presented with a bag, which contained a number of goodies associated with Ed's Diner.

'What's this?' Steve asked.

'We like to give all our out of town customers a little touch of Carolina hospitality,' replied the waitress in her soft North Carolina drawl.

'Thank you,' replied Lucy. 'That's very kind.'

Steve and Lucy walked across the main road towards the hotel. Although it was now getting late, the air was still warm and dry, and the sound of the crickets made a fitting complement to a pleasant evening.

The silence was broken by the deep hollow bellow of a car horn, closely followed by the screech of tyres and a loud shout of 'Get out the god damn road!' Lucy grabbed Steve's arm tightly and the two embarrassed and frightened visitors scuttled quickly over to the curb. 'God damn idiots!' shouted the driver again through his open window before he sped off down the road. Steve and Lucy did not hear his words or notice the customary gesture which accompanied his diatribe. They were conscious that upon reaching the curb their arms were still entwined. Rather than withdraw from their clinch they pulled closer together, and in moments became locked in a powerful embrace, which culminated in a long passionate engagement of their lips. As they kissed Steve's strong arms caressed her head, shoulders and back. Lucy's perfume now seemed even more enticing than it had when she first sat next to him in the hotel lounge.

On many occasions later Steve would try to make sense of how they managed to reach this point. However, at that particular moment their actions seemed not only natural, but also inevitable. Lucy welcomed not only the kiss and embrace but also the movement of his hands across her body. From the first day she saw him from the window of the police station, she had dreamed of his attention and she tingled with delight as his warm tongue probed the depths of her mouth. Eventually their lips parted, and as they did a thin moist tentacle of saliva remained for a split second between them, like an imaginary umbilical cord joining the two would-be lovers. Steve cleared his throat and without a word between them placed his face downwards once more to enjoy the experience for a second time. It was during this embrace that Lucy felt justified in returning the compliment of the caress. At first she satisfied herself with firmly holding his strong broad shoulders, but later she felt safe to run her hands downwards to his waist and to the middle of his back at that tender spot just above the line of his belt.

When their lips parted for a second time Lucy heard herself saying, 'Let's go to your room.' And without another word the two walked slowly arm in arm to the hotel. They did not embrace again until they were alone in the lift. Once the doors had collided shut, the couple returned to a tight and passionate clinch. When the doors finally opened the pair walked quickly down the corridor to Steve's room.

* * * *

When morning broke and Steve opened his eyes, it took him a couple of seconds to realise where he was. Then he started to recall the events of the previous evening with Lucy. He slowly turned to his side expecting to see her lying naked next to him. When she wasn't he was confused. 'Was it a dream?' he thought.

It was the impression of her head on the pillow beside him and the faint sweet smell of her perfume that confirmed that his memory of the night before was no illusion. At that moment Lucy emerged from the bathroom dressed only in a thin T-shirt that she had retrieved from the goody-bag that she had been given at Ed's Diner. As she walked toward the bed Steve looked proudly at the beauty that approached him. Her legs were thin and tanned, and her hair, which she usually wore up, now hung down naturally across her back and shoulders.

She smiled and said, 'Morning.'

It was when she slid into bed beside him that Steve first started to feel the pangs of guilt. He had never been unfaithful to Penny; in fact the thought of being with someone else had never crossed his mind. But at that moment he could not resist Lucy.

Once again he took hold of her and once more took great pleasure in feeling her slight form next to his large body. Fondly she stroked him, like a child with a small pet. Steve enjoyed her intimate caresses and responded by gently feeling her breasts through the cotton shirt with the flat palm of his hand. Gently he moved his hand lower, to her stomach and then lower still to her warm smooth thighs.

Suddenly Steve stopped. 'We had better get up. Sergeant Usselmann is due to meet us here at nine-fifteen.'

Begrudgingly Lucy climbed out of the bed and started to collect her clothes, which had been so wantonly discarded the night before. As she did Steve looked with satisfaction at her compact young body within the skimpy, cheap T-shirt.

'Jesus Christ!' he exclaimed. 'I've got it.'

'Got what?' Lucy asked.

'No time to explain now. I'll tell you later,' responded Steve. 'Get dressed,' he ordered.

By the time Lucy arrived in the hotel lobby it was 9.30 a.m. and Steve was already in conversation with Usselmann. She could not remember the last time that she had managed to shower and change so quickly. Steve however was not at all impressed, given that she was late. 'What kept you?' he snapped.

Lucy had not expected this sort of reception and when the smile she gave to Steve was not reciprocated this only added to her confusion and dismay.

$$* \quad * \quad * \quad *$$

Usselmann, who was a native of the area, took great delight in explaining to Steve and Lucy something of his home town's history. Not that Lucy was that interested.

Winston-Salem was a city created in the early 1900s from two towns which were originally a mile or so apart. Winston had been founded in 1849 as the country seat of the revolutionary war soldier, Major Joseph Winston. Salem was older, having been established by Moravian colonists in 1766. The new city had a population of over 150,000 and was the home of a number of educational establishments, including Wake Forest University and the North Carolina School of the Arts. In recent times the tobacco company R.J. Reynolds had dominated life in Winston-Salem. Since 1875 the Reynolds Tobacco Company has been not only the major employer but also a significant influence on political, social and recreational life in the North Carolina city.

As they sat in the back of the car Lucy put her hand gently on Steve's thigh. 'What was it that excited you so much earlier?' she asked with a wry smile.

Steve pushed her hand away from his leg. 'Not now,' he whispered. At that moment Lucy started to realise that maybe the passions of the night before were not going to be repeated.

'How long have you been in the force?' Steve asked Usselmann.

'Ever since I left school. It will be thirty years next fall.'

'That's autumn,' interjected Lucy coolly as she shuffled away from Steve and turned her head to look out of the window.

'Really,' replied Steve. 'Thank you for that, Lucy.'

By now Lucy was convinced that there wasn't going to be a rekindling of the passion between them. She felt confused, used but mostly angry with herself that she had so easily capitulated to Carmichael.

'You shit,' she muttered as she slid over to the door, which was as far as she could get away from her boss.

Steve heard her but remained impassive, which irritated Lucy even more.

'To the left you can see the local college football field,' announced Usselmann, oblivious to the negative body language in the back seat. 'It was partly funded by R.J. Reynolds you know.'

'Really,' replied Steve for a second time.

Steve had made two telephone calls that morning before going down to reception. The first was to Angela to ask her to arrange early flights back to the UK for himself and Lucy. The second call was to Cooper. As he waited for Angela to text him back the new flight details, Steve could not get Lucy out of his head. It had felt so comfortable being with her the night before, but now that they were back on duty Steve had become riddled with guilt and found it impossible to show any sign of affection to the young officer. His palms had become clammy and he kept saying to himself over and over again, 'What have I done?' The adrenaline that had pumped through his body only a couple of hours earlier had now been replaced. Now all that he could feel was undiluted guilt and an overwhelming sense of fear. Fear of what he had started, fear of what Lucy would now expect, but most of all fear of what Penny would do if she found out.

'Here we are inspector,' said Usselmann as they pulled into the police station car park. 'Winston-Salem police station.'

Once Usselmann was out of the car, Steve grabbed Lucy by the wrist. 'We need to talk,' he said.

Lucy was still feeling angry and hurt. 'Yes we bloody well

do,' she replied under her breath as she pulled her hand free. 'But not now!'

Steve received their revised flight details from Angela by text. He and Lucy then spent the next hour with Usselmann and Arthur Colman, the officer in charge of the investigation into the death of Gary Leeman. Art, as he insisted on being called, was in his late fifties, and was more than happy to share his thoughts about the case with his British colleagues.

'The coroner recorded an open verdict,' Art explained. 'But Gary was a strong swimmer and in my opinion he is unlikely to have drowned in calm, flat water.'

'So you think it was murder?' Lucy asked.

'I can't be certain,' replied Art. 'But on balance I would say yes. He was murdered.'

'To your knowledge did Gary have any visitors from Britain around the time of his death?' Steve asked.

Art shook his head. 'Not to my knowledge,' he replied. 'But it's not something that we investigated at the time. I suggest you ask his little sister when you see her.'

'Talking of whom,' said Steve, 'I think we should go over to meet her.'

Turning to Lucy he said, 'We need to get an earlier flight back.'

This surprised Lucy, however she was in no mood to argue or even ask for an explanation. 'That's fine with me,' she retorted.

'Let's get moving then,' said Usselmann. 'It will take us about two hours to get to Frankie Leeman's place. What time is your flight back to England, inspector?'

'Our connection leaves Greensboro at one-thirty this afternoon,' replied Steve.

'Then you're not going to have time to get to see Frankie Leeman,' said Art. 'Do you have to go back so soon?'

'I'm afraid so,' replied Steve. 'I need to be back in the UK tomorrow morning local time. I've already arranged flights for us out of Chicago this evening.'

'Seems a shame that you have come all this way without meeting Frankie Leeman,' said Art ' It's such a waste of time.'

'Quite the opposite,' replied Steve with a forced smile. 'My journey hasn't been wasted at all.'

'I'll be able to handle the interview with Frankie Leeman,' Lucy announced. 'Why don't you go and I'll follow you tomorrow?'

Steve was surprised that Lucy was prepared to let him go back without her. He correctly concluded that she did not want to spend too much time with him on her own.

Although he tried, Steve was unable to get a moment alone with Lucy. He desperately wanted to talk to her before he left, but she was clearly in no mood to help in this and Usselmann was always in tow. By the time Usselmann had deposited Steve outside Greensboro Airport it was 11:15. 'I'll call you when I get back to Manchester,' Steve said.

'OK,' Lucy replied curtly.

Lucy watched him disappear into the terminal building. It was at that moment that she started to regret not having spoken with Steve before he left. How stupid she'd been, she would now not be able to discover where she stood with him until he called. She took a deep breath and turning to Usselmann she said 'OK sergeant, let's go.' Usselmann sped away.

It took them just under the two hours to reach Frankie Leeman's house, which was located in a secluded lane near a local beauty spot called High Point. As the car pulled into the drive the figure of a tall slim lady with short hair and a suspicious face emerged from the rear of the house. 'Good afternoon,' Lucy said as she walked up the garden path. 'I'm Lucy Clark from Lancashire CID, in England.'

'Pleased to meet you,' replied Frankie Leeman. 'Please come inside.'

It would be over two hours before Lucy emerged from Miss Leeman's house, during which time she would learn a great deal more about Linda Cartwright's investigation and the death of Gary Leeman.

Chapter 19

Steve's connection from Greensboro to Chicago left on time. As the tiny plane struggled over the Appalachians his thoughts again drifted back to Lucy. However, he forced himself to concentrate his mind on the case, in particular how he was to handle the interview the following day.

When Cooper had received the call from his boss that afternoon he could not understand why he was being asked to make the arrest. However, the clarity of Carmichael's order left him in no doubt that he was to carry out the instruction without question, which he did to the letter.

By the time Lucy got back to her hotel room it was around 5:30 p.m. She knew that her information would be invaluable to Carmichael, but she also realised that his flight would not arrive in England for another six hours at least. Having mulled things over, she decided that she should speak to him in person with her new information. She figured that he would be at the station by about 9:30 a.m. GMT, so she decided to stay in her room with a room service dinner, try to get to bed early and set her alarm for 3 a.m. local time to be awake to make the call.

Steve managed to get a couple of hours' sleep on the flight from Chicago to Manchester. When he finally arrived he collected his suitcase from the baggage hall and passed quickly through customs and into the arrivals hall. Marc Watson was waiting for him.

'Morning sir,' said Watson 'Did you have a good flight?'

'Fine,' replied Carmichael. 'Is everything in hand?'

'Yes sir,' said Watson. 'Cooper should be picking him up about now.'

'Fantastic,' Steve exclaimed. 'Let's get to the station. Quick as you can Marc.'

'There's something else that you should know though sir.'

'What's that?'

'We've found another body. It's Robin Mayhew.'

'What?' exclaimed Steve. 'When did this happen?'

'About an hour ago. We found him in Wood Lane.'

* * * *

When Steve entered the interview room David Turner was already seated behind the desk. 'Good morning Mr Turner,' said Steve. 'Thank you for agreeing to help us with our enquiries.'

'I understood that I had been arrested,' replied Turner sharply.

'It amounts to the same thing.'

Watson then turned on the tape recorder and the interview commenced. 'The time is now nine forty-seven a.m. on the twenty-sixth of August 2005,' he said. 'Interview conducted with David Turner. Inspector Carmichael, Sergeant Watson and PC Duggan in attendance. Mr Turner has declined legal representation.'

'David,' began Steve deliberately, 'you are aware of the reason for being here?'

'I am. Although you've got this all wrong.'

'For the purpose of the tape this interview is being conducted in connection with our enquiries into the deaths of Linda Cartwright, Gary Leeman, Clara Applebaum, Sarah McGuire and Robin Mayhew.' As Steve spoke the name of the latest victim, he looked to gauge Turner's reaction.

Turner was clearly surprised. 'What?' he exclaimed.

'Oh yes, David,' continued Steve. 'We've found the body.'

Turner looked down at the table in front of him and shook his head.

'David, can you please tell us where you were on the evening of Sunday August the fourteenth?'

Turner shook his head. 'I was at home,' he replied.

'Was that for the whole evening?'

'Yes.'

'Can anyone vouch for this?' asked Watson.

'No,' replied Turner. 'I live alone so nobody else can confirm it.'

'And in the early hours of the next day?' Steve asked.

'Well, as I told you before, as the school had already broken up for summer, I didn't have any need to get up early, so until Clive called me and asked me to take over in the post office I was in bed.'

'Alone?' asked Watson.

'Alone.'

'And what time did Clive Penman call you?' asked Steve.

'As you already know,' replied Turner calmly, 'it was about nine o'clock.'

'How long did it take you to wash, dress and get down to the post office?' asked Steve.

'Not long. About thirty minutes.'

'Have you ever been to the United States Mr Turner?'

'The United States?'

'It's that big country across the Atlantic,' said Watson.

Realising from the steely glare that Steve gave him that his sarcasm was not appreciated, Watson sensibly decided that he'd let the boss do the rest of the interview.

'Can you answer the question please?' said Steve.

'No, I have not been to America,' replied Turner.

Steve paused for a few seconds before he issued his next set of questions.

'I understand that your father was once the schoolmaster at the Moulton Bank Primary School.'

'That's correct. But I fail to see what dad has got to do with Linda Cartwright's death.'

'In my opinion quite a lot,' replied Steve. 'In fact, in our opinion Linda's death is very closely linked to your father.' Steve paused for a moment before delivering his next question. 'Can you please confirm when and how your father died Mr Turner?'

Turner's eyes looked upwards. 'It was a Sunday when he died. He shot himself while I was out playing cricket for the village team. The thirteenth of June 1976 to be precise.'

Steve could not help recalling how Clive had made an almost identical statement only a few weeks earlier, on the first occasion when he had visited Steve and Penny's house.

'It was my debut in the Moulton Bank cricket team,' Turner continued with pride. 'I was really excited. I must have run almost all the way home. Then when I got to the door there was a note on it telling me not to come in and to go and get PC Watson.' With that Turner looked at Marc. 'Your dad,' he said firmly. 'I guess he must have told you about that day?'

'Actually, not until last week,' replied Watson quietly.

'Well, when PC Watson came he made us wait outside,' continued Turner. 'I never actually saw dad, but I recall the body bag coming out and the crowd of neighbours that gathered across the road.'

'Where were your mother and sister?' Steve asked.

'They had been to Southport for the day. They came back about two hours later.'

'So where did you go?' asked Steve.

'I was taken to wait in Mrs Applebaum's house until mum came.'

'His death must have been a big shock to you,' continued Steve. ' Did you ever find out why he took his life?'

Turner shook his head. 'No,' he replied. 'No we never did.'

'Did he leave any other note?' asked Steve.

Turner shook his head once more. 'No, there was no other note,' he replied, his voice now trembling.

Steve could see that Turner was getting quite emotional. 'Would you like to have a break?' he asked.

'No,' replied Turner. 'Let's get on with this.'

It was at this point that Steve first started to doubt whether they had got the right person. However, he decided to continue. 'I also understand that your sister died fairly recently?' he asked.

'Yes she did,' replied Turner. 'She passed away about two years ago.'

Steve could not help noticing the difference in David Turner's precise recollection of the date of his father's death, even though it happened nearly 30 years before, compared to the vague timing he placed upon his sister's death, though that had only happened two years earlier.

'I realise that this may be awkward for you,' said Steve, 'but it's important that I ask you these questions. I hope you understand.'

'I don't understand what relevance the deaths of my father and sister have to this investigation,' retorted Turner. 'But I'm prepared to answer your questions because I've got nothing to hide.'

'Thank you,' replied Steve who was now very unsure about whether Turner was the killer. 'I understand that shortly before your sister's death she asked for you and a few others to come to her. I further understand that she then confessed that she was the driver of a car that had killed a young girl in 1976. Is that correct?' Steve could see the colour drain from David Turner's cheeks, but he did not answer. 'Mr Turner? I was asking whether it was true that before your sister died she asked for you and some other people to come to her. And that at that meeting she admitted that it was she who was the driver of a car that had killed Gillian Pugh in 1976.'

'That is right,' replied Turner, tears welling up in his eyes. 'She did.'

'Did that surprise you?'

'Of course it did!' snapped Turner angrily. 'We had no idea that it was her, none at all.'

'So why did she confess?'

'I don't know,' said Turner. 'She was dying, so I suppose she wanted to clear her conscience.'

'I can understand that,' said Steve. 'But what I can't quite understand is why she would want to confess to so many people. It's rather melodramatic. And I also can't understand why Mr Pugh was not one of those invited. Surely he was the person she should have told first.'

'I don't know,' said Turner. 'I suppose she didn't feel strong enough to include him. After all, the girl was his daughter.'

Steve paused again. 'I suppose you could be right. But I'm still confused as to why she had to invite so many people.' Steve then pulled out the small scrap of paper that he had been given by Terry Mayhew. 'For the tape can you confirm who was present when your sister made her confession regarding the death of the little girl.'

'There were five of us. Linda Cartwright, Sarah McGuire, Terry Mayhew, Robbie Robertson and me.'

The five names matched exactly the names on Steve's piece of paper.

'Who else knows that Mary killed Gillian Pugh?' Steve asked.

'I don't know,' replied Turner. 'Mary swore us all to secrecy. At least while she was alive.'

'So who was told afterwards?' Steve asked.

'I can't speak for the others but Robbie and I decided that we needed to tell my mum and Reverend Pugh,' he replied.

'I can understand that too,' said Steve, with sincere empathy. 'But did you tell anyone else?'

'No,' replied Turner. 'We didn't.'

'And what about the others?'

'I don't know,' replied Turner. 'But I doubt that Terry or Linda told anyone. I'm not sure about Sarah.'

'And what was the reaction of Reverend Pugh and your mother when they found out?'

'They were shocked,' replied Turner. 'I told them both together about a week after the funeral. They were shocked, but to be honest they were also a little relieved I think.'

'Why do you say that?' asked Steve with surprise.

'Because I think that Mr Pugh was relieved to at last know the truth. And for mum, and I suppose for me too, we were relieved because we had always thought that it was dad who had knocked the little girl down. We never discussed it but I know that mum thought the same as me. That dad had killed himself because he had killed Gillian.' Turner put his head in his hands.

Steve thought long and hard about his next move. He had gone over his strategy while he was on the aeroplane. His questioning so far had gone to plan and it was to be at this stage that he was to bring out his trump card. However, with Turner in such state he felt awkward.

'Go for it,' a voice said in his head, so he did.

'David, at the start of this interview you stated that you had never been to America. Do you remember?'

Without looking up Turner responded, 'Yes I remember. I have never been to America.'

'Well, that's strange,' replied Steve smugly. 'You see, I've just come back from the US myself. I went over to meet a lady called Frankie Leeman. Do you remember her?'

'Yes,' replied Turner. 'She and her brother were at school with us in the seventies.'

'That's correct,' said Steve. 'Well, Frankie lives in a place called Winston-Salem. It's in North Carolina. When I was there I happened to visit a restaurant called Ed's Diner. It's a great little eating-house. Very good food and quite reasonably priced.'

'So what has all this got to do with me?' Turner asked.

'Well the custom of Ed's Diner is to give its out of town customers a goodie bag with some gifts inside. And do you know what I found in my bag Mr Turner?' There was a slight pause before Steve continued. 'They gave me a beautiful T-shirt which is unique to them.'

With that Steve pulled out the T-shirt identical to the one that he had seen on Turner when the family had first met him at the school. It was the same as the one that had been so seductively worn by Lucy less than 24 hours before. 'Does this ring any bells with you?' he asked.

David Turner peered out from between his fingers. He was clearly horrified at seeing the T-shirt. He stood up rapidly, knocking his chair over as he rose. 'I want a solicitor,' he shouted. ' I'm not answering any more questions until I can see a solicitor.'

Steve was delighted with himself. His plan had been executed perfectly. He now dismissed the doubts that he had had earlier about Turner. He knew that he had his man.

*　　*　　*　　*

Steve took the opportunity of the short break in proceedings to phone Penny. 'Hello darling,' she said when she realised it was Steve, 'how's it going over there?'

It was then that Steve realised that he had not told his wife that he had returned to the UK. 'It was fine,' he replied, 'but I had to return rather quickly. I'm actually back at the station.'

'When did you get back?' Penny asked with amazement.

'About two hours ago,' he replied.

'So why didn't you let me know and why didn't you come home?'

'I'll explain later,' said Steve. 'It's all been pretty hectic.'

'I'm sure it has. How much sleep did you get on the plane?'

'I did OK. I got a couple of hours, but I'm getting a little tired now.'

'I bet you are,' she said. 'I don't know what is so important, but surely it can wait until you get a few hours sleep.'

'Yes,' agreed Steve. 'I'm planning to wrap up here in the next two or three hours then I'll come home.'

'Make sure you do,' ordered Penny.

'Look,' continued Steve with care, 'there's been another murder.'

'Who?' replied Penny with concern.

'It's Robin Mayhew,' said Steve. 'He was found earlier today in Wood Lane.'

'Good God,' muttered Penny.

'I have to go, I'll see you later.'

'OK,' replied Penny, who was numb at hearing this latest piece of news.

*   *   *   *

Lucy had spent the previous evening contemplating a number of issues. Not only did she have the information that she had gleaned from Frankie Leeman to mull over, she also thought long and hard about her night with Carmichael and the possible implications that this would have for their professional relationship. It took her until well into the early hours of Friday morning before she managed to finally get to sleep, so when the alarm clock's piercing siren dragged her from her slumbers, she felt dreadful. However, she knew how important her information would be to Steve.

It was Cooper who took the call in the office. 'Hi Lucy! How's the US?'

'Fine,' replied Lucy. 'Is Carmichael available?'

'No, he's with Marc. They're still in with Turner. What did you find out from Frankie Leeman?'

'Turner?' exclaimed Lucy. 'Why are you interviewing him?'

Cooper was taken aback by her remark. He had assumed she knew why Carmichael had come back so suddenly. 'Yes, we arrested him this morning. It was the T-shirt you and Steve got from the diner. Carmichael recognised it as the same one that he had seen Turner wearing, so that proves Turner had also been to North Carolina.'

Lucy thought for a moment. So that was what he had been so excited about.

'Anyway,' said Cooper, 'what have you found out?'

'Quite a lot,' she said excitedly. 'Can you get the boss to call me back?'

'Of course. Where are you?'

'I'm at the hotel.'

'Is there anything that you can tell me?' asked Cooper.

'Only that I know what Frankie Leeman and Linda Cartwright talked about on the night she died,' said Lucy.

'What?' said Cooper excitedly.

Lucy was disappointed that she had not been able to speak to Carmichael, but she realised that he needed her information, so decided to tell Cooper.

'She was very cooperative. She could not shed any light on whether her brother had been visited by anyone from the UK, however she was able to provide me with the details of her relationship with Linda.'

Cooper waited with bated breath for the young officer to continue.

'First of all,' Lucy announced. 'Frankie confirmed that she had been first contacted by Linda some time before. Apparently Linda had got Frankie's telephone number from her mum, whose number had in turn been given to Linda by

Clara Applebaum. Mrs Applebaum had been Frankie's mother's cleaner when they lived in Moulton Bank, and according to Frankie, Clara had always stayed in touch with her.'

'Did Frankie know that Mrs Applebaum is dead?' Cooper shouted.

'No,' replied Lucy. 'That was a real shock to her. She was clearly upset when I told her.'

'So what else did you get from her?' Cooper asked.

'She said that she had spoken to Linda on about three or four occasions. That Linda had told her that Mary Turner had confessed to killing Gillian Pugh and that she was trying to discover more about the reason why Arthur Turner had taken his own life.'

'So why did she think Frankie could help?' asked Cooper.

'Frankie said that she had asked that very question,' responded Lucy. 'She said that Linda always avoided answering her directly, but that she had been particularly keen to talk to Gary.'

'And did she?' asked Cooper.

'No. Gary refused to speak to her. He said she was a crank so Frankie never gave Linda his address.'

'So why did she call Linda on that night?' Cooper asked.

'She had picked up a message on her answer machine from Linda pleading with her to give her Gary's phone number,' Lucy announced with excitement. 'Frankie had been in Harrisburg at a works meeting when she picked up the message. She rang Linda to inform her that Gary had died and to ask her to stop bothering her.'

Cooper paused for a moment. 'So why do you think that Gary was so important to Linda?'

'I've no idea,' replied Lucy.

'Did you find out anything else of interest?'

'No. But tell me, how are you doing with Turner?'

'I wasn't at the interview,' replied Cooper. 'But I

understand that the T-shirt from the Diner was the killer. Apparently he flipped when he saw it.'

'Do you still think he's our man?' asked Lucy.

'Carmichael does I think,' Cooper replied. 'But I'm not so sure. We've not got enough to make it stick so I think we may have to let him go. We need to pin him down to being in the US at the time of Gary's death.'

'Have you found his passport yet?' Lucy asked.

'No,' said Cooper. 'They found nothing at his house, but we're checking with the Passport Office in Peterborough.'

'Look I'm going to have to go,' said Lucy. 'Can you tell Carmichael what I've told you and ask him to call me later? I need to know if he wants me to do anything more over here. Tell him that my connecting flight is not for another nine hours or so.'

Cooper had only just put the receiver down when Carmichael and Watson entered the room.

Steve felt exhausted. The lack of sleep and subsidence of his adrenaline flow had suddenly taken its toll on him. 'Are you OK boss?' asked Cooper.

'I'll be OK,' replied Steve. 'Especially if we can get Turner to start telling us the truth.'

'That may take a while yet,' interjected Watson. 'I've just spoken to Turner's solicitor. He's tied up in court this afternoon. He won't be able to get here until at least six o'clock this evening.'

'Bugger,' said Steve with a sigh. 'OK,' he continued, 'you guys make sure he gets here and spends some time with Turner. We'll reconvene tomorrow morning at nine o'clock.'

'Right you are sir,' said Cooper. 'But before you go I've had Lucy on the phone. She's briefed me on her meeting with Frankie Leeman but she wants you to call her.'

Steve rubbed his eyes. 'I'm going back home to get some sleep. Cooper, why don't you drive me home and you can tell me what Lucy has found out on the way.'

Cooper nodded in agreement.

Steve then turned to Watson. 'Make sure that Turner and his brief know what the score is,' he said. 'And don't forget to check with the Passport Office at Peterborough to see if they have a passport on record for Turner. I can't believe that a man in his forties has not got one.'

'OK sir,' responded Watson. 'See you in the morning.'

Steve smiled and departed.

It was just after 1:30 p.m. when Cooper's car arrived at the Carmichael house. Penny saw the car pull into the drive and rushed to the door to greet her husband. 'Hello darling!' she said. 'You look shattered.' She grabbed his arm and the two of them walked into the hall.

'Where are the kids?' Steve asked.

'Robbie's at a friend's house, Jemma is with her young man Jason, and Natalie is in the garden,' replied Penny. They walked into the kitchen where Steve crumpled into a chair. 'So what's been happening?' asked Penny. 'And why are you back early?'

'We've arrested David Turner for the murder of Linda Cartwright,' replied Steve.

'No!' exclaimed Penny in amazement. 'There must be a mistake. David couldn't hurt anyone. You're kidding me.'

Steve was surprised and a little hurt by his wife's reaction. 'No, I'm deadly serious,' he said. 'We've interviewed him once this morning and I'm going back tomorrow and will be interviewing him again.'

Penny was stunned. 'What evidence do you have?' she asked.

'Well, we have connected him to Winston-Salem. He owns an unusual T-shirt that is only given out by a restaurant in Winston-Salem. He is refusing to give us any explanation of where he got it from so my guess is he got it when he went to the US and killed Gary Leeman. He was one of only a handful of people who knew his sister had killed the vicar's girl and it's

206

my guess that he killed Linda because she had found out something about his father's suicide which he didn't like.'

Penny said nothing, but she could not help feeling that Steve had got it wrong. Steve said nothing either, but when he reflected on the evidence that he had just shared with his wife he started to have doubts about his chances of making a case stick against Turner. Eventually Penny broke the silence. 'Do you want anything to eat?'

'A sandwich would be nice,' he replied.

'Why don't you go into the other room,' she said, 'I'll bring you something through.'

Obediently Steve got up from his chair and trotted off into the next room. 'Fantastic!' he shouted. 'At last that lazy sod's finished.'

Penny had followed Steve into the room to see his expression when he saw the building work had all been completed. 'Well,' she said, 'what do you think?'

At first Steve was speechless. He surveyed the work with a critical eye before declaring once again, 'Fantastic.'

Penny smiled from ear to ear. 'He's done a great job Steve, doesn't it look fabulous?'

'He may be the most annoying, unreliable pain in the arse, but he can't half do a good job when he puts his mind to it,' he said.

Penny's smile suddenly slipped. 'Does Clive know you've arrested David?' she asked.

'I don't know,' replied Steve. 'I suspect not as they pulled him in pretty early this morning. Why?'

Penny shook her head with total exasperation. 'Because,' she said, 'they're close.'

'I know they're friends,' replied Steve, 'but everyone seems to be in this village, so why should Clive be especially bothered about Turner?'

'You really are the most unobservant person I have ever come across,' said Penny. 'And you a top detective too.'

Steve was now not only tired but also utterly confused. 'What *are* you talking about?' he snapped.

'They're not *just* friends,' said Penny slowly. 'They're an item.'

'You're joking?' Steve spluttered. 'Bugger, we've got the wrong man. It's Penman that's the killer not Turner.'

Steve rushed past his wife and ran upstairs to his study.

Chapter 20

Steve's throat was dry and his heart pounded heavily as he entered his study. He sat behind his desk and picked up the telephone receiver. The first call that he made was to Cooper who had not yet got back to the station. But before Steve had a chance to say anything Cooper announced that he had some bad news.

'What's the problem?' Steve asked.

'There's no chance that Turner is our man, sir,' he said. 'Marc's been on the phone. First of all Peterborough have never issued him with a passport, then Turner takes a size nine shoe and the footprint in Clara Applebaum's garden was a size eleven. Lastly the fingerprints that were found on the patio door at Mrs Applebaum's are not Turner's.'

'That's pretty conclusive,' Steve said. 'I've also just found out that Turner is gay. He has been having a relationship with a local builder called Clive Penman. I think that it was Penman who gave Turner the T-shirt. I think it's Penman that's our killer.'

After a brief pause Cooper asked, 'What do we do with Turner?'

'You'll have to wait till his brief arrives, but as soon as he does you need to speak to Turner and advise him that we believe that the person who gave him that T-shirt is the killer,' replied Steve. 'He knows that, I'm sure. That was why he reacted so angrily earlier. Until we informed him of the significance of the T-shirt I'd bet he had no idea that Penman was the killer. But he does now and we need to let him know that unless he cooperates fully then we will continue to hold him on suspicion of aiding and abetting the murders. We'll see how he reacts to that.'

'Right you are sir,' replied Cooper. 'I'll do it as soon as I get back.'

'Call me if he says anything that you think I should know,' said Steve. 'But don't let him out and don't allow him access to anyone outside the station. I don't want him getting a message to Penman before I have a chance to talk to him.'

It was just before two o'clock when Steve dialled Lucy in Winston-Salem.

'It's me,' Steve said. 'We've made a breakthrough.'

Neither Steve nor Lucy heard the click as Penny picked up the receiver in the kitchen. She had not intended to eavesdrop on Steve's call. She was merely trying to call Jemma on her mobile. However, as soon as she heard Lucy's voice on the other end of the line she couldn't bring herself to replace the receiver.

'It's a bad line, what's that you said?' asked Lucy, who was straining hard to hear her boss.

'We've made a breakthrough,' repeated Steve. 'It's not Turner who is the murderer, it's his lover.'

'Who is she?' Lucy asked.

'He's gay,' shouted Steve. 'It's Clive Penman. If you remember he was at the barbecue and at Linda's funeral.'

'I remember him,' replied Lucy. 'He was the tall skinny bloke that Marc spoke to at the barbecue.'

'Yes that's right,' continued Steve. 'He's a builder, in fact it was him that did our alterations.'

'So how do you know it's him?' asked Lucy.

'We've nothing concrete, but it all stacks up,' Steve said excitedly. 'I'm sure that it was him that must have given Turner the T-shirt. And it was Penman who first indicated to me that Linda was seeing Matt Talbot. My guess is that he did that to throw us off track for a while. Also, when I interviewed Talbot he said that his builder had been at his house on the evening that Linda was killed. He said that the company was called CAP Building Contractors. Don't you see that must stand for Clive Penman, his middle name must begin with A.'

It's Alan, thought Penny, but of course she did not say anything.

'My bet is that it was when he was with Talbot that he got the call from Linda Cartwright,' continued Steve. 'I also suspect that she wasn't calling to ask him to mind the post office for her the next day, my guess is that she told him that Frankie Leeman had called her and informed her that Gary was dead.'

'I see,' said Lucy. 'And I guess if Linda had called Penman on his mobile while he was at Talbot's it would make sense for him to call her back a few minutes later from the phonebox at the end of Wood Lane. But why did he kill Gary Leeman, Sarah McGuire and Linda Cartwright? And what about Clara Applebaum and Robin Mayhew?'

'I don't know why he killed any of them Lucy, but I'm sure he did,' Steve said. 'As for Mrs Applebaum he could easily have got in and out when I was there. He was doing some work at my house at the time. My guess is that he knew that Clara would expose him so he must have climbed out of the back of my house and slipped back in afterwards. She was just about to tell me something when she left the room. I've been trying to remember if she said anything that could help. Until just now I couldn't recall anything that she said that had any relevance to the case. But I remember now that she called Linda's accomplice the "queer one". At the time I thought that when she said queer she meant strange, but she didn't mean strange at all, I'm sure she meant gay.'

'Wow,' said Lucy. 'That makes sense, but it's still all speculation.'

'I know,' said Steve. 'That's where you come in. I need you to get to Usselmann, and get him to check the hotels in Winston-Salem to see if it was Penman who stayed there when Gary Leeman was killed.'

'I'll call him straight away,' said Lucy.

'Good. Make sure that you get him to call the station if he discovers anything.'

'I will,' said Lucy. 'Is that all?'

'Yes,' said Steve 'I think that's all.'

'Steve,' said Lucy nervously. 'We need to talk when I get back. I need to know where I stand with you.'

'Yes, you're right,' Steve said gently. 'We do need to talk. We should do that as soon as you get home.'

'Good,' said Lucy. 'I'll see you soon.'

Lucy replaced the receiver first, followed shortly by Steve. It was a further few seconds before Penny replaced her receiver.

Steve's next call was to Penman's mobile. It rang for a couple of moments before Penman answered. 'Clive Penman,'

'Hi Clive,' said Steve. 'It's Steve Carmichael here.'

'Oh, hi Mr Carmichael,' responded Clive. 'What can I do for you?'

'We need to meet so I can settle up with you for the building work,' said Steve.

'Sure,' responded Clive. 'How do you like it?'

'It's fabulous,' said Steve trying to sound as calm as possible. 'You've done a great job. So when can we meet?'

'I'm at another job at the moment,' said Clive. 'But I could come round this evening if that's OK.'

'Why don't I drop into your house on my way back from the station?' asked Steve. 'I could be at yours at around six o'clock this evening.'

'I'm not sure I'll be through by then,' replied Clive. 'Make it seven o'clock, that should be OK.'

'That's fine,' said Steve. 'Where do you live?'

'Station Road,' replied Clive. 'Number nine, it's the middle house in the terraced row opposite the hairdressers.'

'I know the houses you mean,' said Steve. 'It's £1,000 that I owe you isn't it?'

'£1,000 in cash we agreed,' said Clive.

'Cash is fine,' said Steve. 'I'll see you this evening.'

When Penman was safely off the line Steve let out an audible sigh, before making his fourth and final call. This was to Marc Watson.

'Marc, I'm going to pick up Penman tonight, meet me here at home at six-thirty.'

'Fine,' replied Watson. 'Cooper's just told me that you think he's our man. Why don't we pick him up now?'

'He's not going to be home until around seven,' said Steve. 'He doesn't suspect anything. He thinks that I'm going round to settle up for the work he did here.'

'OK,' replied Watson. 'I'll see you later.'

As soon as Steve ended the call he collapsed back into his chair and fell into a deep slumber. He had only had a couple of hours sleep in the last 24, and he just couldn't stay awake any longer.

Chapter 21

In all the years that Penny had known Steve, she had never once contemplated the prospect that he would be interested in another woman. Even the uneasy feeling that she had harboured for Lucy Clark at the barbecue could not dent the trust she placed in her husband. She knew Steve well enough to realise that he admired his young junior officer and after meeting Lucy she had no doubt that the admiration was reciprocated. However, even this had not perturbed Penny when she was told that Steve would be travelling to the US with Lucy. In short she trusted her husband, and she had thought that he was far too preoccupied with the case to take an interest in anything or anyone else.

When Penny replaced the handset she was shaking. For the first time in over 15 years she craved a cigarette. Although neither Steve nor Lucy had said anything that was in any way incriminating, Penny had no doubts about what they were going to sort out on Monday. Various emotions welled up inside her. She was shocked, hurt and angry, but most of all she felt betrayed and was anxious about what was to become of a relationship which, up until that point, she had taken for granted as being rock solid.

As often in times of trouble, Penny retreated to the sanctuary of her garden. For half an hour or so she wandered around the flowerbeds, occasionally stopping to stoop and pluck a weed or dead-head a wilting flower. Penny was always good in a crisis, and after the initial emotional surge had subsided she calmly pondered about what course of action she should take. Having decided upon a strategy she returned to the kitchen to make her husband the sandwich which she had offered him earlier that afternoon.

*   *   *   *

It was shortly before six when Steve awoke. For a couple of seconds he forgot where he was. Wiping his eyes he looked at the cheese sandwich and mug of tea that Penny had rested next to him several hours before. He pushed open the lid on the cheese sandwich and although he was quite hungry he decided to leave it and the tea, which was now cold and had a thin film of skin forming on top.

Steve gazed at his watch. 'Bugger,' he muttered when he realised the time. Why the hell didn't she wake me, he thought to himself as he rushed towards the bathroom. Twenty-five minutes later, Steve rushed down the stairs, having showered and changed for the first time since he left the US. 'Penny? Where are you?'

After a brief pause Penny emerged from the kitchen. 'Do you feel better after that nap?' she asked, trying hard to appear as normal as usual.

'Yeah,' replied Steve. 'But I'm meeting Marc in five minutes, so I haven't time to chat.'

Right on cue the doorbell rang. 'I'm not sure what time I'll be back,' said Steve as he pecked Penny on the cheek. 'See you later.'

Penny managed a forced smile as her husband disappeared through the front door. As soon as he had left the house Penny picked up the phone and the first phase of her plan started.

*   *   *   *

Steve and Watson parked their car about 50 yards away from Penman's terraced house roughly 20 minutes before the prearranged time.

'He doesn't suspect anything,' said Steve. 'We don't need any backup, but I want you to arrive no later than five minutes after I go in. By that time I'll have him under arrest.'

'Are you sure sir?' enquired Watson. 'I really think that it would be safer if we had a couple more officers with us.'

Steve smiled. 'Don't worry Marc, it will be OK.' For the next 20 minutes the two officers waited in silence.

Clive Penman's suspicions had started when Carmichael suggested that they meet at his house to settle the bill. Having spent numerous hours in Carmichael's study during the previous couple of weeks, Penman had read all the papers that Steve had brought home and had kept himself up to speed on the progress that Carmichael and the team were making in the case. Then when he had learnt from Penny, earlier in the week, that Carmichael was *en route* to North Carolina, he knew that the net was closing in on him. Although Penman did not know Carmichael well, he felt he knew him well enough to understand that the suggestion of a meeting at his house was not the sort of thing Carmichael would do, unless of course he had an alternative reason to pay him a call.

After receiving the call Penman had decided not to go home. Instead he had parked his van a couple of streets away and had made his way to Tan House Row and the Carmichael house. Once outside Penman hid himself in the shadows in an alley across the road. From that position he had a clear view of the Carmichaels' front door. He had waited for about an hour before Watson arrived. From that moment he knew that the game was up for him. There was no way that Carmichael would take another policeman with him if all he was doing was clearing the balance of cash that he owed him, particularly as it was a cash in hand job.

Penman spent a few moments trying to work out what he should do next.

*　*　*　*

It took Penny only a few minutes to glean from the duty officer at Kirkwood the flight details of Lucy Clark. It was certainly not in keeping with her character to create such a false pretence. The story she invented, namely that Steve wished to meet his colleague as she arrived, and had mislaid the information, had done the trick. She did feel a little guilty that she had found it necessary to resort to such measures to gather this information, however her desire to know when Lucy was arriving back in the UK was overwhelming.

*　*　*　*

Steve strode purposefully up to Penman's front door and banged the knocker a couple of times. He waited for a few minutes then repeated the exercise. After a third unsuccessful attempt he decided to peer through the front room window. Inside, the house looked neat and tidy. A small two-seater settee took up most of the room, and on the wall were a couple of undistinguished prints. Steve looked down the road towards Watson, and shrugged his shoulders, before making one last attempt to summon Penman with an inordinately loud rap on the front door.

At about that time Robbie Carmichael returned home. As he walked up the path, the fragrant rampaging tentacles of lavender brushed against his feet and ankles. It was then that Clive Penman made his mind up what to do.

When Penny answered the door the first thing she saw was Robbie in his red Liverpool shirt. 'Hello darling,' she said with a broad smile. However, her smile evaporated when

217

Clive emerged into view. 'Hello Penny,' he said, 'I've arranged to meet Steve, is he in?'

Before Penny could answer Penman was inside the hallway and had closed the front door behind him. 'I think there must be some mistake,' spluttered Penny, who had put her arm around Robbie and was trying hard to act normal. 'Steve has just left.'

'Oh,' said Clive. 'I'm certain we agreed to meet here. Never mind, I'll wait. He's sure to come back when he realises I'm not there.'

'Yes,' responded Penny. 'I'll tell you what, I'll call him on his mobile and let him know you're here.'

It was at this point that Clive's expression changed. 'I don't think so,' he said in a controlled whisper. 'Get over there.' With that he pushed Penny and Robbie through the open doorway, which led into the newly-refurbished morning room. Once inside the room Penman pulled out a Stanley knife from his pocket and slowly and deliberately pushed forward the lever, which extended the sharp blade.

Penny pulled Robbie close to her. 'What do you want from us Clive? I don't understand. What's the matter?' she said, her voice shaking with fear.

'Don't bullshit me Penny,' came back the reply. 'I know what's going on. I may not have a degree like you and your smarmy husband, but I'm not stupid.'

'Clive,' pleaded Penny. 'I really don't know what you're talking about.'

Clive grinned. Although he was very scared, outwardly he remained calm. 'Who else is in the house?' he asked.

Penny thought for a while before deciding to be honest about her reply. 'Just us and Natalie,' she replied. 'She's in the toilet at the moment.'

'What about the other one?' Clive snapped.

'Jemma's out with her boyfriend,' replied Penny. 'She won't be back for a couple of hours.'

Clive pushed forward the knife in his outstretched right arm. 'You,' he said to Robbie, 'get your sister and bring her here.'

'Do as he says,' said Penny, as calmly as she could. 'Don't be scared.' With that she kissed his head and then pushed Robbie towards the door.

Robbie walked slowly to the door without taking his eyes off the knife in Penman's hand. Once he reached the door he looked back towards his mother before making his way down the hall to the downstairs bathroom. After a short while they heard the lavatory flush, followed by the click of the bolt as Natalie unlocked the door. The bathroom was the last door along the corridor from the kitchen. Penny counted to ten in her head before shouting loudly, 'Run children! Run! Get help. Run as fast as you can!'

Penman had not expected this. Panic overwhelmed him. He grabbed Penny and threw her into the corner of the room before making his way to the hall. Down the other end of the hall Robbie was dragging his confused little sister into the kitchen. 'Quickly Natalie,' he shouted, 'He's coming!'

By the time Penman made it to the end of the hall the two children had already reached the back door and were making their exit. Penman stopped and looked back towards the front door where Penny was struggling to release the Yale lock. 'No!' he shouted and started to run back towards where Penny was frantically trying to open the door. When Penny saw him coming she realised that she was not going to get out before he caught her. With that in mind she started to climb the stairs two steps at a time. She had just reached the top when Penman's arms clamped her legs and he brought her down to the floor with a loud thump.

Once out into the garden Robbie and Natalie scaled the fence at the back and ran screaming across the open fields that lay behind. As soon as they had cleared the fence, Robbie realised that they were no longer being followed, but he still kept running. It took him only a matter of minutes to reach the road where he waited for his sister. Even though he knew they were safe from Penman this seemed to have little effect on the fear and adrenaline which continued to pump through him.

When Natalie reached where he was standing she was crying. He cuddled her in his arms and said, 'We've got to get help. He's still got mummy. You have to be brave Natalie.' Natalie nodded and the two children ran down the road which led to the WI hall where they knew there was a public phone-box. It seemed to take them an age to get to the box, but once inside Robbie dialled 999 and waited for the operator.

Penny was only unconscious for a couple of minutes. But that was long enough for Penman to drag her into Steve's attic and to tie her hands tightly behind her back with the cord from Steve's desk-side light.

'That was a stupid thing to do,' he said when she came round. 'You'll regret it I promise.' With that he grabbed her hair, pulled back her head and pushed the point of the blade of the Stanley knife into the soft tissue beneath her chin. Penny swallowed hard. She could feel a small trickle of blood run down her neck, a little of which ran over the tip of Penman's blade. 'Now,' continued Penman in a low calm voice. 'If you know what's best for you just do what I say from now on.' Penny nodded but did not reply. By now she was very scared. 'I'm going downstairs,' continued Penman. 'I'll be gone for a couple of minutes. If you utter one word or move one inch before I get back I'll kill you. Do you understand?' Again Penny nodded. She had no doubt that Clive meant what he said. However, knowing that the children were safe and also accepting that she would be unable to break free from the tight knots which bound her hands, she decided that her best course of action would be to wait for the police, who would surely come in numbers once Robbie had raised the alarm.

Penman was away for just a few moments. Just long enough to lock all the doors and windows downstairs and to draw closed all the curtains.

* * * *

When Chief Inspector Hewitt was informed of the situation he quickly decided to assume command himself. Within minutes of receiving Robbie's call, armed officers had been despatched to Moulton Bank. Hewitt, clad in full armoured gear, was among them. Hewitt called Steve from the police van as it sped through the country lanes. His final words before hanging up were, 'Under no circumstance do I want you going near your house until we arrive. You will not help Penny by attempting to restrain Penman by yourself.'

Steve heard the words, but he never had any intention of following his superior's command. Being only a short distance from home it took him and Watson only a few minutes to get their car close to Steve's house.

'Park down Broadhurst Lane,' Steve barked as they neared the house. He had chosen Broadhurst Lane as it was just around the corner from the house but was completely hidden from view from any of the windows. 'There's the bastard's van,' shouted Steve as they turned into the lane. 'Pull up behind it.'

Marc parked behind Penman's van and the two officers got out of the car. Steve's face was grey and sullen. He leant against the side of Penman's van to consider his options. As he did so, Watson opened up the unlocked cab door and rummaged through the contents of the glove compartment. Once he had satisfied himself that he could see nothing there of value he climbed up into the back of the pickup.

At first he saw nothing other than a set of ladders, some half-used bags of cement and sand, a tarpaulin and a whole load of tools. Then he saw it. Glinting away in the evening sunshine, a tiny object caught his eye. 'My God,' he said as he picked it up. 'I think this is Linda's missing earring.'

Steve glanced up at his junior. 'Well I think we've got enough to nail him, but it's not that which worries me at the moment,' he said.

After a further moment's contemplation Steve decided what he should do. 'Marc,' he said, 'I want you to meet up with Hewitt at the front of the house as we agreed. I'm going to go through the fields at the back and take a look through the kitchen.'

'Do you think that's wise, sir?' said Watson. 'The chief was quite clear when he called.'

'Bugger him,' said Steve. 'His wife's not being held hostage by some nutcase. Look Marc,' he said. 'I'm not stupid. I'm not going to try and get in, I just want to make sure that he doesn't try to take her out the back.'

Watson was not sure he believed him, but he nodded and walked away towards the front of the house. Steve threw off his jacket and tie and made towards the field that lay behind his house, oblivious to his younger colleague's expression.

After making the call, Robbie and Natalie waited outside the phonebox, just as the operator had told them. In a matter of minutes the local village policeman arrived. PC Newman was surprised how calm the children appeared to be. His instructions from Chief Hewitt were to collect them, locate their elder sister and then to bring all three of the children back to Kirkwood. At first Robbie did not want to be taken to the station. He wanted to stay close to the house and their mother. It took Newman several minutes to persuade him that their mother would be fine and that he and his sisters would be more help at the station, where they could provide valuable information about what had happened earlier that evening. Eventually, albeit still quite reluctantly, Robbie agreed that Newman was probably right.

222

* * * *

When Penman returned to Steve's study, Penny was exactly where he had left her.

'Good girl,' he said in a way a dog is praised for sitting neatly at the curb. 'You're being smart at last.'

'Clive,' Penny said, 'why are you doing this?'

'Doing what?' replied Penman.

'Holding me hostage like this,' responded Penny.

'I'm not stupid,' said Penman. 'I know that your husband and his colleagues will be outside now. They know that I killed Linda, Sarah, Leeman, that meddling old bag next door and that drunk Mayhew.'

'I see,' she said. 'But why?'

Penman sat down in the large leather chair behind Steve's desk. 'Have you ever seen a dead body?' he asked. Penny shook her head. 'You're lucky. I hadn't until that day I came back to David's house.'

For the first time since Clive had returned to the room, his glare moved away from Penny. 'David had just played his first cricket match for the village team. He had played really well. He was so keen to tell his dad. We must have run almost all the way to David's house. When we got there we found a note on the door. It said DON'T COME IN GET PC WATSON. DAD. It was Mr Turner's writing. So David ran over to get PC Watson. I said I would wait in case Mary or Mrs Turner returned. Well I waited for a few minutes, then for some reason I decided to go in. The front door was locked so I went round the back. The kitchen door was open. I went inside and walked carefully through towards the stairs. My heart was pumping and my legs were like jelly.' Penman took a deep breath before continuing. 'As I reached the top of the stairs I could see that Mr and Mrs Turner's bedroom door was open slightly. I pushed it open and there, laid across the bed, was Mr Turner. He'd blown half his head away. There was blood all over the place and on the floor was the shotgun.' Penman was almost in a trance as he recounted precisely what had happened almost 30 years earlier. 'I touched it,' he continued. 'It was still warm. Then I saw the note in his hand. It had blood on it. I took it from him, read it and then decided to keep it.'

'Why did you keep it?' asked Penny.

'Because it said that *he* was the driver of the car that killed the Pugh girl. I couldn't let David know that. He idolised his dad. It would have killed him.'

'So what did you do next?' said Penny.

'I left the same way I had come,' responded Clive with a wry smile. 'By the time I got back to the front David and PC Watson had still not arrived. They came about two minutes later.'

'And you kept quiet about the note all this time?' exclaimed Penny.

'I thought it was the kindest thing I could do. That's until that selfish cow decided to come clean and confess to being the driver. I had no idea that Mr Turner was just trying to protect his daughter.'

'But why did you kill all those people?' asked Penny.

'Shortly after Mary died I foolishly showed Linda the suicide note. She then became obsessed with finding out why Mr Turner had committed suicide. At first Terry helped her with her digging. When he had had enough and moved away, she asked Sarah and I to help her. We both agreed, but we made her promise to keep our involvement quiet from the rest of the village. We didn't want to receive the same level of ridicule that she was getting. Also I didn't want David to think I was involved in dragging up the past. I think Sarah wasn't that keen on Ken knowing either.'

'But why did you kill them?' asked Penny.

'Before Mary died, Linda had got quite close to her. Funny really, as Mary was cruel to her when they were kids. Anyway,

Mary let slip that she thought that her dad was being blackmailed over Gillian Pugh's death. Linda thought that if that was the case the most likely person would be either Robin Mayhew, Ken McGuire or Gary Leeman. She spoke to Robin and Ken about it but of course they both denied it. But she could not locate Gary. He'd gone back to the States years before and nobody had his address. Or so we thought. Then a little later I was doing a few jobs at old Clara Applebaum's. It was there that I found a letter from her to Gary Leeman's mother. I took down the address and wrote to her.'

'Did Linda know you were doing that?' Penny asked.

'No, I kept it to myself,' replied Penman. 'After a few weeks I got a call from Gary. He told me that he was now living in North Carolina and invited me over.'

'So you went,' prompted Penny.

'Yes,' Penman said. 'I booked a flight and went out there in March.'

'And what did you find out from Gary?' she asked.

'At first nothing,' said Penman. 'In fact he seemed a really nice bloke. However one night we had a few beers and got talking. I brought up the subject of Mr Turner's death and the fact that it was still a mystery why he had killed himself. It was then he confessed to the blackmail.'

'What?' interrupted Penny. 'He just said "I blackmailed him".'

'No,' snapped Penman. 'He didn't say that. He just let it slip that he knew that Turner had killed Gillian Pugh. He called Mr Turner a murdering coward.' Penman again fixed his gaze on Penny. 'I couldn't let him get away with that now could I?' Penny remained silent. 'So later that night when we were driving home I asked him to stop the car. We were by a lake. It was all so easy really. Once we were out of the car I pulled his own gun on him, led him down to the water's edge, tied his hands behind his back and when he couldn't put up a struggle I held his head under the water. He

225

thrashed around a bit, but it was easy. It took just a few moments and I can honestly say that I felt nothing.' Penman paused. 'Then I untied his hands, removed his trousers, shirt and shoes, which I folded neatly and put on the passenger seat in the car. I then loaded him into a rowing boat. I rowed out for a few hundred yards and slipped him into the water.'

Penny felt a cold chill at the calm and calculated way that Penman was reciting the story. 'How did you get back to your hotel?' she asked.

'I walked,' replied Penman. 'It took me most of the night, but that was no problem. Then I checked out of the hotel and took the next flight home.'

'I can understand why you killed Leeman,' Penny said, trying to sound as sincere as she could. 'But why kill the others? Surely they had not done anything to harm Mr Turner?'

Penny's question seemed to snap Clive out of his trance. 'I've said enough. I've said too much already,' he replied firmly. 'Anyway, it's none of your damn business.'

Chapter 22

It took Steve only a few moments to reach the broken wooden fence at the back of his house. He crouched down amongst the brambles and stinging nettles, straining his neck to see if there was any sign of Penny or Penman. All he could see were closed curtains at all the windows. He wasn't sure what he should do next. While he was considering his options his mobile phone rang. 'Inspector,' said Hewitt, 'what the hell do you think you are doing? I specifically told you to wait at the front of the house out of sight until backup arrived. Why did you take it upon yourself to ignore my instructions?' Steve switched off the phone.

'Inspector Carmichael!' shouted Hewitt. He removed the phone from his ear in total disbelief. 'He's hung up on me,' he said in amazement.

'I'm sure there is a perfectly good explanation sir,' Marc said in as reassuring a voice as he could muster. 'Maybe his batteries are running low.'

'Maybe,' responded Hewitt. 'But I don't want him round there on his own.' Turning to a group of armed officers he shouted, 'You four, go round the back and await my instructions. If you see Inspector Carmichael make sure that he does not try to enter the house or engage in any way with Penman. Do you understand?' The four officers nodded and made their way down the road, following the route Steve had taken a few minutes earlier.

Hewitt had no reason to worry about Steve entering the

house. He had already decided that his best course of action was to remain well out of sight. He had no intention of provoking Penman and risking any harm to Penny. He did however want to ensure that Penny was OK. With that in mind he keyed in their home telephone number.

The sudden ringing of the telephone startled Penman and Penny. They both stared in silence at the phone in Steve's study until finally, after about six or seven rings, Penman picked up the receiver. 'Hello,' he replied in a whisper.

'It's Steve Carmichael. Can we talk?'

'You talk, I'll listen,' responded Penman.

'OK,' Steve said, his heart pumping loudly. 'I need to know that Penny is safe. Can I speak to her?'

'She's safe,' responded Penman without any emotion.

'Can I talk to her?' repeated Steve

'Why?' said Penman curtly.

'To make sure she's safe,' echoed Steve as calmly as he could.

'She's safe,' replied Penman who was by this time starting to get agitated. 'I've told you that already.'

'OK,' replied Steve, trying hard not to annoy his wife's jailer. After a brief pause he asked, 'What are you planning to do now?'

'Call me back in half an hour and I'll tell you,' Penman retorted. 'No funny business in the meantime or she gets it.'

Steve was consumed with fear. 'Don't hang up,' he pleaded. 'I understand, but I need to know she's fine. Please let me talk to her. Just for a few moments. That's all.'

Penman thought over the suggestion. He moved the receiver near to Penny's head, and with his hand over the receiver he said to her, 'Tell him you are OK. But also tell him that I am armed and that if they try anything silly I'll kill you.'

Penman lifted his hand from the mouthpiece and nodded at Penny to talk.

'Steve,' said Penny in a shaky voice. 'I'm OK. He won't

harm me if everyone stays away. He's got a knife and he says he will kill me if you try anything silly.' At this point Penny's courage stared to wane and she sobbed uncontrollably.

'Don't worry Penny,' shouted Steve. 'It will be OK, be brave.'

Penny did not hear Steve's words as Penman had already taken the receiver from her. 'That's enough,' he snapped. 'She's alive and unhurt. Now no messing about or I'll kill her. Call me back in half an hour and I'll tell you what I want.' Penman slammed down the receiver.

By the time the conversation had finished, Carmichael had been joined by the four armed officers. 'He's got a knife,' Steve said anxiously.

Upon hearing this the first officer spoke into his radio. 'Inspector Carmichael's spoken to him sir.'

Before he could say anything more Steve snatched the receiver from the hand of the officer. 'It's Carmichael here. Listen carefully. My wife is unharmed. Penman's ordered us to call back in thirty minutes. He's made it clear that if we try to do anything to gain entry he'll kill her.'

'This is Hewitt,' responded the voice at the end of the line. 'We have no plans to aggravate the situation. But it's important that you return to me at control. I understand how you must be feeling Steve, but I need you here. I need your knowledge of the layout of your house, your perception of the mind of Penman and I also need to know how Penny will be coping.'

Steve listened in silence. 'I'll come round now sir,' he eventually replied. He then handed the radio back to its owner and retreated back through the brambles and gorse, and onwards towards the road.

Penman looked at his watch. It was 8:13 p.m. 'Right,' he said pointing the knife at his prisoner's face. 'I need to think so I want you to just sit there and be quiet.' Penny was still sobbing. She had no intention of disobeying his instructions.

Penman sat himself down in Steve's leather chair. With repeated strokes he started to systematically carve huge chunks out of the top of the desk as he plotted his next move.

It took Steve only a couple of minutes to reach Hewitt's control centre, which was a large police van parked just out of view of the front of the house. All down the street he could see armed police officers crouching behind walls and bushes. There must have been at least a dozen of them, with their guns trained on the front of his house. Inside the control centre were Hewitt, Watson, Cooper and three other officers. 'Thank God,' exclaimed Hewitt. 'I'm pleased that you've decided to follow my orders for once.' Then to everyone's amazement, Hewitt threw his arm around Steve's shoulders and grasped him tightly. 'Don't worry Steve,' he said with genuine sincerity. 'I've no intention of doing anything that will in any way frighten Penman into hurting Penny. You have my word.'

This was the first time Steve had encountered a human side to his boss, and the only time he had ever felt any true respect for him. 'Thank you sir,' he said wearily.

'Now,' said Hewitt, ' what exactly did he say?'

For the next 20 minutes Steve provided Hewitt and the rest of the team with as much information as he could about his conversation with Penman and the personality of both of the remaining occupants of his house. He also provided them with a detailed drawing of the layout of his home.

* * * *

Penman carved away at Steve's desk for a further 10 minutes before he spoke again. 'You were asking me why I killed Sarah, Linda, old Clara Applebaum and Robin Mayhew,' he said with an air of calm authority. 'Then let me tell you.' Penny had gained her composure. She listened with interest.

'When I got back from America I tried to carry on as normal. Only David and Sarah knew I'd been in the US. David knew because … well he's my friend and Sarah because it was she who drove me to the airport. David never learnt to drive you see. For a couple of weeks everything was OK. Then Mrs Applebaum got a letter from Leeman's mother telling him that her son had died. The old busybody told Sarah. When Sarah told me that she was going to tell Linda, I just panicked.' As he spoke he fixed his gaze on the knife. 'We were in Sarah's house when she told me. I tried to persuade her to keep quiet, but she was insistent. Then she suddenly put two and two together. You could see it in her eyes.'

Penman was silent for a moment before continuing. 'All she kept saying over and over again was you killed him. I could see that she wasn't going to keep quiet. What choice did I have, but to kill her?'

After a short pause Penman smiled. 'I just tied her up like I've tied you up. Then I got some sleeping pills from her bathroom and a bottle of vodka from her husband's plentiful supply and gave her most of them. It didn't take long for her to descend into a deep sleep. Then when she was unconscious I untied her hands and put her in the back of her car and we drove to Wood Lane. I grabbed some of her shoes on my way out of the house, so that when I dumped her people would think that she had driven herself down to Wood lane and had taken the overdose herself while she was down there. Once there I put her in the driver's seat, poured a little more vodka down her, put a couple more pills in her mouth and then scattered the rest of the pills on the floor. I poured some of the vodka over her clothes and the car seat and just left her. It was a stroke of genius and so simple to execute.'

It was clear to Penny that Clive was getting quite excited reliving the details of the murder. He was clearly mad. 'But why did you kill Linda?' she asked.

'Linda just couldn't stop meddling,' he replied. 'She had somehow got Frankie Leeman's address and had been writing to her. Then on that Sunday evening she called me. She said that she had spoken to Frankie who had informed her that Gary was dead. As soon as she said that I knew she would be on to me fairly soon. She was very persistent. I was at a customer's house when I took her call, Matt Talbot in Wood Lane, so I couldn't ask too many questions. So I called her back from the phonebox at the end of the lane. I knew that I would have to kill her and I knew that when the police got involved they would check her calls in and out, so I made the call from the box. She agreed that I could come round that evening. Before I arrived she had no idea that it was me who had killed Leeman, she just thought I was coming round to help her with her investigation. But she was smart and I knew she would work it out sooner or later.'

'So you killed her in her own house?' Penny said.

'Yes,' replied Penman. 'But this time I couldn't risk taking her body out that night. She lived in a busier part of town to Sarah, so I waited until just before dawn. I wrapped her in my tarpaulin from the van and took her down to Wood Lane and dumped her. It was only when I dumped the body that I realised that she had no shoes on. But I couldn't risk going back so I just had to leave her. Anyway, I needed to be back at the post office if my alibi was going to be believed.'

'So David knew nothing of all this?' Penny asked.

Penman smiled. 'David is one of life's innocents,' replied Penman. 'He always thinks the best of everyone. That's why I love him and why I have to protect him from life's darker side.'

For the first time since her capture, Penny sensed some compassion coming from Penman. 'But what about Mrs Applebaum?' she asked.

'To be honest,' responded Penman in a very blasé manner, 'by her turn I was quite getting used to the act of murder. I

232

wasn't sure if she suspected me, however when you told your husband that she wanted to see him I knew that I had to make sure that she said nothing. So I climbed out of the back bedroom window and got in through her patio door. I listened at the door and when I heard her call me Linda's "queer friend" I knew she was about to say something. I ran to the front door and knocked as if there was someone there. Then I hid behind the long curtain that she used to pull across the door when it was closed. Once she had opened the door a little I hit her with my hammer. It happened really quickly. I caught her as she fell so she would not make a noise, and then gently laid her body on the floor. Then I returned back the way I came, using her ladder to get back through your bedroom window. I had to kick it over once I was in, but that was easy.'

'And Robin Mayhew?' Penny asked. 'Why did you murder him?'

Clive shook his head. 'He had it coming.' He looked Penny straight in the eye before continuing. 'He was smarter than your husband, he worked it out. Although he was pissed ninety per cent of the time he was nobody's fool. He knew what Linda was doing and when they found her body he went looking for clues. He found an empty packet of Hamlet near the body. I must have dropped it there by mistake when I dumped her. He knew it was mine because I'd written something on it and he recognised my handwriting.' Not for the first time Penman decided to take a pause while he gathered his thoughts. Then with the hint of a smile he continued. 'He thought he could blackmail me. He sent me an anonymous letter first. In it he asked for £3,000. I didn't know it was from him until that day I took him home from your barbecue.'

Penny was speechless. The calm and precise way that Penman was re-living his murders started to terrify her.

'When I got him home that evening he was so pissed that

he couldn't get himself into the house,' continued Penman. 'At least that's what I thought. But I was wrong. As soon as we got in the house he miraculously sobered up. He told me he had the cigar packet. He also told me that he now wanted five grand to keep quiet. So you see I had no choice. I wasn't going to be blackmailed like Mr Turner had been. No way.'

'So how did you kill Robin?' asked Penny.

'He was easy to kill. I had no trouble strangling the life out of that miserable waste of a man.'

Penny was shocked. She found it almost impossible to reconcile the man who was holding her captive with the gentle boy she had known so well in her youth or even more recently the builder who had worked so cheerfully on her house. What she did know was that she was in grave danger of being his next victim. She was in no doubt about that.

Chapter 23

At precisely 8:43 p.m. the phone rang in Steve's study. It continued to ring for a few minutes before Penman picked up the receiver.

'Hello Clive,' said the voice at the other end of the line, 'my name's Chief Inspector Hewitt.'

'I don't want to negotiate with you,' snapped Penman. 'Get Carmichael on the line.' Hewitt did not argue. He simply passed the phone to Steve.

'It's Carmichael here Clive.'

'How many coppers have you got out there Carmichael?' demanded Penman.

'About a dozen,' replied Steve. 'They have the house surrounded front and back.'

Penman was not surprised to hear this news. He'd fully expected that by now he would be trapped. 'Listen to me Carmichael,' he said, 'I want to speak to David and I want a car delivered to the front of the house.'

'OK,' replied Steve. 'I can arrange that but it will take me an hour or so.'

'You've got twenty minutes or I start hurting your wife,' he said.

'That's not going to be easy,' responded Steve calmly. 'David is at the station in Kirkwood. It will take longer than that to get him here.'

Penman was shocked by this piece of news. 'Why is he there?' he asked.

'We arrested him this morning,' replied Steve. 'We thought that he had killed Linda and the others.'

'Arseholes,' snapped Penman. 'He had nothing to do with it. Do you understand? He's totally innocent.'

'We know that now,' replied Steve. 'But all I'm saying is that it will take longer than twenty minutes to get him here.'

Penman looked at his watch. 'OK,' he said. 'I want to speak to him before nine o'clock at the latest. Then I want him here by a quarter past with a car full of petrol.'

'That's fine Clive,' said Steve. 'We'll get him to call you while he's travelling here from Kirkwood.' Penman hung up.

Hewitt had been listening into the call. 'Get Turner here as quick as you can,' he barked at the nearest officer, who immediately picked up the phone to call the station, 'and make sure he calls Penman before nine from the car.'

'Right sir,' responded the officer.

'This is the number,' Steve said as he scribbled down his telephone number on a piece of paper and handed it to his colleague.

'Let's get some air inspector,' said Hewitt. 'You two can come as well.'

Hewitt, Cooper, Watson and Carmichael clambered down the short stairway from the control vehicle and wandered up the lane. 'What do you think gentlemen?' Hewitt asked once they had stopped walking.

'I don't know,' replied Steve. 'He's very keen to see Turner. My guess is that he wants to explain to him what he's done.'

'Yes,' replied Hewitt. 'If they are in a relationship my guess is that Turner's probably the only person that he'll listen to. Maybe that's our opportunity.'

'I agree,' said Cooper.

'Me too,' concurred Watson.

'What are you proposing?' asked Steve. 'That we use Turner to persuade Penman to give himself up?'

'That's exactly what I'm thinking,' replied Hewitt. 'He

must know the game's up. But he's obviously planning to depart from here in the car he's ordered. Presumably he wants Turner to be with him. So we need to get Turner to talk him out of it or at least let Penny go as part of the deal. Once Penny is safe we will easily take control of the situation.'

'We should speak to Turner before he makes the call to Penman,' Steve said. 'I'm sure Turner will help us. He seems a decent man.'

'Yes,' agreed Cooper. 'We need to get him to start working on Penman from the word go.'

'I agree,' said Hewitt. 'I only hope that you're both right and that Turner is willing to play ball.'

*   *   *   *

In many respects it had been Clive who had suffered most from the suicide of David's father. Since that day in 1976, his life had changed irreversibly. Everything he did in the intervening years had been influenced by his fondness and sense of duty to David. He saw himself as not just a friend but also a surrogate father. He admired David and would do anything to protect the man he saw as a near perfect albeit vulnerable human being. The rumours that had circulated in the village about their relationship were in truth a little off the mark. Theirs was not a physical union. However their bond was as deep and caring as any could be between two people.

For his part David's feelings for Clive were undoubtedly strong. He would never have said or done anything to damage their friendship, even though at times he found it suffocating in its intensity. On numerous occasions over the years David had felt trapped and to some extent controlled by his friend. In spite of this David was largely comfortable with their relationship, so much so that he had given up on the thought of marriage or even any normal relationship

237

many years before. In his heart he knew that Clive would never permit any other individual male or female to usurp the position that he had created for himself with David.

When David was informed that Clive was holed up in Carmichael's house with Penny as his captive, he did not believe it. However, as soon as he received the call from Carmichael asking him to talk his friend out of his role as hostage-taker, he rapidly became reconciled to the facts. Although his loyalty to Clive was unquestionable, David was a practical human being, so his overriding instinct was to assist an innocent person, an impulse that was far too great for even his deep affection for Clive to stifle. Without hesitation he agreed to try and persuade his friend to release Penny unharmed.

'Clive is that you?' he said when Penman picked up the phone. 'It's David.'

'I'm afraid, David,' replied Penman. 'I need you with me. Please come as soon as you can.'

'I'm on my way,' responded David. 'Now just relax and stay calm. Don't do anything silly and certainly don't harm Penny.'

'I've told them to get us a car,' interrupted Penman. 'I've got a plan. When you get here I'll share it with you.'

'Fine,' replied David coolly. 'That's fine. Just stay calm. I'll be there in about fifteen minutes.'

'When you get here come alone, David. I don't want anyone else coming with you, just you.'

'Don't worry Clive, I'll be alone. I promise.'

Penman hung up and made his way to Steve and Penny's bedroom, which overlooked the front. He moved the curtain a couple of inches and peered out to try and see his friend arriving.

When the car carrying David arrived it pulled up outside the control room, out of view of Penman. Steve rushed down to meet David Turner. 'Did you speak to him?' he asked.

'Yes,' replied David, who was surprisingly composed for someone who had just learned that his closest friend was a murderer and a hostage-taker.

'What did he say?'

'He's very scared,' explained David. 'I'm sure that he will not harm your wife inspector, but I do think that the sooner I go in to see him the better.'

By this time Hewitt was also outside the control van, with Cooper and Watson in tow. 'Did he mention the car?' asked Hewitt.

'Yes. He did. He thinks we will both be able to escape in it.'

'Look,' continued Hewitt, 'if you are willing I'd like you to go in there and explain to Penman that he can have the car only if he agrees to let Penny go.'

'No!' shouted Steve. 'Penman's cornered, he's likely to do anything if we intimidate him like that. We should give David the keys and park a car outside for him. We stand a much better chance of getting Penny out alive if we just do as he says.'

'I agree,' said Watson. 'He's a nutcase, we shouldn't do anything that will push him over the edge.'

'He's not a nutcase,' snapped Turner. 'He's *scared*. He's not a bad person, he's just got out of control and he doesn't know what to do.'

The five men stood in silence for a moment until Hewitt spoke again. 'OK, we won't make it a condition,' he said. 'You can go in David, with the keys to this car. Watson, you drive Mr Turner to the front of the house and then retire immediately. Try to persuade your friend to release Penny before he gets into the car.' David nodded and got back into the passenger seat. A rather nervous Watson climbed into the driver's side and slowly drove round to the front of Carmichael's house.

Marc deliberately parked the car so that the passenger side was nearest to the house. He was determined to let Penman see Turner before he saw him. The ploy worked perfectly. Penman was totally disinterested in the slight figure that got out of the driver's door and made a speedy exit across the road and out of sight. He was only interested in seeing his friend. A broad smile of relief travelled the width of Penman's face as he rushed downstairs to let David in.

'What the hell are you doing?' said David. 'Why have you kidnapped Penny? Are you mad?' Clive didn't answer. His face was pale and he was clearly worried about his predicament. 'Don't worry, It will be OK,' said David in a quiet and controlled tone. 'Where's Penny now?'

'She's in Carmichael's study in the attic,' replied Clive.

'OK,' said David. 'This is what we'll do. You go into the front bedroom and make sure that nobody approaches the house. I'll take care of Penny.'

Clive nodded his approval. 'Don't leave me,' he pleaded, 'I'm really scared.'

David embraced his friend. 'I won't leave you Clive,' he replied, 'I'll never leave you, I promise.'

For the next five minutes the police waited quietly outside the house. Nobody spoke in the control room, as they waited for a sign from David Turner. Then suddenly the radio crackled into life. 'The back door is opening,' came the call from the officers at the rear of the house.

Hewitt said, 'Don't fire unless you have a clear sight of the suspect and you have reason to believe that he will harm either one of his hostages.'

There was a brief silence. Then an excited voice made a significant announcement. 'It's the female hostage, she's leaving the building. She's running towards us. She's alone and she looks fine.'

Steve's relief was plain for all to see. 'Thank God.'

'She's clear,' came the voice. 'She's clear and safe.'

'Bring her to control,' ordered Hewitt.

When Penny arrived it was only 9:20 p.m. Her time as a

captive had been less than three hours, however to Penny and Steve it had seemed like an eternity. Shaking and sobbing, she threw herself into her husband's arms.

'I was so scared,' she said.

'Me too,' replied Steve.

'Are the kids OK?' she asked.

'They're fine, Mrs Carmichael,' replied Hewitt. 'They're back at the station, safe and well.' Steve and Penny continued to embrace tightly. 'How did you get free?' Hewitt asked.

'I was tied up in the attic. In Steve's study,' she said. 'Then David Turner came in and untied me. He told me to go downstairs and out of the back door. I didn't stop to ask questions, I just ran as fast as I could.'

'Did you see Penman?' Steve asked.

'No.'

'Where are they in the house?' Hewitt asked.

'They're in our bedroom,' Penny replied.

'That's at the front,' said Steve. 'It's the main window on the first floor.'

Hewitt thought for a moment. 'Steve, you and your wife need to go back to the station to be with your children. We'll take it from here.'

'No. This is my case, this is my house and he has held my wife hostage. I'm in to the finish on this one.'

Hewitt nodded. 'OK inspector,' he said. 'That's understandable. But I insist that Penny goes back to the station to be reunited with your children and to give a full statement.'

'That's fine,' Penny said. 'But before I do you need to know that he confessed to all five murders. He told me chapter and verse about them all.'

'Did he say why he did them?' Steve asked.

'He killed Leeman first,' she replied. 'He had been blackmailing David's father about Gillian Pugh's death. I think that he blamed him for driving Mr Turner to kill himself.'

'What about the others?' asked Watson.

'He was just covering his tracks with them,' replied Penny. 'I think he simply lost control of events and just killed anyone he feared was on to him.' She paused, then she said, 'But I think he started to get a taste for it. He really enjoyed telling me about it. Every little detail was recounted with calm, cold precision and no remorse. I'm no psychologist but I'd say he got off on the adrenaline rush and the power it gave him.'

Watson put a consoling arm around Penny. 'I'll take her back to the station sir,' he said.

'Thanks Marc,' replied Steve.

Penny and Watson left the control room and got into a marked police car, which quickly sped off in the direction of Kirkwood.

'What do we do now?' asked Cooper.

'I'm not sure,' replied Hewitt.

With Penny now safe Steve was much more lucid in his thinking. 'I think we should give David about ten minutes more. Then if we still haven't heard from him we should try to make contact with them.'

'I agree,' replied Hewitt. 'Penman won't harm Turner, that's for sure, and I'm sure that they'll be ready to come out soon. So let's just wait and see.'

After 15 minutes had elapsed Hewitt was becoming impatient. He had spent virtually all that time pacing up and down inside the small control vehicle. 'I don't like this at all,' he said at last. 'Let's give them a bit of a push. Make the call inspector.'

The phone rang for a good three minutes, before Steve replaced the receiver.

'What now?' Cooper asked.

'We need to make contact,' said Hewitt. 'We'll loud-hailer them. If they don't respond we'll have to gain forced entry.'

Steve nodded his agreement, but his announcements through the loud-hailer received no reply, and Hewitt, who was now very uneasy ordered his officers to break down the front door. Once inside they searched the ground floor, and once this yielded nothing they made their way upstairs. Having done a fruitless sweep of that floor the officers, joined now by Hewitt, Cooper and Steve made their way up to Steve's study. The door was closed. Pinned to the outside was an envelope. On the front in red ink David had written the following words:

FOR INSPECTOR CARMICHAEL: PRIVATE AND CONFIDENTIAL

The sight of the note sent a chill down the necks of Steve and his fellow officers. Steve carefully extracted the yellow drawing pin from the door and prised open a tiny scrap of paper from the envelope. David Turner had found some paper and the envelope in Steve's desk drawer, and using the only pen in Steve's office that he could find, he had attempted to provide some reason for Clive's actions and to explain why he had done what the officers were shortly to discover in Steve's study.

Steve read the note carefully. When he had finished he pointed at the door. 'Break it down.'

In a moment Hewitt and three officers entered the room and were confronted by the gruesome spectacle of Clive Penman lying face up on the floor with a knife handle sticking out of his chest. His hands were carefully folded across his stomach and his eyes had been closed tight shut. Above his body dangled the limp body of David Turner, suspended by the same cord that earlier had bound Penny's hands so tightly.

David had managed his own execution with precision. He had carefully fastened the long nylon cord to the exposed roof joists using a reef knot similar to the one that his father had taught him to tie many years before. At the other end he had created a noose with an improvised slipknot. He had then placed his head into the noose, pulled down the slipknot behind his neck and without any hesitation launched himself from a chair into open space.

In contrast to his friend, David's face was contorted and full of pain. His eyes bulged almost clean out of their sockets and his bitten tongue protruded from his gaping mouth.

'It's ended as it all started,' Steve said. Then turning to Cooper and Hewitt, he smiled and shook his head. 'I suppose that's the only way this was ever going to end.'

Steve left the others in his study and walked slowly down the stairs. He had no need to remain in the room. For him the case was now over.

Chapter 24

The Carmichael family were not allowed to go home until the SOCOs had finished their work. So on Hewitt's instructions they were to spend the next two nights in a large family room at a five-star hotel. The hotel chosen for them was built into the Red Rose Stadium, the ground of Kirkwood Town, the local football team. Their suite was large and sumptuous, with two large bedrooms attached to a large lounge area with windows which looked out over the football pitch.

It was after midnight before Steve finally caught up with Penny and the children. When he arrived at the hotel the children were all asleep and to his amazement Penny was calm and collected. In fact he found her busily typing away on a laptop computer, which she had borrowed from the hotel manager.

'What are you doing?' Steve asked.

'I'm just trying to record all that Clive told me this evening,' she replied. 'I don't want to forget anything.'

Steve smiled and flopped down into a large sofa. 'I'm really proud of you,' he said. 'You were fantastic today.'

'I understand that they're both dead,' she said quietly.

'Yeah,' sighed Steve. 'It's all over.'

Steve had no trouble sleeping that night, unlike his wife. Penny still had to attend to some unfinished business.

* * * *

245

Lucy's return flight from Greensboro to Chiago O'Hare and then her flight from Chicago to Manchester were both on schedule and she arrived in Manchester on time. By 8:40 a.m. she had collected her bags at Manchester airport, loaded them onto a trolley and was heading for the exit, oblivious of the happenings in Moulton Bank on the previous evening. She did not see the person standing in her path. It was only when she heard her name that she realised who had come to meet her. 'Good morning Lucy, I think we need to have a little chat, don't you?'

Lucy gave Penny a forced smile. She had been hoping that maybe Steve would meet her at the airport. Not for one moment did she expect to be confronted by Penny. She tried to maintain some control, but her blushing pink cheeks only confirmed her guilt.

Penny was surprised at the ease at which she had managed to convince Steve to remain at the hotel with the children while she popped out to buy some bits and pieces. She had always considered herself to be a formidable foe when she was determined to do something, but even she had been taken aback by her powers of persuasion on this occasion. As she had expected Steve did at first object when his wife had suggested that she go out shopping by herself, particularly at such an early hour. However, Penny's insistence eventually won the day.

Penny was not in the habit of lying to her husband, so she did feel a little guilty, however given the circumstances she had convinced herself that her 'little white lie' was quite acceptable. When the alarm rang she had gently kissed her husband's forehead and quietly left. Steve was totally unaware of the time. He grunted a muffled but audible, 'See you at lunchtime,' and went back into a deep sleep. In truth he was happy to remain at the hotel. He was totally exhausted, and was relishing the prospect of spending most of the morning in bed and the rest of the day with the children.

Lucy followed Penny as she strode towards the nearest coffee bar. She had been so surprised at seeing her lover's wife that she had temporarily lost her poise. In her confusion she had allowed herself to be dragged along by Penny, like an obedient child. Penny on the other hand had planned her campaign in some detail. She was in full control and she knew it. In a perverse way she found herself enjoying the experience.

Under normal circumstances Lucy was a confident creature. She had been taken by surprise by Penny, but it took just a few moments to regain a degree of composure and shake off her acute guilt complex. 'Hang on a minute,' she said as she tugged at Penny's sleeve. 'What's all this about?'

This was the reaction that Penny had been expecting all along, so again she was fully prepared. 'This is about you and my husband,' she said quietly. 'It's about his family and it's about both of your careers.'

It was the final couple of words that registered with Lucy. At no stage had she thought that her liaison with Steve would adversely impact her career. 'What the hell do you mean?' she retorted angrily.

'Look,' said Penny, in a tone normally reserved for addressing the children when they had been particularly wayward. 'We can discuss this here in front of everyone or we can go somewhere a bit more private.'

Lucy stared at her while quickly considering the options. She could see that Penny was taking them towards the coffee bar and out of sheer bloody-mindedness she decided to at least take some control. 'I don't want a coffee. Let's sit over there.' Lucy pointed to a couple of seats that were located in a relatively quiet corner of the lounge.

'That suits me fine,' Penny said. 'After you.' Penny made a sweeping motion with her hand and Lucy and her trolley trundled across to the vacant seats. Penny calmly followed close behind.

It took them no more than 15 minutes to conclude their business. When they had finished there were no handshakes or pleasantries, they simply parted and separately made their way out of the terminal building.

As Lucy stood quietly at the taxi rank a loud voice rang out from across the sliproad. 'Lucy!' She turned to face the direction of the caller. 'Lucy!' shouted Marc for a second time, 'over here.' Lucy walked over to his car. 'Where have you been? Your plane arrived ages ago. I thought you'd missed the flight. I was just about to abandon you and make my way home.' Lucy forced a smile but said nothing.

Marc did not see Penny's car leave the car park or the triumphant expression on its driver's face.

*   *   *   *

Having successfully completed all her objectives for the morning, Penny returned to the hotel room to be greeted by Jemma, Robbie and Natalie, who had been waiting anxiously for their mother's return. Steve, on the other hand, had only just risen from his bed when his wife came in.

'Morning!' Penny shouted. 'I'm back.'

'Are we going home today?' asked Robbie.

'No not today,' replied Penny. 'But maybe we will tomorrow.'

'Cool,' he replied. 'The later the better as far as I'm concerned. This place is luxurious and there's World Cup qualifying games on TV today.'

Penny laughed. 'Trust you,' she replied, as she gave him a massive hug.

It was at this point that Steve emerged from the bedroom. 'Hi darling,' he said. 'Did you get everything sorted out that you wanted?'

'Yes,' Penny said. 'I got everything done.'

For the rest of the day the family relaxed and enjoyed the

fine facilities that were available in the hotel. Jemma and Penny spent most of the afternoon in the beauty parlour. Penny enjoyed a back, neck and shoulder massage and they both took advantage of free steam facials. Natalie spent her day in the pool. For their part Steve and Robbie took advantage of a free afternoon to watch the football on TV.

At half time Steve tried calling Lucy on his mobile. He knew that by that time she would be home, and he was very concerned about meeting her in front of the rest of the team without first having a chance to talk to her. The phone rang twice before kicking into Lucy's answering machine. Steve had no intention of leaving a message so he quickly hung up.

'Who are you calling?' Robbie asked.

'Nobody,' replied Steve, 'just the office.'

That evening, for the first time in years, the entire family had a meal out together. For Penny and the girls this was the highlight of the day. Steve and Robbie also enjoyed their meals, but for them the highpoint had to be England's impressive win. Once the kids were safely tucked up in bed, Steve and Penny decided it would be a good idea to take a stroll and take in some of the warm evening air. Penny held tight to Steve's hand. 'I can't come to terms with what happened yesterday,' she said. 'I still can't accept that Clive could have harmed anyone, but to be the murderer … I just can't believe it.' Penny threw her arms around Steve's neck. 'Do you still love me?' she asked.

'Still?' Steve said. 'That makes the assumption that I once loved you.'

'Don't evade the question. Do you love me.'

Steve was suddenly consumed with guilt. Somehow could not bring himself to tell his wife that he loved her. He knew that he did but for some reason he could not utter the words she wanted to hear. 'Come on,' he said eventually. 'It's getting late, let's get back.'

On the way back to the hotel, not one word was exchanged

between them. However, before they entered the foyer Steve grabbed hold of Penny's hand. Pulling her close to him he looked into her eyes and said, 'I do love you Penny.'

For the next few minutes Penny and Steve embraced each other in a way they had not done for many years.

'We are OK aren't we?' Penny asked.

'Too right we are,' replied Steve.

'We have no secrets from each other do we Steve?' Penny asked.

'No, not any,' replied Steve, who was now once again feeling decidedly guilty.

Penny's strategy was working. She was sure that now her plan could not fail. As they embraced she allowed herself a small grin of satisfaction.

Chapter 25

'Shall we go to church today?' Penny asked as she sat up in bed, coffee cup in hand.

'Absolutely,' said Steve. 'I see no reason for us to shy away, just because of David and Clive's unfortunate and untimely end.'

'I thought you'd say that,' she replied. Penny would have preferred the family to keep a low profile for a week or so, however she was not in the mood to be confrontational.

The SOCOs had spent the whole of the previous day at the house. So when Sunday morning arrived they had finished their work, and Steve and the family were told that they could move back home. The Carmichaels packed up the small number of possessions they had with them and left the hotel in plenty of time to get to the church for morning service. They had decided to go straight to church from the hotel rather than go first to Tan House Row. On the way Steve called into the newsagents to get a couple of Sunday papers, which he planned to read later that day.

By the time that the family entered the church a large number of the usual Sunday morning regulars were already in their pews. With the exception of Beth Turner, it appeared to Steve that the whole village was there. This surprised him as they had arrived at church much earlier than usual. As they walked slowly towards a vacant space big enough for all five of them, he could feel that the eyes of the whole congregation were upon him and his family.

The church proceeded to fill up even more, until there were hardly any free spaces left. 'It's never been this busy before,' remarked Steve to Penny in a whisper.

'I suspect the events of Friday evening have something to do with it,' Penny replied. 'I also suspect that our presence here has been a factor too.'

'Do you really think so?' asked her bemused husband.

'Yes I do,' said Penny. 'They will all have suspected that we might turn up, and they want an opportunity to see how we act. Also, they'll be expecting the vicar to deliver one of his moralistic addresses which they will use as a guide as to how they should behave following all the recent goings-on.'

'You're joking!' exclaimed Steve in a tone that was a little louder than he had planned. 'I'm sure he'll mention what's been going on, but it surely won't be the basis of his sermon, will it?'

Penny raised her eyes to the heavens. 'You really don't understand village life do you?'

'Obviously not,' replied Steve, who was now even more pleased that they had decided to go to church that morning.

The service began as normal, and before the Reverend Pugh had climbed up to his pulpit, nobody would have guessed that two of the community's most popular members had died only a couple of days before. However, Pugh's sermon was to change all that.

'Ladies and gentlemen of Moulton Bank,' Pugh announced in a loud clear voice. 'We are today a village in mourning. Sarah McGuire, Linda Cartwright, Clara Apple-baum, Robin Mayhew, Clive Penman and David Turner, were all beloved members of this congregation. They were wives, a mother, sisters and brothers. They were friends, neighbours and they all supported our community with their skills. Whether at the post office, at our school, cleaning our houses, driving our village taxi or simply arranging the flowers in this very church. All of these people contributed

252

much to make Moulton Bank a better place. They leave behind them relatives and friends who are desperately trying to come to terms with what has happened. It is only right and proper for us, their friends and neighbours, to first of all praise God for sending these fine people to live with us, and whilst we cannot begin to understand why he chose to take them from us in such a way, we must also accept that this is his will and ask him to give us the strength to overcome our grief and to ensure that their memories are not diminished through the tragic circumstances of their departure from this worldly existence.'

Pugh then turned his gaze to the direction of the Carmichaels. 'I am sure that Inspector Carmichael and his colleagues will discover and make public the reasons why these deaths occurred, and while we can never condone the taking of a life, I urge you all to try to show compassion and forgiveness to those who are found culpable in these acts of true evil.' The vicar was by now in full flow. 'When we do this we should not only forgive those who delivered the fatal blows, but also those of us who bear guilt in this affair through our actions or reluctance to act. For in a small village like ours, very little goes on without someone knowing or suspecting what is happening. As such those of us who turned a blind eye, those of us who kept quiet and those of us who foolishly believed that the lies that we told ourselves or others were justified, must also accept our rightful share of blame for this tragic chain of events.'

Pugh took this moment in his address to pause. 'I myself am not without blame in this respect. As your chosen pastoral leader I have a duty to ensure that the spiritual well-being of our community is preserved and cherished. However, I have another duty. A duty to act as a good citizen. In that role I have been found wanting. Like many others in this community I did not act as a good citizen. When I should have made public my concerns about Clive and when I should have cooperated fully with the authorities, I chose to remain inactive and was less than frank in what I disclosed. I justified this to myself as being the act of a spiritual leader whose prime responsibility was to those whose motives and actions were in question, rather than the community as a whole.'

Pugh again turned his gaze on the Carmichaels. 'Over the last twenty-four hours, I have been in conversation with the bishop, who agrees with me that the best course of action for me to take under the circumstances is to retire and leave this parish. Therefore after thirty-nine years, I will humbly and quietly take my leave from you after today's service.'

At this point audible gasps could be heard from the normally quiet congregation.

'I wish you all well and I hope and pray that all of you who have been touched by the traumatic deaths of Sarah, Linda, Clara, Robin, David and Clive will soon be reconciled with the consequences of this tragedy. I am convinced that God will forgive all of you, who like me have been in some way responsible for what has happened, and I sincerely hope that your consciences will soon feel reconciled and that you can all move forward in a positive direction.'

As the now forlorn figure of the vicar descended the steps of the pulpit a couple of members of the congregation stood up and started to clap loudly. They were quickly joined in their applause by about half a dozen other people. By the time Pugh had reached the bottom of the steps almost all the congregation were applauding.

As usual, Pugh waited at the church gate to shake hands with the congregation as they departed. It took over 20 minutes before it was Steve and Penny's turn.

'We will all be sorry to see you go vicar,' continued Penny. 'I wish you well.'

Penny put her arms around Natalie and Robbie, and then walked slowly down the path, followed closely by Jemma.

Steve paused for a while to continue the discussion with the vicar.

'Don't chastise yourself too much Mr Pugh,' Steve said. 'I doubt that you could have done anything to prevent any of the murders.'

'Possibly,' replied Pugh. 'But when you came to see me I could have told you more. And I cannot help feeling that if I had then maybe I could have helped you thwart more unnecessary deaths.'

'Unless you knew that Clive was the killer, and I suspect that you did not, then I doubt that you could have prevented any of the deaths,' said Steve, in an attempt to ease the vicar's obvious pain.

'But neither of us will ever know,' replied Pugh, 'and regrettably it is I who have to live with that. Linda knew who the killer was that night when she called me.'

'How can you be sure?' asked Steve.

Pugh's eyes descended to the ground. 'She asked to meet me, as I told you, but what I didn't tell you was that she told me that she had received a call from Frankie Leeman and that as a result she now knew who the killer was. She wouldn't tell me who it was over the phone, which led me to believe that it was someone I was close to.'

'But what I can't understand,' said Steve, 'is why you didn't tell me all this when I interviewed you.'

'Because my sense of duty to my flock clouded my sense of duty to society,' replied Pugh. 'I convinced myself that in misleading you by not telling you all I knew it would allow me to identify Linda's killer and in so doing help him to repent his sins and to turn his energy away from evil.'

Steve could not believe his ears. He shook his head and strode away to catch up with the rest of his family. 'Can you believe that man?' he snarled as he reached the car. 'He's just had the audacity to admit that he withheld evidence from me.'

Penny shrugged her shoulders. 'He's just announced that he's leaving, what more do you want!' she whispered. The Carmichaels all clambered into Steve's BMW and made their way towards home. For a few moments the car was silent. However, Jemma was confused by the vicar's sermon. 'Why does the vicar feel he should retire?' she asked.

Steve looked at Penny.

'Well,' Penny said. 'He feels that he could have spoken out about things he knew, which could have helped the police in their investigations into Linda Cartwright's murder.'

'But he didn't lie,' replied Jemma.

'No, he didn't lie,' interrupted Steve, 'but he withheld evidence from the police, which might have prevented some of the other deaths from happening. It's that which he was referring to in his sermon. He now regrets what he did and he feels that the honourable thing for him to do is leave.'

Again the car fell silent for a few moments. 'Mum,' said Natalie, 'would it be wrong for someone not to tell if they knew that someone else had lied to their parents?'

'That depends,' replied Penny with a smile.

'What if someone had sold their bike and had told their parents that it had been stolen,' announced Natalie, much to the horror of her brother, who sat open-mouthed.

'Well dear,' replied Penny as she fixed her gaze on her son. 'It would not be wrong for that person to keep that a secret. But it would be wrong for the person who said he had sold the bike to lie like that.'

Robbie's heart sank. He knew full well that this would not be the last he would hear of this particular misdemeanour.

The family arrived back at Tan House Row at lunchtime, and having missed his weekly Saturday liquid lunch, Steve suggested that the whole family should have their Sunday lunch at The Railway Tavern. As he had expected, this was warmly received by all concerned, so the family set off on foot to the pub.

'I don't see why we have to walk,' moaned Robbie.

'Because I would like to have a drink,' replied Steve.

'Perhaps we should have cycled down,' said Penny sarcastically. 'Oh I forgot,' she continued dramatically. 'You had your bike stolen didn't you?'

Robbie's cheeks reddened, and he exchanged a threatening look with Natalie, who grasped tightly to her father's hand for safety.

When they arrived at the pub they went straight into the taproom, which was fairly empty. There were only a handful of people in the bar, none of whom Steve knew. The Carmichaels found themselves a table and started to study the menu. They where soon joined by Katie Robertson. 'Hello,' she said with a smile. 'What can I get you?'

Steve looked up from the menu and smiled at Katie. 'Can you give us a moment?' he asked.

'Certainly,' replied Katie. 'Take all the time you need.'

'Thanks,' said Penny, who was amazed by the lack of tact being shown by her husband. 'And I'm really sorry about the death of your Uncle David. If there's anything we can do ...'

'That's OK,' replied Katie with a forced smile. 'We weren't really close, but thanks anyway.' Katie paused for a moment. 'How about I get you some drinks while you choose?' she asked.

'Yes,' replied Penny. 'We'll have three cokes, I'll have a white wine spritzer and Steve, what will you have?'

'I'll have a pint of best,' replied Steve, timidly.

Katie departed, leaving the Carmichaels to make their choices, but not until Penny had cut her husband down with her best 'I'm really not that impressed' stare.

In under the hour they had all finished their meals. 'Fantastic,' Steve said as he picked up his newspaper. 'That was an excellent meal.'

'It's always better with two or three pints as well,' commented Penny sarcastically.

However, Steve's relaxed mood changed dramatically after he read an article on page five.

'High Flying Police Chief Names Names' was the headline. The story was about his old colleague Chief Inspector Butler. It alleged that Butler was about to name other officers guilty of taking bribes.

'What's wrong?' asked Penny when she saw Steve's expression. 'You look as though you've seen a ghost.'

'Let me pay the bill and we can go,' replied Steve, trying hard to change the subject.

'Pay the bill?' boomed the voice of Robbie Robertson from behind the bar. 'I will hear of no such thing inspector. This one's on the house.'

'That's very kind,' Penny said with a smile.

'But it's really not necessary,' said Steve. 'We can pay our own way you know.'

The publican was clearly hurt by Steve's abrupt refusal. 'I'm sorry if I offended you,' said Robbie. 'But I would like the meal to be a gesture of my thanks to you for finally bringing this nightmare to an end. It's also a sign of my sincere regret at the terrible ordeal that Penny and the children went through on Friday at the hands of a man that we all considered to be a friend.'

Steve looked at Penny, who quite clearly wanted him to accept the gift. 'Thank you,' said Steve with true humility. 'If you put it like that I can hardly refuse.'

Robbie, who had now made his way over to their table, was beaming from ear to ear. 'Also it's probably the last freebie anyone will get in The Railway from now on,' he continued.

'What do you mean?' Penny asked.

'Well that conniving young lady over there has been plotting and scheming behind my back,' as he spoke he was joined by Katie, who was also grinning.

'I'm confused,' Penny said with a frown.

'With a little help from Adrian Hope, my little girl has bought this place from the brewery.' Robbie's smile seemed to encircle his head with delight. 'With the help of a small legacy from her mum's estate, which she inherited at her last birthday, and a loan from the bank, we are now the proud owners of The Railway Tavern.'

'Congratulations,' said Penny as she gave the burly landlord a hug.

'Yes,' echoed Steve, 'congratulations.'

It took a few more drinks before the Carmichaels finally left. When they arrived home Cooper was waiting for them outside. 'Cooper,' said Steve, who by now was clearly a little worse for the drink, 'what are you doing here?'

'We've finished searching Penman's house sir,' he replied. 'We found this.' Cooper handed Steve a folded piece of paper faded yellow with age.

'What is it?'

'It's Arthur Turner's suicide note from 1976,' replied Cooper. 'It was in a drawer in Penman's bedroom.'

Steve carefully read the note. 'Thanks Cooper,' he said. 'I'll see you tomorrow.' Cooper departed, leaving Steve to rejoin his family who had already entered the house.

For most of the afternoon Steve lay in his favourite chair snoring loudly. However, that evening, he sat alone in his study, with three notes laid out in front of him. The first was Arthur Turner's suicide note, the second contained the five names that Terry Mayhew had written down for him earlier in the week. The last note was the one that David Turner had scribbled and pinned to that very door two nights before. Steve spent a good hour reading and then re-reading the notes with care.

Arthur Turner's letter

13th June 1976

Dear Beth

Please forgive me for leaving you in such circumstances. I can no longer continue with all the gossip relating to my involvement in Gillian's tragic death.

I am truly sorry that I have left you to care for our two beloved children, but I believe that it is better for all concerned that I do this.

Please tell the children that I love them dearly and that I am sorry that I have let them down so badly, and let Pugh know that I am truly remorseful for Gillian's death.

All my love

Arthur

Terry Mayhew's note

Those present when Mary confessed to Gillian's death were Robbie Robertson, myself (Terry Mayhew), Linda Cartwright, David Turner and Sarah McGuire.

David Turner's note

August 26th 2005

For the attention of Inspector Carmichael.

It may be difficult for you to understand what you find behind this door. Please believe that I had no idea that Clive was behind the murders of Linda and the others. If I had known I would have made certain that he gave himself up before we got to this stage. I know that he acted out of love for me and while I cannot condone his actions, I do not feel that he is a bad person.

However, what he has done cannot be altered or forgiven; and like all of us he must accept his punishment for his crimes.

I have thought long and hard about how this should end. I've no doubt that if he is arrested he will be tried and imprisoned for life. I am sure that some would say that this would be a light sentence for someone who has murdered five people. But believe me, knowing Clive as I do I can tell you that this would be a cruel existence for him and one which he would be unable to bear. As such I have taken the decision to end his life today.

My life without him is meaningless and as his executioner it is only right that I should join my good friend at the same time. Although you may not condone my actions today I expect that you understand why I have done what I have done.

My only regret is that in taking my life I will again cause my mother the sorrow of dealing with a family bereavement. Please tell her that I am truly sorry and that I love her.

David Turner

Also on Steve's desk was the Sunday newspaper, open at the article about Butler. Steve must have read each of the notes at least a dozen times before he carefully folded them up and placed them in his jacket pocket. In spite of this his mind was still more preoccupied with the article about Butler and what he was going to say to Lucy. He decided that the worst thing he could do with either of his dilemmas would be to allow others to dictate the pace of events. So in typical style he decided that it was up to him to take control. He picked up the phone and dialled Lucy's mobile.

'Hello,' said Lucy.

'Hi,' responded Steve. 'It's Steve here.'

'Oh hi. It's a bit late for you to be calling me.'

'Yes. I'm sorry about that. I just needed to speak to you before tomorrow morning.'

'I see,' replied Lucy.

'We need to meet before we go to the office,' continued Steve. 'We have to talk.'

'Yes, we do need to meet,' agreed Lucy. 'But where do you have in mind?'

'How about your place?' he suggested.

'No,' replied Lucy. 'That would be awkward.'

'Where then?' Steve asked.

'How about Wood Lane?'

Lucy's suggested location surprised Steve, however he was desperate to meet her before they reached the station. 'Sounds fine,' replied Steve. 'How about seven-thirty?'

'That's OK with me.'

After a short pause Steve said, 'Good, I'll see you then.' Both Lucy and Steve hung up at about the same time.

Lucy was pleased that they would have a chance to talk privately. She cared deeply for Steve, but her meeting with Penny had been a major jolt to her. She spent an uncomfortable night deliberating on what she should do the following day.

Steve was also relieved that he had managed to arrange the meeting. The last thing that he wanted was to meet Lucy for the first time after their US trip surrounded by Watson, Cooper and the other officers.

As he climbed into bed next to his wife he whispered, 'Are you asleep?'

'No. I can't get comfortable.'

'Can we talk?' Steve asked.

'Yes of course,' said Penny. 'But do you mind if you talk and I listen? I'm shattered.'

'I have a confession to make,' he boldly announced.

Penny's heart leapt into her mouth. She had not expected this at all. 'What sort of confession?' she asked as she turned on the bedside light.

Chapter 26

Steve rose bright and early. He was able to shower, have a cup of coffee, eat a bowl of cornflakes and take Penny a cup of tea in bed, all before leaving the house at 7:15 a.m. He was in a good mood, mainly because Penny had reacted so positively to his confession of the night before. In fact to his amazement she appeared downright amused.

'Now's the tricky one,' he whispered to himself, as he approached Lucy's parked car. He had already decided to make it clear to Lucy that their brief although passionate encounter in America was a one-off. Even though he had thoroughly enjoyed the experience, he had no intention of allowing the events of the previous week to develop into a serious affair. He had no desire to compromise his relationship with Penny or to do anything that would adversely affect the family. 'Be firm and business-like,' he kept saying to himself. 'If she gets emotional, don't cave in.'

It was a pleasant sunny morning. Lucy, who had arrived 10 minutes earlier, had already got out of her car when Steve arrived.

'Morning,' said Steve. 'How are you?'

'Fine,' replied Lucy nervously. 'I'm fine.'

Steve took a deep breath and was just about to launch into his well-rehearsed monologue about how they needed to forget what had happened in Winston-Salem, when Lucy thrust an envelope into his hand. 'I'm no good at this sort of thing,' she said clumsily. 'It's all in there.'

Steve could see that Lucy was finding it difficult to look him in the eye. He decided it would be wise to open the envelope and read the note inside. The first thing that struck Steve when he looked at the note was that apart from the signature at the bottom, it was typed. It was not even addressed to him. There was no 'Dear Steve' at the top. In fact without reading the contents, anyone who saw the letter could have been forgiven for believing that it was a formal letter rather than a note from a passionate lover. When he had finished reading the note he looked at Lucy. 'I see,' he said.

'It's for the best,' replied Lucy, who was now close to tears.

'Well, if that is what you want,' continued Steve, 'I understand.'

Lucy rushed forward and kissed Steve's cheek before darting back to her car and driving away. Steve remained rooted to the spot. He was stunned. Not for one moment had he expected to get a 'Dear John' letter from Lucy. Although the outcome of the meeting had been exactly what he wanted, his pride was severely dented by the fact that it was Lucy who had ended the relationship and not him.

* * * *

Penny remained in bed for a further hour after Steve had gone. At first she had not been sure whether she should be angry or amused at Steve's confession. However, it did not take much deliberation for her to come to the conclusion that this was probably a good thing. The truth was that when she began to realise that the confession was going to be about borrowing money from Butler all those years ago, to pay for Jemma's operation, rather than the affair with Lucy, she had felt very relieved.

The irony was that she had known all along that Butler had loaned Steve the money. Butler had taken great pleasure in letting her know that fact many years before. In her eyes her husband had done no wrong. When Steve took the money he had no idea that it had been acquired from payments made by criminals, and in her view this had in no way incriminated her husband in Butler's shady business practices. What she hadn't fully realised was that Steve had been prevented from exposing Butler by being worried about the threat of being implemented in his activities, and she had certainly grossly underestimated how the whole affair had preyed so heavily on Steve's mind.

She was pretty confident that her scheme was unfolding to plan, nevertheless she was still a little unsure as to whether Lucy would sign and deliver to Steve the letter that she had painstakingly typed at the hotel and had presented to Lucy at the airport. Penny did not know Lucy well enough to be certain as to how she would react when she met with Steve at the office that morning. However, the expression that she had seen on Lucy's face at the airport when she had threatened to make the affair known to Hewitt had made her quite confident that if push came to shove her rival would choose her career over Steve.

Penny then started to wonder what would have happened if she herself had chosen a career in preference to Steve and her family. 'Stupid girl,' she said out loud to herself. 'That's where we differ my girl. That's where we differ.'

*   *   *   *

After Lucy's car had disappeared Steve read her letter once more before placing it in his jacket pocket. He decided that he would destroy it in the shredder at work, to avoid it being seen by unwanted eyes. Not for one moment did he suspect that the business-like way the letter had been drafted, with neither the slightest sign of passion nor any hint of emotion, had been crafted in such an expert and calculating way by his own wife.

266

He arrived at Kirkwood and was at his desk much earlier than he had anticipated. His first task for the day was to get the team together to perform a concluding debrief on the Linda Cartwright case. This was then to be followed with the careful dismantling of the paraphernalia associated with the case.

All the charts, photographs, reports, statements and exhibits would have to be recorded and filed away, before they could move on to the next case. This was the part of the job that Steve hated. The degree of care that the police have to take when completing the paperwork to a case was always something that made him feel frustrated, even though he knew it was a necessity. However, one of the perks of being an inspector was that he could now delegate the majority of this work to others in the team. His strategy for this case was to grant Lucy, Cooper and Watson the privilege of preparing most of the final written submissions and ensuring that all the loose ends were tidied up.

Steve was the first to enter the incident room. He glanced casually at all the exhibits and papers that were fixed to the wall or arranged in neat piles on the various workstations. It always amazed him how much paper a criminal investigation generated. Even now, with the advent of computer technology, there was still a vast amount of paperwork accompanying even the most minor case.

After a few moments Watson and Cooper entered the room. 'Morning sir,' Watson said cheerily.

'Morning,' replied Steve.

'Chief Inspector Hewitt wants to see you,' Cooper announced.

'Now?' Steve said, with no attempt to disguise his irritation.

'He said as soon as you arrived,' Cooper replied.

'OK,' he said. 'You two get started packing up all this. Make sure it's all carefully marked and logged and filed neatly.'

Watson and Cooper exchanged an exasperated look. 'Right you are sir,' replied Cooper.

Steve was surprised that Lucy had not made an appearance. She'd left Wood Lane well before him, so she should surely have arrived before him. 'Where's Lucy?' he asked.

'Don't know,' replied Cooper.

'She was in here earlier,' Watson declared. 'Last time I saw her she was heading towards the ladies. To be honest she didn't look too happy.'

'I see,' said Steve.

When he reached Hewitt's office, Angela greeted him warmly. 'Inspector Carmichael,' she said, 'how are you and Mrs Carmichael? It must have been a terrible ordeal for you both. I'm so pleased that you are both safe and well.'

'Thank you Angela,' replied Steve. 'We are fine thank you.'

At that moment Hewitt appeared at the door. 'Come in Steve.'

Steve smiled at Angela. He then went into his superior's office and sat down in the same low chair that he had occupied on the day he arrived.

'Great to see you Steve,' boomed Hewitt. 'How's the family?' Before Steve had a chance to reply Hewitt had moved on to a new subject. 'I need to have a word with you,' he continued. 'I've decided to ask Inspector Pearson to lead the team we discussed.'

'You mean the internal corruption assignment?' asked Steve.

'That's correct.'

'But I thought that I was to lead this new team?'

'I never actually promised you the position inspector. I did consider you as a strong candidate. However, on reflection I decided to ask Pearson to take this on. I'm sure you understand.'

'No I don't,' replied Steve.'What has made you change your mind?'

Hewitt adopted a more stern appearance. It was clear that he felt awkward and a little threatened by Steve's abrupt response. 'Now listen to me inspector,' he announced in a clear authoritative voice, 'I am responsible for making this appointment and in my view Pearson is better suited to the role. I am not obliged to explain my decision to you and quite frankly your aggressive reaction only confirms to me that I have made the right choice.'

Steve was angry. However, he managed to remain calm. 'It's your decision sir,' he replied. 'Will that be all?'

Steve rose from his chair and made his way to the door. Before he left he turned round to face Hewitt. 'For the record sir, although I was involved with Butler when I was at the Met, at no time did I do anything that I am ashamed of. I am not a corrupt officer. You asked me on the day I arrived why I chose to leave the Met for provincial Lancashire. The answer is quite simple. I left to get away from officers like Butler. However, to be honest sir, at least in London you know where you stand. There's no hidden agenda. Everything is quite simple.'

Hewitt had expected Steve to be upset, but he had not anticipated such an outburst, particularly as the link Steve had made between him losing the assignment and his association with Butler was way off the mark. When Steve had applied for the post at his station Hewitt had checked his background thoroughly and following these checks had been in no doubt that Carmichael was an honest and capable officer. The simple truth was that Hewitt did not like officers who disobeyed his instructions and Carmichael, however good he may be, had chosen to ignore his orders on at least two occasions. In Hewitt's opinion, although Carmichael had eventually got to the bottom of the case, he could not ignore the fact that Steve had taken almost two days to get a SOCO to carry out a forensic investigation in Mrs Applebaum's house and he had abandoned a junior officer in America to interview an important witness, while he raced back to arrest the wrong man. Also, by jumping to the wrong conclusion in this way he had allowed two further deaths to occur and had put his own family in danger. With all these errors, Hewitt could not reconcile himself to allow Steve to be given charge of such a high profile job. However, after all that Steve had been through in the last few days he decided that he should spare him a reprimand. He would leave any further discussion about these matters for his next appraisal.

As Steve made his way down towards the incident room, he passed by Inspector Pearson's office. The door was slightly ajar and he could see Pearson behind his desk chatting to someone who was out of Steve's view.

'So what do you think?' Pearson said. 'If you're interested you can be part of the team.'

'Sounds interesting,' replied a familiar voice.

'It will be far more interesting than the normal run of the mill work that you'll get under Carmichael. At your age this will give you a great deal of experience. In my view there's no reason why you couldn't make sergeant within a year to eighteen months.'

'Do you really think so?' said Lucy. 'In that case you're on.'

Pearson's grin stretched from ear to ear. 'I'll tell the Chief right away,' he said.

Steve had heard enough by now. 'Bloody mercenary,' he said under his breath as he made his way down the corridor.

For the next few hours Steve helped Watson and Cooper dismantle the incident room. This uncharacteristic move was quite therapeutic for him. Although he would never admit it, he actually quite enjoyed himself. Lucy had decided not to join the rest of the team. As soon as Hewitt had received the call from Pearson confirming that Lucy was to be part of his crack team, her involvement with Carmichael, Cooper and Watson had been severed.

Steve took the four pieces of paper out of his pocket. After reading them all once more he handed Watson the note from Terry Mayhew and the suicide note that David Turner had written. 'Bag these up carefully Marc,' he said. He made two photocopies of Arthur Turner's note and handed Watson one. 'Put this on file,' he ordered, 'I'll replace it with the real one tomorrow.' He placed the original and the second copy in his jacket pocket. He read the note that Lucy had given him earlier in the day one more time before carefully folding it in half and running it through the shredder.

'What was that?' asked Watson.

'It's of no consequence Marc,' Steve replied. 'It's nothing of any worth whatsoever.'

Chapter 27

Carmichael's BMW pulled up outside Beth Turner's house at a little after three. He climbed out of the car and walked slowly up the drive.

Mrs Turner had lived in that house for over 45 years. She and her husband had arrived there just after Mary had been born. It was the first house that they had owned and although it still had some painful memories, it was also a place that had seen great happiness. On that particular day Mrs Turner had spent the morning with the Reverend Feeney, the vicar of Newbridge, discussing plans for David's funeral. Since Reverend Pugh's sudden retirement, the Newbridge minister had been asked to look after both parishes, until a replacement could be appointed. It had been an arduous task for the old lady to arrange her son's funeral, particularly with a cleric that she hardly knew.

Alone in her home she had sat motionless in her armchair for two hours before she was interrupted by the sound of the doorbell. Although she was now getting on in years, she was still fairly sprightly and it took her no time at all to answer the door.

'Good afternoon,' Steve said as the door opened. 'I hope you don't mind me coming over to see you unannounced like this.'

She returned him a faint smile. 'Not at all inspector. It's nice of you to call. Please come in.' Steve entered the house and followed Mrs Turner into the living room. 'Please do take a seat,' said Mrs Turner. 'Can I get you some tea?'

Steve sat down in the same armchair that had just been vacated by Mrs Turner. 'I won't have any tea,' he said, 'I just wanted to show you something which I feel you should see.'

Mrs Turner lowered herself into the other armchair. 'Thank you inspector,' she said, 'but I cannot think what you can show me that is so important.'

Steve pulled a note from his pocket and handed it to Mrs Turner. 'It was found in Clive Penman's bedroom,' he said.

Mrs Turner opened the folded note. 'I recognise the writing inspector,' she said, 'but I regret that I cannot read what has been written without my glasses. Could you be a dear and get them for me? They are in the kitchen on the table.'

'Of course,' replied Steve, who immediately rose from his chair and made his way to the kitchen.

Upon his return he handed the spectacles to Mrs Turner and returned to his armchair while the old lady read the note. Although the note was quite short, it took Mrs Turner some moments to raise her eyes from the paper.

'Thank you for bringing this to me,' she said. 'I'd always pondered why Arthur never left a note. That was certainly not like him. But how did Clive come to have it?'

'It would appear that when he and David saw the note on the door that day, Clive remained at the house while David went to fetch the police. He went inside and found your husband and this note. Thinking that the note would incriminate Mr Turner as the driver who killed Gillian Pugh, Clive took the note and kept it. For almost thirty years he kept it without ever telling another soul about it.'

Mrs Turner nodded. 'That would explain it I suppose,' she said.

'I'm sure he acted only out of kindness to you, to Mary and David and also to your husband's memory,' Steve continued, 'but I'm equally sure that your husband would have wished you to see the note.'

'Can I keep it now?' Mrs Turner asked.

'I'm afraid not,' replied Steve. 'It's now evidence in the case. However, I've made a copy, which I can certainly leave with you until all the legal aspects of the case have been concluded. I'm sure that then you will be able to have the original back.'

'Thank you,' replied Mrs Turner. For a moment they both sat in silence until Mrs Turner said, 'Are you sure that I can't make us both a cup of tea?'

'Actually Mrs Turner, that would be nice,' replied Steve. 'But only if I can help.'

'It's a deal,' she said. 'And please call me Beth.'

For the next hour the two engaged themselves in largely meaningless conversation. Beth was very keen to learn about Steve's family and of course Steve was very keen to learn more about Arthur Turner. When at last he had made his way to the door and was about to walk back to his car, Steve turned to face her.

'When we met before you indicated that you had promised not to discuss why your husband took his life. You also asked me to what lengths I would go to protect my children.'

She nodded. 'And if I remember I also said that if you could prove to me that Linda's death was connected to Arthur's I would reconsider.'

'That's right.'

'Well I see no reason not to let you into the secret now,' continued the old lady. 'Arthur and I both suspected that Mary and Robin had taken the car and that it had been the car in the accident. Arthur was very proud of the car and he would polish it religiously every weekend. It was when he was cleaning the car a few days after Gillian's death that he found some scratches on the wing. He knew it had not happened while he was driving so we became suspicious. We confronted Mary with it, but she denied it.'

'But I still don't see how you could be sure it was Mary or

why your husband felt he had to take his own life as a result,' Steve said.

Mrs Turner sighed. 'After a few weeks we started receiving letters saying that there was a murderer in the house. As I'm sure you can imagine we were both distraught. At first we ignored the notes, but as time went on they turned into blackmail. At first it was £50, but after a while the demands grew to £100, then £200. We were terrified that the person would go to the police and that Mary would be found out.'

'Why did you not go to the police?' Steve asked.

'Because we loved Mary, she was just eighteen with her whole life ahead of her. If we had gone to the police then the chances are she would have gone to prison. Could you let your daughter go to jail over a dreadful mistake?'

Steve nodded, 'I see,' he said quietly. 'But that still does not explain who the blackmailer was and why Mr Turner took such a desperate step.'

'All the payments were made in the same way,' continued Mrs Turner. 'We would leave the cash in a bag in a dustbin up near the old basketworks. After we had made four or five payments we decided that we needed to find out the identity of the blackmailer. So on the next occasion I made the deposit as usual while Arthur hid in the bushes. He waited for about an hour before Gary Leeman arrived and collected the money. The next day Arthur confronted Leeman, who admitted that he was the blackmailer. However, he also made it clear that he thought Arthur was the driver, not Mary as we had previously thought. This changed everything as far as Arthur was concerned. Once he knew that Mary was not suspected he became much more relaxed about things. Then after a few days Arthur realised that on the day that Gillian died we were both away in Manchester on a two-day seminar with some of Arthur's colleagues from school.'

'So?' replied Steve. 'I fail to see the significance.'

'Well if the police did find out that it was our car that killed Gillian,' replied Mrs Turner, 'we would have an alibi that we could never refute. If that did happen then it would be no time before Mary became the main suspect. I think that Arthur figured that Mary would never allow him to take the blame for her and go to jail. You see just as he loved her, she idolised him. It would be inconceivable for her to allow him to take her punishment.'

'I see.' said Steve. 'So your husband took his own life so that the police would believe that it was he that was guilty and stop their investigations.'

'Yes,' replied Mrs Turner. 'That's what I've always thought and this note confirms it.'

'I suppose you are right.'

Mrs Turner nodded. 'Of course Arthur did not discuss it with me, he knew I would have stopped him. However, it always puzzled me why a note had not been found because Arthur was a very intelligent and meticulous man. It is inconceivable that he would have not left a note, but until you gave me this I could not be sure.'

'But what I still find hard to understand is how Gary Leeman knew that it was your car that was involved,' Steve said.

'I don't know. Mary's pals were always popping by. Maybe he saw the scratches on the car as we had, or maybe Robin Mayhew let something slip when he was drunk. I really don't know. And now that Gary Leeman is dead I guess we'll never know.'

Steve smiled. 'And to be honest I suppose that little piece of information is now totally irrelevant.'

'I agree. It has been the absence of a note that has concerned me these past years. I no longer care about any of the other missing details.'

After a short pause Steve shook Mrs Turner's hand and turned to depart. However before Mrs Turner had a chance to close the door, behind him, he stopped and spun round slowly. 'Someone once said to me that your husband was a remarkable man,' he said. 'At the time I did not understand what he meant. However I do now. I really would have liked to have met him.'

'Oh,' she replied, 'he was certainly remarkable. You would have liked my Arthur.' With that she smiled again and closed the door. 'And he would have liked you,' she said to herself as she strolled back towards the comfort of her chair.

*　*　*　*

Penny was delighted to see her husband return home so early. She saw this and the warm embrace he gave her in the kitchen as sure signs that Lucy had delivered the letter as instructed. 'It's nice to have you home before five,' she said. 'What sort of day have you had?'

'Oh fine,' he said sarcastically. 'But Hewitt's given that bloody assignment to Pearson.'

'What, the internal corruption thing?' Penny asked. 'But I thought it was already yours?'

'It was,' retorted Steve angrily. 'But apparently I was just in the frame. It was that Butler thing in the papers. He didn't say so but I could tell. He thinks because I knew Butler that I'm bent too.'

'I'm sure that's not the case,' Penny said, trying hard to comfort her husband.

'Believe me, it bloody is,' replied Steve.

'Oh dear,' continued Penny. 'Never mind, it's not the end of the world.'

'I suppose not,' he grumbled. 'But what really pisses me off is that smarmy sod Pearson is already pinching people from my team to join him.'

'Who do you mean?' asked Penny.

'Lucy Clark,' snapped Steve.

This was music to Penny's ears. 'Well I'm not surprised,' she replied. 'I never took to her. From what you said about her and from what I saw at the barbecue, she's an ambitious young lady who is well prepared to use all her talents to get to where she wants to go.'

This comment made Steve pause for a while. Until that moment he had never considered that the passion that he had shared with Lucy could have been a carefully planned exercise on her part. His ego would not allow him to accept this view so he quickly dismissed the thought. 'I'm not sure that's true,' he said, 'but her sudden desire to join Pearson's team was a real bolt from the blue.'

Penny laughed. 'You are really so naïve sometimes' she said. 'Believe me, that young lady not only knows what she wants, but also knows how to get it. The problem you men have is that she's young and pretty and you can't cope with her tactics. You're fine with rough and dangerous blokes, but the gentle sex is alien to you, and girls like Lucy are just capitalising on this. And frankly you can't blame them.'

'Well she's had it as far as I'm concerned,' announced Steve through clenched teeth. 'I'm through with her. She can bugger off.'

Penny felt a gratifying warmth course through her body. She gave Steve a massive hug. 'Mission accomplished,' she said to herself.

'Anyway, enough of her,' said Steve. 'I also went to see Mrs Turner today.'

'How is she?' asked Penny. 'She must be distraught.'

'Actually she's bearing up pretty well, all things considered. We had a long chat about her husband. I showed her his suicide note and well, it did seem to ease her mind a little.'

'Oh good. I must go to see her myself.'

'She admitted that Gary Leeman had been blackmailing her and Arthur over Gillian Pugh's death. And she believes that the reason Arthur killed himself was to deflect suspicion away from Mary.'

'How awful. That's real love for you.'

Steve's arms engulfed his wife again. 'Yes,' he replied. 'That's exactly what I thought.'